A GOD IN CHAINS

MATTHEW HUGHES

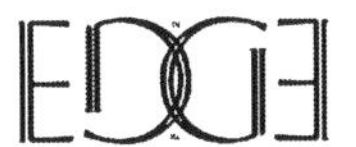

EDGE SCIENCE FICTION AND FANTASY PUBLISHING
An Imprint of HADES PUBLICATIONS, INC.
CALGARY

A God in Chains

This is a work of fiction. Names, characters, places, and incidents are the products of the author's imagination or are used fictitiously and are not to be construed as real. Any resemblance to actual events, locales, organizations, or persons, living or dead, is entirely coincidental.

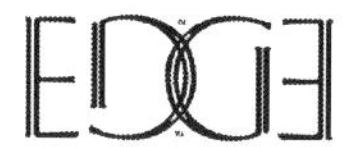

EDGE SCIENCE FICTION AND FANTASY PUBLISHING
An Imprint of HADES PUBLICATIONS, INC.
P.O. Box 1714, Calgary, Alberta, T2P 2L7, Canada

The EDGE Team:
Producer: Brian Hades
Acquisitions Editor: Michelle Heumann
Edited by: Shannon Parr
Cover Design: beti bup
Book Design: Mark Steele

ISBN: 978-1-77053-203-8

EDGE Science Fiction and Fantasy Publishing and Hades Publications, Inc. acknowledges the ongoing support of the Alberta Foundation for the Arts and the Canada Council for the Arts for our publishing programme.

Library and Archives Canada Cataloguing in Publication
CIP Data on file with the National Library of Canada
ISBN: 978-1-77053-203-8
(e-Book ISBN: 978-1-77053-202-1)

FIRST EDITION
(20201104)
Printed in USA
www.edgewebsite.com

Publisher's Note:

Thank you for purchasing this book. It began as an idea, was shaped by the creativity of its talented author, and was subsequently molded into the book you have before you by a team of editors and designers.

Like all EDGE books, this book is the result of the creative talents of a dedicated team of individuals who all believe that books (whether in print or pixels) have the magical ability to take you on an adventure to new and wondrous places powered by the author's imagination.

As EDGE's publisher, I hope that you enjoy this book. It is a part of our ongoing quest to discover talented authors and to make their creative writing available to you.

We also hope that you will share your discovery and enjoyment of this novel on social media through Facebook, Twitter, Goodreads, Pinterest, etc., and by posting your opinions and/or reviews on Amazon and other review sites and blogs. By doing so, others will be able to share your discovery and passion for this book.

Brian Hades, publisher

Part 1

Farouche speaks

As if half-waking from a dream, I found myself walking along a dirt road scored with wagon tracks and hoof prints, with occasional deposits of animal dung. Something about the combination said *caravan* to me. To either side of the road was a flat and level plain covered in dry grass, with clumps of some kind of prickly bush I couldn't name. Farther off in one direction was a line of hills with patches of stumpy trees; in the other, the plain continued, unbroken.

The sun was over the hills, so they were either west or east, depending on whether the sun was coming up or going down. After I'd walked on a ways, I looked again and decided it was higher than when I'd first observed it; that meant it was morning and I was walking south. By the freshness of some of the dung, I decided I wasn't far behind the caravan. When I looked ahead, I thought I could see dust on the horizon.

It occurred to me that I should walk a little faster. A man alone on an empty savanna would be in trouble if he ran into the kind of people who haunted empty spaces. An image came into my mind: men on shaggy ponies, hung about with lances and swords, bolt-throwers in their hands. I looked down at the broad belt that confined my upper garment and, seeing not even a dagger, I started to trot toward the dust.

Now it was like coming all the way out of a dream. I'd been walking, now I was trotting. The exercise seemed to clarify my mind. I stopped and turned around. The grassy plain stretched on to the north, broken only by the scar of bare earth I'd been following. There was nothing to suggest where I'd come from or how I'd got here.

I did another, more comprehensive self-examination and found nothing: no purse, no wallet, only me in a shirt and trousers of good-quality cloth, with well-made boots on my feet, but no hat or neckcloth. No pack or water bottle. Like a man who had stepped out into the street on some mundane errand.

So, I'm not a tramp, I thought. Which, of course, raised the fundamental question: *What am I?*

That led to other questions: where was I and how did I get here? And why didn't I know the answers? I felt my head, but encountered no bruises or sore spots. That eliminated one possibility, which left only two others: magic or the ingesting of some drug that removed memory.

I started to jog south again. The problem with those two remaining possibilities was that I was unlikely to have done them to myself. That meant someone had done this to me, and probably not for my benefit. I had an enemy or, at least, someone who didn't wish me well.

I increased my pace. After a few footfalls, I added two new items to my skimpy store of knowledge: I wasn't particularly old and I was in good physical condition.

«»

The plain turned out to be high plateau, as I discovered when the road began to zig-zag down a long incline. Below me, I saw the land rumple and fold, copses of trees sprouting around meadows of grass that was properly green. The bare dirt of the caravan trail met a stone road where the forest thickened and stretched unbroken to the horizon.

Civilization, I thought, *and maybe not far ahead.* I jogged on down the slope.

By the time the land leveled out again, I was walking a broad causeway cut through the forest. The stone road was wide enough for two full-sized carts to pass each other and the land to either side had been cleared the width of a bowshot. That had all sorts of implications, the upshot of which was that, as an unarmed man on his own, I needed to catch up with the caravan as soon as I could.

I set myself a pace of fifty steps walking followed by fifty jogging. I wasn't sure why that was a familiar mode of covering distance, but my body's response said I had done it before. I wondered how long it had been since I had eaten, since that would determine how long I could keep it up.

But I wasn't hungry, which was a good sign, although as the day warmed, I was getting thirsty.

In the mid afternoon, I saw more light in the sky ahead. I slowed and approached with caution. If there was a clearing ahead it might be occupied. If it was occupied, there might be sentries watching the road, and sentries tended to have a jaundiced view of strangers who came running toward them. I didn't know how I knew that, but I wasn't prepared to question my own judgment.

The road entered a wide, open space and ran across it to where a wooden stockade built of upright logs stood in the middle of the clearing. The road ended at a pair of tall wooden gates flanked by timber towers. There were men in the towers, and the moment I came out from the shade of the trees I saw one of them pointing at me. A moment later, a horn sounded and all along the wall facing me heads and shoulders of armed men appeared.

I approached at a walking pace and, when I got within range of a bolt-thrower, I spread my arms to let all the eyes on me see that I was unarmed. I stopped in front of the gate and turned a slow circle.

A helmeted, red-bearded man in one of the towers said, "What do you want?"

"To come in."

"And do what?"

"Get a drink of water," I said. "I'm hot and thirsty."

The guard spat and said nothing to me, but spoke over his shoulder to another man. *Waiting for someone who has the authority to make the decision,* I thought.

In a little while, another man came up beside Red Beard, this one with a softly rounded hat instead of a helmet and a black beard streaked with gray. He gave me a good looking-over, then said something I couldn't hear. The red-bearded guard disappeared and moments later one side of the gate swung inward just wide enough for a man to get through.

The older man up above beckoned with a finger. I went forward and squeezed between the unfinished wood of the gates' edges. A splinter caught in my sleeve just below the shoulder and I reached to pull it out.

A hard hand grabbed my arm, pushed me so I was off-balance, and thrust me against the inner surface of the gate. I put my hands out to keep from crashing into the timbers and felt my ankles being roughly kicked apart. I was then subjected to a search that seemed unnecessarily rough.

"Easy," I said. "I'm not—"

That got me a hard slap against the side of my head and an order to, "Shut it!"

I turned around. The red-bearded guard moved in close enough that I could smell the onions and garlic that had been part of his midday meal. A couple of others, similarly clad in leather jerkins and conical helmets, were there to back him up.

"Try that again," I said.

Instead of another slap, he went for a short, sharp punch aimed at my floating ribs. But he was one of the kind whose eyes let you know when it's coming. I blocked the blow, stepped inside his reach, and took hold of his wrist. A half-second later, he was flying over my shoulder to land hard on the packed dirt in front of the gate.

Well, I seem to know how to do that, I thought.

Give him credit, he didn't lie there looking up at me for long. He got up fast and swung a haymaker at my head. It would have been a painful experience if I hadn't leaned back, let it go harmlessly past, then stepped in again and given him three sharp blows to his prominent nose, the third of which broke the bone.

Blood spurted and his eyes watered with the pain. I turned to see what his two friends might be good for and saw them giving each other the kind of sideways looks that said neither one of them wanted to be the first to come into range. But, if they could coordinate effectively…

"That's enough," said an authoritative voice.

The dark-bearded man who had ordered the gates opened had come down from the tower. He was dressed in a merchant's robe, yellow silk with a broad green sash of braided cloth from which hung a ring of heavy keys. He was regarding me with a gaze that said I was being weighed up.

Then he indicated the two guards with a motion of his chin and said, "Could you take the two of them together?"

I gave him an honest answer, "Think so."

He considered me for a few more heartbeats. Finally, he gave a nod that said he was making a decision. "Could you teach them how to do it?"

I didn't know if I'd ever been an instructor, so I hedged my bet. "If they're willing to work at it," I said.

He nodded again. "They'd be willing," he said. He spoke to the three guards. "Get better at your jobs, you'll get better paid."

The two who hadn't been touched let their faces say they were all right with that idea. Red Beard was looking at me in a way that told me he would be all right with the idea of bashing my brains in when I wasn't looking.

"You'd need help," I told him, "and I think your friends would rather have the extra pay."

He said something I didn't catch. I didn't ask him to repeat it. I turned my back on him.

The merchant was watching this bit of byplay with a half smile. "What's your name?" he said.

I opened my mouth to answer, but nothing came out. It should have occurred to me when I didn't know *what* I was that I also wouldn't know *who* I was.

"Ah," I said, after a moment, "that seems to be a problem."

«»

His name was Nulf Bernaglio and this was his caravan. It consisted of twenty high-sided, canvas-topped wagons, each drawn by six mules, with a human complement of one muleteer for each vehicle and ten guards. The caravanserai had its own small garrison of twenty men. Eighteen of the wagons were loaded with valuable goods — silks, unguents, spices, and steel weapons — from the bazaars at Ur Nazim. The remaining two carried fodder and water for the stock, and food for the men. There were also two additional wagons belonging to taggers-along whose owners, I later learned, took their chances at the rear of the procession where an attack by reivers was most likely to come.

As I followed Bernaglio to his capacious tent, I surveyed the layout of the camp. The wagons were formed into a circle, with the animals tethered to picket lines on either side of the space the vehicles enclosed. The master's tent, with an armed guard at each corner, was in the center of the circle, next to a covered well. In the event that an attack penetrated the stockade, the wagons would make a redoubt for the defenders to fall back to.

As I told that to myself, I realized that I must have had some experience in assessing military situations. *Maybe I was a soldier,* I thought.

Bernaglio led me into his tent, which was surprisingly cool. He made himself comfortable on a brocaded divan but left me standing. A servant appeared from behind a hanging divider. The master gestured for him to withdraw.

"Wait," I said. "I need a drink of water."

The man hesitated, looking to Bernaglio, who made another gesture. The servant left and came back with a jug. I drank half of the contents in four gulps and when the man reached for the container, I said, "I'll keep it."

When we were alone again, Bernaglio said, "You have no idea who you are?"

"I'm beginning to think I might be a soldier. Or have been one."

"Come closer," he said. "Show me your hands."

I did as he wanted. He studied the backs of my hands briefly then said, "What is this scar?"

I looked and saw an irregular splotch of white cicatrice tissue on the webbing between the thumb and forefinger of my right hand. "I hadn't noticed it," I said.

"A burn," he said, thoughtfully. "Maybe a caustic substance."

"I don't know," I said.

"Turn them over." When I did, he rubbed his thumb across the base of my fingers. "Those are the callouses a sword's hilt makes. Though they are not recent."

"More evidence," I said.

"What do you remember?"

I told him about walking the trail, the way it felt like waking from a dream. He scratched his beard and called for the servant, gave him an order. The man left and came back with a small coffer of chased copper. Bernaglio used a small key on his ring to open it and took out a silver brooch set with a polished stone. He stood and brought the gem close to my chest then turned it in his hand and looked at it.

When he had taken it from the coffer, the stone had been green. Now it was a fiery red.

"You have been in contact with magic," he said, "but the contact was negligible. It was near you, but you were not its focus. It's doubtful that is the cause of your forgetfulness. You are not now under a spell or geas."

"What does that mean?"

"I'm not a thaumaturge," Bernaglio said. "You could possibly consult one after we reach Exley."."

"Exley," I said. A picture came into my head: a sprawling town on either side of a wide river crossed by two stone bridges. I saw walls and towers and streets of stone, a big white dome.

Bernaglio was watching me. "You've been there?"

"I think so."

He scratched his beard again. "But you haven't been here before."

"Not that I recall," I said.

"Or Ur Nazim?"

No image came to me. "Don't think so."

He was thinking again, then he reached for a slate and chalk on a nearby table. He wrote a word and showed it to me, asked me to pronounce it.

"Saskardia," I said.

He put away the slate. "You're not from Ur Nazim. You're from the south. Old Almery, probably."

He must have read the question in my face because he explained. "If you're from the north, the word starts with *suss*. If you're from the south, you say, *sass*. You're a *sasser*."

"All right," I said. "I'm in no position to argue."

"The question is, what is a Southron doing on the road from Ur Nazim to Exley?"

"That's just one of the questions," I said.

He made a two-handed gesture that said that didn't matter for now. "From Exley you can go to Vanderoy and ask a wizard," he said. "By then you will have earned enough to hire one."

I didn't comment, but something in the back of my mind told me I didn't care to be in the company of wizards.

«»

"I'm not going to turn you into experts," I told the men gathered in front of me. "I'm just going to teach you enough to be dangerous."

Four of the guards had been sent to my class. Five more were on the stockade walls, watching. Bernaglio had kept just one to guard his tent. A dozen or so muleteers had also come to watch, whether to learn something or just to be entertained. Once the animals had been fed and watered, and their manure shoveled into a pile, there wasn't much amusement in a caravanserai.

I showed them the basics: the soft parts you could hit to do maximum damage with no risk of hurting your own hands or feet; the simple throws, like the one I'd used on the red-bearded guard, whose name turned out to be Gashtun; the upthrust heel of the hand to the nostrils that could drive the nasal bone into the brain; and the side of the hand into the larynx, to crush it and cut off the windpipe. I instructed them, then I divided them into pairs and let them practice on each other. Some of them showed an aptitude. With more practice, they would be dangerous.

Gashtun kept putting too much into it, as if he was showing off for an easily entertained audience.

"No," I told him. "Less is more. Get in close, do the damage. The shorter the blow, the less chance the enemy can block it."

But he wouldn't listen, at least not to me. Then, after one of the talented muleteers threw him the way I'd thrown him the day before, he got up swearing and left the session.

«»

We stayed at the camp another day, until the mules were fully recovered from the long trek across the savanna. I got in some more teaching, then left it to them to practice in their own spare time. Most of the guards caught on quickly. By the end of the second day of instruction, they could receive a thrust from a spear, disarm the attacker, reverse the weapon, and deliver a killing thrust. Some of the muleteers were also coming along nicely.

Bernaglio watched the last session. Afterward, he said, "I hope I'm not training and motivating bandits."

"Pay them extra," I said. "They'll fight if the time comes."

"Speaking of which," he said, "these are for you."

He beckoned to a servant waiting behind him who brought up a spear, sword, and helmet. They were of better quality than what the guards had.

I drew the sword from its scabbard. It had a fine balance and the tracing on the blade said it was of Ur Nazim manufacture.

"To keep?" I said. "Or for the duration?"

He had been watching how I handled the sword. Now he made an ambiguous gesture. "We'll see."

«»

The caravanserais were sited an easy day's travel from each other, with garrisons jointly paid for by the Margrave of Ur Nazim and the Oligarchs Council of Exley. Experienced travelers like Bernaglio knew that the likeliest spot for an ambush was when the mule train was close enough to shelter to make a run for it, but not so close as to encourage the garrison to make a sortie. The spoliators would try to separate the rearmost wagon from the rest and once the main body of the caravan had whipped up its mules to race for the caravanserai, they could loot the cargo and run off the stock.

We were an hour's trek from the caravanserai when the merchant called a halt. He selected four of his own guards and sent them back to the rear, telling them he was putting me in charge. We were armed with bolt-throwers, only good at short range, but the kind that can be quickly cocked and loaded. I suggested short thrusting swords, and the merchant ordered them distributed from his cargo.

"It offends me that this filth think they can play me for a noddy," Bernaglio said. "It's time they met with a surprise."

His plan was simple: we would hide in the last wagon and, when the robbers came running out of the trees, we would let them get close then give them a volley of darts tipped with razor-sharp iron.

"There should be time to reload and give them a second dose," I said. "Then we come over the sides of the wagons and go at them with the sword."

Bernaglio nodded. "They're used to frightening the wagon drivers, who don't put up much of a fight and often jump down and run. Kill a few of them and they might think twice about it next time I come this way."

The owners of the last two wagons were a pair of brothers, wiry little Ur Nazimites whose cargo of dyed woolens and soft leather boots, hats, and gloves represented every groat they had. They would join us in the rearmost vehicle, whose canvas covering was rigged so that a hard tug on a rope-and-pulley arrangement would suddenly lift the cloth and give us a clear field to shoot into.

"You approve?" Bernaglio asked me.

"The trick," I said, "will be in the timing. We want them close enough to do them damage, but not so close that we can't get off a second volley."

"That depends on the man in charge keeping a cool head," he said.

"So it does." I couldn't remember having done anything like this before, but somehow I wasn't unduly concerned.

"Motion in the trees," said Besserine, the elder of the Ur Nazimite brothers. He was peering through a loophole cut in the canvas.

"What about the other side?" I asked his brother, who was looking through his own hole. I hadn't learned his name.

"Nothing," he said. "They usually attack from one side or the other."

"Right," I said and spoke through the opening at the front of the wagon to tell the driver to slow it down a little. I wanted our vehicle to be the reivers' sole focus.

The rest of the caravan pulled away.

"More movement," said the elder brother.

"Nothing," said the younger one.

"Let me see." I put an eye to each of the loopholes in turn. "Right," I said again, keeping watch on the action side. "Ready on the rope, prepare to receive on this side."

The men with bolt-throwers kneeled and cocked their weapons, each with a second missile in their off-trigger hand.

"Here they come," I said, as I saw a double line of men — between fifteen and twenty of them — come out of the trees. They ran bent over, long knives, swords, and spears in their hands. One big one carried a heavy cudgel.

The men in the wagon shifted. "Wait for it," I said.

A shout came from somewhere up the line of wagons and I heard the crack of whips and the voices of muleteers urging their animals to make speed. The driver of our wagon made a show of doing likewise, but still we fell farther behind.

"Ready on the rope," I said.

"Just tell me when," said Besserine. He sounded calm enough.

"Still nothing this side," said his brother.

"Steady," I said. "Almost there."

The bandits were not crouch-running anymore. They came on fast, and I heard an ululating sound from several of them, an eerie wail they surely intended to unsettle the driver and make him jump down and run to catch up with the departing caravan.

They were close, then closer, then...

"Pull!"

The pulley worked well. The wagon's canvas top lifted smoothly and suddenly there was a rising gap between the sides and the cloth. The spoliators kept on coming.

"Take time to aim," I said. "Ready! Loose!"

The driver had dropped his reins and picked up his own thrower. He shot with the rest of us, and eight missiles went thrumming across the cleared ground. Seven of them hit flesh, mostly in the first line of attackers. I heard screams and a groan.

"Reload! Hit 'em again!" I called, even as I yanked back the action of my thrower, set the dart in its slot, and let fly.

But the targets were crouching now and some in the second line had turned to flee. I caught one of these, the dart piercing the left side of his back below the shoulder blade.

"Swords!" I shouted. "At them!"

I vaulted over the side of the wagon, drew the sword Bernaglio had given me, and charged. They were all running away now. Besserine had taken up a light javelin. He threw it and hit one of the runners in the back of his thigh. The man went down and before he could pull the point free, the other Ur Nazimite was upon him. A quick motion of a curved dagger and the reiver's throat was cut.

One of the pursued was an older man, his hair a mass of gray bound up in a filthy ribbon. I caught him before he could make it to the trees and slid the point of my sword into his lower back. He screamed and I twisted the blade and thrust it higher. He fell forward, hands spasming at the grass, his weight pulling him free of my weapon. I put the point on the nape of his neck and pushed it home. He stopped moving.

None of the guards had been unwise enough to go into the trees. I turned back to survey the fallen ambushers and was in time to see Besserine's brother finishing off the last of the wounded. All of the men I had commanded were unhurt, though the wagon driver was shaking with after-action tremors. Abruptly, he bent over and spewed out the contents of his stomach.

I had seen that before, somewhere, though the memory would not come. But that realization made me take stock of my own state of mind. I found myself untroubled by what I had done. *I've done this before,* I thought.

We had killed ten of them. One or two more might have got away with light wounds. We searched the bodies for valuables, and that too struck me as nothing out of the ordinary. The older man I had killed had a pouch at his waist with some gold and silver coins, and he had worn an arm ring of heavy silver set with garnets. None of the others had carried as much and I thought he might have been the leader.

I told the guards they were entitled to keep what they found. I gave the arm ring to the driver — it was probably worth a month's wages to him — and said, "You did well. Don't let it bother you. The man you killed would have cut your throat and smiled."

He wiped the traces of vomit from his lips and tried a smile of his own. I'd seen that look before, too.

«»

If there were other gangs operating in our vicinity, they didn't try their luck with us on the rest of the journey to Exley. *Word might have spread*, I thought.

Four days after the fight we came down onto the flat land of a wide valley and saw the walls and towers of the river town in the distance. Before evening, the wagons were in the yard of a walled compound not far from the docks, Bernaglio supervising as his goods were unloaded and carried into a pair of large warehouses. The mules were herded into a corral on a piece of open ground next door, the drivers rewarding them with rubdowns and grain. A wheelwright and a blacksmith began looking over the rolling stock.

It was a well-organized operation, I thought, which argued for Nulf Bernaglio's intelligence and experience. So I wasn't surprised when, after paying off the guards, he called me over and said, "The journey is over. I have no more need of you."

He handed me a purse that was heavier than the one I'd lifted from the bandit chief. "I'll be on my way, then," I said.

"Have you anywhere to go?" he said.

I shrugged. "No."

"Then come have dinner with me. I will introduce you to someone who can offer you work."

"Killing work?" I said. Some part of me felt a twinge of resistance. It had not bothered me to kill the robbers; it had had to be done, and they would have killed me. Still, the thought of deliberately putting myself in harm's way again did not appeal.

But Bernaglio said, "I shouldn't think so. More the kind of work done by someone who can manage men and knows something of the ways of the world." He smiled and added, "Even if he can't remember where he learned it."

And so I accompanied Bernaglio to his house in a tree-shaded quarter near the civic basilica, where the leading citizens of Exley met to decide how the city would be run. He had his servants show me to a suite of rooms and bring hot water for a bath. When I was clean again, a soft-handed servitor trimmed my beard and nails, while another laid out an array of fresh garments and a pair of boots of supple leather.

Beside the feather bed was a strongbox built into the wall and hidden behind a decorative panel. Bernaglio's majordomo, Izmah, a sharp-eyed man with precise gestures, showed me how to lock away my valuables and handed me the key.

"The staff are not to be trusted?" I said.

"The servants are well-paid and well-trained," he said, "but it is never wise to leave the thieves guild of Exley out of one's calculations."

I rested until the sun had gone down and a mellow gong sounded. A servant came to lead me down to supper, the merchant's manse having enough rooms and hallways to lead a stranger astray. I was brought to an airy room overlooking a perfumed garden where Bernaglio waited for me, along with a mature woman of strong character he introduced as his spouse, Philaria, and a short and sturdy-looking man who was the wife's brother, Vosko.

As was traditional in Exley, the conversation over dinner was confined to the food and the setting, both of which were exceptional. It occurred to me that my knowledge of the local customs probably meant that I had been here before. Perhaps there was someone in the town who could tell me who I was.

I wished to tell this to my host but had to wait until the last course had been praised and consumed, and the servants had whisked the dishes away and lit the lamps. Bernaglio suggested we repair to the garden to take glasses of fironche, the local liquor distilled from a plant that grew only in the valley. There was an item of business he wished to discuss. Philaria declared her lack of interest in such matters and withdrew. By the time we were settled on padded, cast-iron chairs among the blossoms, we could hear the mellow chimes of a harpsichont.

I knew the peppery taste of fironche, though no specific memory accompanied the familiarity. I said as much to the merchant, adding my thought that someone in the town might know me.

He waved away the subject and said, "I wished to discuss with you not your past, but your future."

"It seems as blank to me as the empty years behind me."

"Yet you must do something," he said, "unless it turns out you have a fortune somewhere. Although it would do you no good if you didn't know where."

"You have something in mind," I said.

He did. And that was why he had invited his found-brother, as brothers-in-law were known as in Exley. Vosko, it turned out, captained a packet boat owned by Bernaglio, that regularly plied the river between Exley and Vanderoy. Besides goods, it carried passengers, many of whom indulged in games of brag, follow-the-fox, and panacho, sometimes for high stakes.

"The pots are large, and that draws gamblers, some of whom are less than honest. The money also attracts an element who are prepared to separate the unwary from their funds by more direct methods," Bernaglio said. "The situation cries out for a man of resource and accomplishment."

"A watchdog," I said.

The merchant nodded. "Who bites."

"You think there is someone who needs biting?"

"I have a suspicion. I need a clear-eyed man to take a look and tell me if my mistrust is justified."

Vosko had said nothing. I glanced his way and saw him quickly raise his glass to his lips. But on his face I had caught the tail end of an expression that had formed while his found-brother was speaking and Vosko was unobserved.

He does not favor the idea, I thought. That did not bother me. Apparently, I was not the kind who let others' judgments determine how I conducted myself.

Bernaglio saw the direction of my gaze. He said, "My found-brother asked the first mate to keep an eye on the gambling room. She discovered nothing actionable."

Vosko kept his head down. "None of the gamblers profited unduly," he said. "When there is a big winner, it's always some passenger."

"There is another consideration," Bernaglio said. In a few months, Exley would conduct its ratherings, the process by which the town decided which of its leading citizens would be named to the Council of Oligarchs.

"My name has been put forward and it was met with favor by some of the senior councilors. But the sons of two of them, traveling down to Vanderoy on my boat, have lately suffered heavy losses playing brag. Opponents of my election to the Council have spread rumors that I was complicit in the fleecing."

I looked again at Vosko. His shoulders lifted and fell while he kept his gaze on his glass.

The conversation lapsed while I thought about what I had heard. Finally, I said, "What would such a position pay?"

Bernaglio mentioned a number. I suggested a different one. A discussion ensued, in which it was established that I would have my own cabin on the boat as well as free meals from the commissary and a reasonable number of drinks at the bar. Finally, we settled on a figure for my remuneration and performed the mutual gestures that pledged our honors to the agreement.

Bernaglio displayed satisfaction. Vosko's face was a careful mask of disinterest. The merchant now said, "My found-brother and I have some other matters to discuss that would bore you."

I rose and said, "Would your lady mind if I listened to her playing? I like the music."

"Do you recognize it?"

"What she is playing now is the chorus from Urdefoll's *Farouche*," I said. "Before that, there was an air from Chao-Zin's *A Gentleman of Om*."

Bernaglio's brows rose. "Whoever you are, you have had some education. Who wrote *Principles of Applied Metaphysics*?"

"Bistrum," I said, without thinking.

"Just so. If you wish to consult a therapeutic practitioner, I can make an introduction."

I thanked him and said I would consider it. I had been finding that I did not much mind having no past. My thoughts about my condition did not trouble me, which in itself was something to think about.

I left the two of them and went back up to the house, then allowed my ears to lead me to the salon where Philaria was playing. She caught sight of my entrance by way of a mirror behind the harpsichont and nodded her acceptance. I sat on a chair at the side of the room and listened. She had a sensitive touch on the instrument and could infuse the music with delicate emotion.

When she lifted her fingers from the last notes of the final arpeggio, I applauded. She turned to me and said, "Is it true that you do not know who you are or where you come from?"

"Yes, though your husband says my accent has traces of Old Almery."

"Do you feel an affiliation for that county?"

"No, nor for anywhere else."

"Some might count that an affliction, others a blessing."

I smiled. "To me, it is neither. It is just a lack."

"If you wish to investigate, I can recommend a firm of inquiry agents. Chadroyds, they're called. In the Biswant Building."

"Thank you. I'll consider it."

She turned back to the harpsichont. "What would you like to hear?"

"A rondelo," I said. "Or anything sprightly."

"Fair enough," she said, and launched into a lively air that I immediately recognized. I tapped my foot to its rhythm.

When she finished, she rose from the bench and said, "That will do, I think." She looked at me closely and added, "Did my husband persuade you to go to work on his boat?"

"I needed no persuasion. It sounds like interesting work, and I must do something to support myself."

"You've had enough of slaughtering reivers?"

"I think I have. Card cheats and purse snatchers won't need such harsh treatment."

I saw amusement in her face. Then she turned serious. "My brother," she said, then seemed to be uncertain how to continue.

I said, "He showed no enthusiasm for the thought of my coming aboard his boat."

"It is not his boat," she said. "You might have to remind him of that."

"Ah," I said and left a silence she was invited to fill.

Finally, she said, "I hope you can do so… gently."

"Harshness is not my first recourse," I said.

That appeared to satisfy her. She bid me good night and left the salon. A moment later, while I was mulling what she had said, as well as my own impression of Vosko, a servant came to see me to my room.

I slept well and without dreams. In the morning, I dressed in the clothes I had traveled in, now cleaned and pressed by Bernaglio's servants. The majordomo brought me a ditty bag with changes of garments and a few other necessities. I breakfasted in my room, then a footman came to guide me to the packet boat's berth on the docks. Partway there, I discovered that I already knew the way. I gave the servant a coin and sent him back.

«»

The boat's name, in blue paint on her transom, was the *Regal Swan*. She was broad-beamed with several decks, each smaller than the one below. When I arrived, stevedores were loading her with general cargo: crates and bales and barrels, as well as the trunks of the more affluent passengers. A board affixed to a post on the dock said that she was bound for Vanderoy with stops in between and would depart that evening. Would-be passengers were directed to the office of the wharfinger, where tickets for first- and second-class passage could be purchased. There was also a lower rate for on-deck passage, though those passengers must carry their own luggage with them.

A gangplank led from the dock to the lower deck. A man stood sentry at it. As I approached, my ditty bag slung over my shoulder, I was surprised to see it was Gashtun, his eyes still shadowed from the damage I had done him. He had exchanged his helmet and leather jerkin for the short trousers and striped jersey of a riverboat man, but his truculent expression had not altered.

When I came near, he moved to block my passage. "Where do you think you're going?"

"On board."

I could see he felt he had the advantage. He spoke conclusively, "Not without a ticket."

"Does your captain tell you everything?" I said.

Gashtun, I had learned, was easily confused. He mulled my question for several heartbeats, looking, I supposed, for a trap. In the end, he was forced to say, "No."

I said, "I'm your new chief of security."

He wanted to say, "No, you're not," but it was dawning on him that I would always be one too many for him. Finally, he said, "I'll have to call Reder." I let him see a question in my face. He said, "She's the mate."

"Call her, then," I said.

"You wait here."

He turned and went up the gangplank, then aft to where a crane was lowering a net of heavy rope laden with cargo into the hold. He spoke with a lean, middle-aged woman.

Meanwhile, I ascended the gangplank and stood on the walkway where a team of polemen would later strain to move the boat along the river, helped by the mild current. I saw the woman Gashtun was talking to look at me. Her strong face grew harder. She put down onto a bollard the noteboard on which she had been tallying the cargo and came toward me.

"What do you want?" she said.

"To see my cabin," I said.

"Where's your ticket?"

I told her I was not a passenger; I was crew, hired by the owner. And that Vosko ought to have mentioned it.

"The captain slept ashore. He has sent no message." The mate turned to Gashtun. "Do you know this man?"

The guard told her about my time with the caravan. He reflexively touched his nose, which had developed a sideways bent. That caught the mate's attention. "Did you do that?" she asked me.

"Our relationship got off to an uneven start," I said.

"And you evened it?" The question came with the hint of a smile.

"It's all forgotten now," I said, looking directly at Gashtun. He looked away.

"There'll be no trouble on my boat," the mate said.

"I won't start any," I said, "but as security chief, I may have to end some."

The woman made up her mind. She named herself and said, "I'm first mate. There is no second or third. I run the crew. You'll jump when I say jump, or you'll leave the boat. Whether or not it's at the dock or out on the water."

"If I have to brace somebody," I said, "I don't want to have to come running to you for an assent. Circumstances may not allow for it."

She agreed to that. "We'll have to sort you out a cabin," she said.

I had been thinking about it and told her a berth among the second-class passengers would most likely put me among those most likely to draw my attention. "Thieves and cardshifters don't usually travel first class."

«»

After I'd stowed my few possessions in the small but clean cabin, I surveyed the boat from bow to stern. The craft had two passenger decks: the lower range encompassed the cabins, with first-class accommodations facing outward, while second class were windowless cubicles along two internal corridors; steerage passengers huddled on the bare boards behind the blunt bow and were forbidden to go anywhere else once the boat had left the dock. They were expected to relieve themselves in a bucket and toss the contents over the side.

Above the passenger deck was a refectory divided by a curtain into two sections: the front was a saloon for first-class travelers, the rear was for second-class. Both served food, ale, and strong drink, and both featured round tables and packs of cards and tokens for gaming. No one was allowed to use any other cards than what the *Swan* provided.

Aft was the cargo hatch, sealed by a canvas cover stretched taught when the boat was underway, and along the gunwales were the parallel narrow walkways along which the polemen would tread to keep the *Swan* in motion. The current was enough to move the craft downstream, but having it propelled faster than the river's mild flow allowed the captain, up in the forward wheelhouse, to steer the *Regal Swan* around sandbars, snags, and smaller craft that wandered into the main channel.

I had seen all I wanted to see, though I wanted to take a look at the refectory staff. If there was cheating going on, they could be part of it. But they wouldn't come on board until shortly before the launching.

The lock on my cabin door was rudimentary. I didn't fancy leaving my valuables here, nor wearing them in the money belt I had acquired from a vendor on my way down to the docks. I had time to fill, so I decided to seek out a branch of a fiduciary pool, open an account, and deposit unneeded funds.

Holfman Brothers was the name of a pool that had offices in Varderon Square, in a reputable part of the town. The building was clean, the guard at the door looked sober and competent, and the clients I observed going in and out showed a prosperous, respectable air. I went in and approached a counter with a sign that said *Welcome*.

A bright-eyed young woman asked how I was going, the usual informal greeting in Exley. I told her what I wanted and she produced a paper form and dipped a pen into an inkwell.

"Name?" she said.

"Ah," I said, "does it have to have a name?"

The question did not come as a complete surprise to her. "We need to identify the account holder by some signifier," she said, "but it can be anything you choose."

I remembered the piece Philaria had been playing last night. Indeed, I had been humming it as I made my way to Holfman Brothers. "Farouche," I said.

She smiled. "A romantic, are you?"

"I may be," I said.

"Farouche, it is. Address?"

"Care of the *Regal Swan*, Berth Four, River Port."

She noted that down without comment, then asked me how much I wished to deposit. I removed the money belt, counted out coins and scrip, and handed all of it to her except for a few silver and brass pieces of specie. She counted the funds herself and confirmed the amount.

Our business was done. She asked if there was anything else she could do for me. The question seemed deliberately ambiguous.

"I'm afraid the boat sails just before supper time," I said.

Her mouth formed a *too-bad* moue. "Still, it comes back again, doesn't it?"

"It does."

"Well, there you go." She smiled. It was a very warm smile.

I would have continued the conversation, but an overly plump indentor wearing a complex hat of embroidered stuff stepped up beside me and said, "There is a problem with my statement."

He brandished a piece of paper in a show of umbrage. I turned to him and said, "Wait your turn."

His face clouded and reddened as he turned to me. But when I met his gaze he decided his issue was not as pressing as he had thought. I turned back to the young woman.

"Your name?" I said.

"Amalthea."

"I'll be back," I said, and gave her a smile of my own.

I went out into Varderon Square, wondering what I might do to pass the time before I had to be back at the *Swan*. It crossed my mind that I might seek out the Biswant Building and the investigators Philaria had mentioned, but whatever memories I had of Exley did not extend to its location.

I looked about the square, now beginning to fill with persons heading for the outdoor and indoor restaurants that occupied the lower floors of most of the surrounding structures. As well, someone had set up a hustings with banners and bunting of white and purple, Exley's civic colors. A crowd was forming. I presumed it was part of the ratherings for the Council of Oligarchs.

I was hoping to see a member of the Town Watch who could give me directions. Instead, my gaze intercepted that of a man some distance away. In the midst of the crowded square, with so many people moving in so many directions, he stood out by standing stock still. More than that, he was staring at me, a look of startlement on his face. When he saw that I had seen him, the surprise became alarm. He turned away and hurried off in the opposite direction, forcing his way among the passersby.

I found myself following him even as the significance of his behavior was sinking in. He had known me, that was certain, and the knowledge had not comforted him. I needed to know why. And what he knew.

I pushed through the moving crowd, trying to keep him in view. But he wasn't very tall and he had ducked as he scuttled away, like a man who expects a blow. I found my way blocked by a knot of middle-aged women who hoved into my path and immediately stopped to discuss the merits and failings of one of the bistros across the square. One of them, a well-fleshed matron in a multiplaited hairpiece, suggested that the eatery's sauces were far too bland and pointed instead to another establishment whose spit-turned meats really sizzled.

I could not push through the women. Expressions of male privilege in Exley were often met with physical punishment, with all females within range feeling entitled to join in. But by the time I had got around the disputants, the man I was chasing had disappeared down one of the side alleys that fed into Varderon Square.

I noted my reaction: frustration, but with a tinge of relief. I went to a café, sat at a small table, and ordered a mug of punge from the young man who came to take my order. While I waited for the drink to arrive, I considered what I had learned from the almost-encounter with the startled man.

First, I was known in Exley, at least to someone. That was understandable. I knew enough of the place to argue for my having spent some time here. Second, I inspired fear in at least some who knew me. That was not unexpected either. Third, when confronted, I pushed back. So, I had never been like one of those plants that roll themselves up when touched.

A soldier, perhaps. I had handled a sword long enough to have developed callouses, now softened by time. Who else handled swords? I made a mental list: bandits, though usually badly; Town Watchmen, though their preferred weapons were the tipstaff and the slapjack; bodyguards and guardians of the elites; and, in some places, swordsters who risked their lives for fame and fortune in sand-floored stadiums.

None of those rang a chime for me. Upon reflection, I decided I had never been so brainless as to fight in the arena, Old Almery accent or not.

I finished my mug of punge, disappointed the server when he suggested various items from the restaurant's menu, and paid him. I added a small gratuity and asked if he knew the Biswant Building.

He didn't, but he had only come down to Exley from farther upriver a little while ago. "Ask a Watchman," he said. "There's usually a couple over by the clock tower."

He pointed with his chin, the way people do in the high country. As I crossed the plaza, dodging more hungry Exleyans, I wondered why I knew that about highlanders. I certainly seemed to be a well-traveled sort.

Two Watchmen sat on a low wall that enclosed another bistro, this one next to the base of the tower. They were eating meat-filled pastries and sharing a bottle of what was probably ale — they had the red faces and rounded bellies of lifelong imbibers of yeasty beverages.

They watched me approach and each glanced briefly to their sides, where their tipstaffs leaned against the wall. I put on a smile and spread my hands to show I was harmless though they continued to eye me in that evaluating way that police operatives develop early in their careers.

I asked them if they knew the way to the Biswant Building. The older of the two finished chewing what was in his mouth, took a pull from the bottle, and said, "You're new in town? Where do you hail from?"

"I came down with Master Bernaglio's last caravan," I said. "Now I'm chief of security on his packet boat, the *Regal Swan*.

The merchant's name went some way to moderating the man's suspicions, but he followed up with, "You don't look like you're from Ur Nazim. Or sound like it."

"I come from the south," I said, "but I've been traveling around." That was a guess, but I suspected it was true.

He gave me another up-and-downer, then said, "For the Biswant, you want to go up Idderlond," — he gestured to a street a couple of dozen paces away — "then turn right at the Temple of Efferion. You can't miss it. Got a red roof, lots of columns."

"The temple or the Biswant?" I said.

But he had returned to his meat and ale. I went in the direction indicated.

«»

At Chadroyds Investigations, I was ushered into a well-appointed office where a partner in the firm, Tolderman Ufretes, a small man with a fringe of white hair around a pink dome of a skull, greeted me with a politeness that verged on caution.

"You don't recognize me, do you?" I said.

"No, should I?"

I told him of my situation and the reaction of the man in the square. He nodded in understanding and led me to a set of chairs surrounding a small, round table. I declined the usual Exleyan's offer of punge or apple tea, and we got down to business.

He examined my hands, as Nulf Bernaglio had, and said he came to the same conclusions as the merchant. He asked me what skills I had discovered were mine and I told him I appeared to be more than competent in unarmed combat. He asked a few more questions, including some I found surprisingly tangential, while jotting down some observations on a pad of paper.

"A man saw you and showed fear, but the Watchmen did not arrest you," he said. "So, I conclude you are not a wanted desperado whose image adorns the walls of the Watch headquarters."

I agreed that seemed likely.

He then said, "You are acquainted with centuries-old musical compositions, and when I asked you about celebrated works of fiction and history, you knew their contents. That argues for several years of education beyond the elementary."

It had not occurred to me, but I saw he was correct.

"You also know the basics of Exley's layout and economy, but had to ask directions to this building."

"Just so," I said. "Which means?"

He said it meant I had lived here, but not later than sixteen years before, because the Biswant Building had been constructed on the site of an edifice that had been torn down. Also, the temple dedicated to Efferion was the product of a recent enthusiasm for deities imported from the Shen Ten Peninsula.

"What does that tell you?" I said.

"That you are a Southron who probably came here to study at the Comprehensive Institute, possibly as a cadet in the Faculty of Military Sciences, and departed after your matriculation. You may have gone back to your home county to pursue a soldier's career, or you may have joined one of the free companies that recruit from the Institute."

I was impressed. His theory offered promising lines of inquiry as to my identity and background. But there was a more pressing issue.

"What about my memory?" I said. "Can it be restored?"

He steepled his fingers and gave me a searching look. "That might depend on whether or not you want to know what you have forgotten."

"Why would I not?"

"Because you, yourself," he said, "may have arranged for your past to be washed away. You may have done things, and been someone, you could not bear to have done and been."

"Is that likely?"

"It is possible. I say it because when you told me about having lost your memory you displayed the affect of a man who has misplaced something trivial, rather than a man who has lost a treasure."

The possibility had not occurred to me. I had been operating under the assumption someone had inflicted amnesia upon me. Ufretes had given me something to think about.

"Here is what I suggest," he said. "I will have an artist take a likeness of you as you would have appeared twenty years ago and use it to make inquiries at the Institute. If I pick up a sense of who you might be, I will endeavor to discover the 'doing and being' that followed your matriculation. We can then discuss further steps.

"In the meantime, you have an occupation, a source of income, and a residence, of sorts. I recommend you go downstream and come back up, and then we will see what I've been able to find."

I agreed to the plan. I asked about the cost, prepared to indulge in a haggle, but Ufretes showed me a card with rates and conditions that he said were unalterable. I had enough confidence in his abilities to accept the terms. I made out a bank draft for a retainer and he sent me to an office on another floor of the Biswant, where a young woman with charcoal-stained fingers rendered a portrait of me with somewhat more hair and fewer lines to my face.

«»

I ate lunch at the same restaurant in Varderon Square, positioning myself at an outdoor table where passersby could get a good look at me and watching to see if I attracted any responses. No one paid me the slightest heed.

Two hours later, after shopping for some items I thought I would need, I was back at the *Regal Swan*'s berth. The general cargo was now loaded and the stevedores were bringing aboard the trunks and cases of the passengers. I asked Gashtun, still at the foot of the gangplank, if the refectory's crew had come aboard and he told me they were setting up for the first service.

I went to my cabin, stowed my purchases, then ascended the companionway to the upper deck. Outside the door to the first-class refectory, I heard a clatter of dishes and a musical rattle of cutlery. I slipped in and stood quietly, watching the activity. No one paid me any heed until a plump fellow who had been directing the white-jacketed staff spotted me and came bustling over, making shooing gestures.

"We are closed until—" he began.

I raised a hand and spoke over him. "Farouche," I said, "new chief of security."

He identified himself as Brode Verhessian, the maître d' of the first-class refectory. It turned out Reder had told him to expect me. He apparently resented the very thought that the *Swan* might need a watchdog. "We adhere to the highest standards," he informed me, speaking from a great height although he barely came up to my shoulder. "The very highest."

"Excellent," I said. "I will be delighted to find my skills unnecessary. Now please acquaint me with the routines."

He did so in a manner both haughty and perfunctory, which I overlooked. If he turned out to be an honest fussbudget, his attitude did not concern me. If I discovered him to be a pilferer or an abuser of the passengers, I would see that his attitude took a sharp correction.

There were two servings, the first coming immediately after the boat left the dock, the second an hour later. After the second seating, the dishes were cleared away, liquor service was added to the wine and ale that had accompanied dinner, and cards and gaming tokens were distributed.

"And who does that?" I said.

"Basteen, the barkeeper."

I looked around. "And which is he?"

Basteen was not in sight. Verhessian told me he was filling the dispensary shelves with the wine and strong drink brought on board and putting some of the vintages on ice that had been brought down from the snowheights packed in sawdust.

"I will not disturb him, then," I said, and went to look over arrangements for feeding the second-class passengers. They were much the same as for the wealthier travelers, but everything was of cheaper quality. Gambling was not encouraged, and the second-classers were offered only board games and a skittles frame for their amusement.

A whistle sounded, signaling that passengers could begin to board. I went down to the main deck and watched them come out of the wharfinger's waiting area — also divided into two sections — and climb the gangplank. Stewards directed those who had not previously traveled on the *Swan* to their cabins.

Now out of the wharfinger's office came a figure I recognized. Captain Vosko appeared, a sheaf of papers crumpled in his hand, and crossed the dock with head bent. Gashtun, at the bottom of the gangplank, stopped the upward flow of passengers so that Vosko could brusquely insert himself in the queue and come aboard.

By the time he reached the lower deck, Reder was on hand to salute him. I was standing a short distance nearby and I saw her point toward me with a flick of her chin. Vosko looked my way. I inclined my head and took a step forward, but he turned his back and went to the roped-off companionway farther forward and began to climb to the wheelhouse.

The boat's controls were housed in a glass-windowed compartment at the front of the second deck. Reder had reattached the rope that barred the companionway after she had followed Vosko up to the wheelhouse. I now moved it out of my way and climbed the several steps. At the top, I was faced with a solid wooden door. I knocked, then pulled down the handle and opened it.

Vosko was standing at a shelf that extended from the bottoms of the windows that overlooked the bow, his attention, and Reder's, on the documents he had brought aboard. When I stepped over the raised sill of the doorway, they both turned toward me.

I saw anger on the captain's face, though whether it was on my account or from whatever unhappiness might be in the papers he had been perusing, I could not tell. The mate's face was neutral but her tone was firm as she said, "No one enters here without an invitation."

"Good to know," I said. "I just wanted the captain to know that I am ready to assume my duties."

Vosko grunted and turned back to the papers. Reder nodded and said, "Dismissed."

It was only as I turned to leave that I recognized that my right hand had automatically begun to rise in a motion that would have ended in a fingertip's touch to my forehead. *Another piece of evidence to support Ufretes's theory*, I thought as I descended to the lower deck. Then my thoughts turned to the question of whether my memory loss was self-actuated. Did I feel good or bad about being a man without a past? That ought to give me a clue as to whether or not I was the author of my own erasure.

But pressing myself for an answer didn't work. The fact was, I didn't care who I had been. Sure, I would be interested to know, but I did not feel a burning need to find out.

Maybe I have always been the type who lives in the moment, I thought, *so the past and the future mean nothing to me.*

I put the matter aside. I had a job to do, and I was fairly sure I was the kind who took responsibility seriously. I continued to my cabin and lay down for a nap. The gambling would start after supper and go on into the small hours. I would need to be rested.

«»

I was awakened by a voice shouting. As I sat up, I recognized it was Reder ordering lines to be cast off. Then I heard the rattle of wooden poles against the boat's gunwales and felt the deck lean slightly as the *Regal Swan* was pushed away from the dock.

The fact that I had fallen asleep quickly and woken instantly and with a clear head was another point in favor of the argument I had been a soldier. I gave that some thought as I left my cabin and made my way to the outer deck. I leaned on the railing and watched the heavy-shouldered men on the port side of the boat as they dug their long poles into the river bottom, leaned on them, then walked forward along the sideway to keep the craft in motion.

Not far aft of where I was standing, Reder was watching the polemen too, though with a more critical eye than mine. After the men had filed forward to where a barrier separated their path from the open deck where the steerage passengers stood or sat, they lifted their poles from the water then walked aft again, only to turn around and begin the operation anew.

Reder glanced at me but said nothing. She went around the cabins to the boat's other side, to inspect the polemen on the starboard walkway, I presumed. I found the companionway leading to the upper deck and climbed. I entered the second-class passengers' refectory and gave the people inside a looking over as I passed through toward the curtain that separated the room from the first-class space.

I saw no one in second class who looked like trouble. They were mostly men, though there were some couples, and only one or two young bucks. Many were lining up to get their meals from the servers behind a long counter on one side of the room, then carrying their plates to rectangular tables where they would sit on benches rather than chairs. The mood was orderly. No one was drunk, although there were several men leaning against the bar on the other side of the refectory, mugs of ale in their hands or at their lips.

A few men were gathered around the skittles table, swinging the wooden ball on its tether to knock down the wooden pins. I saw a few coins on the lip of the table: small bets that were unlikely to lead to trouble. I pushed through the curtain and entered the first-class space.

Here the passengers were seated at the round tables, and servers were whisking plates from the swinging kitchen doors to the diners. I saw right away that this was a more refined crowd than in the other room; both Exley and the *Swan*'s downriver destination, the city of Vanderoy, had stratified social structures. The passengers here were representative of the indentor and commerciant classes, wealthy and accustomed to being served — and deferred to. I was the object of a few glances as I made my way among them; I was being evaluated by the quality and accouterments of my attire, which indeed marked me as *not one of them*.

But when I did not sit at one of the rounds but settled at a small square table at one end of the bar, I was revealed to be staff and therefore unremarkable. I looked to see, however, if I was singled out for attention by anyone — perhaps someone who had known me in my Institute days, if such had ever happened — but no one showed any interest.

I beckoned a server, asked what the menu offered, and chose a dish of fish stew and a glass of Immelstone wine. I realized as I waited for the meal to arrive that I associated Exley with good piscine cuisine — another indication I was, or once had been, familiar with the place.

The food was good, the wine properly chilled. I finished with a mug of punge and watched as the room made its transition from dining room to gambling hall. In stratified Exley and Vanderoy, gaming for money was mainly a masculine pastime, so most of the women withdrew to one end of the room and settled into plush couches and chairs in pursuit of conversation. A few sat at one round table apparently reserved for them and called for cards and tokens. They played panachio, with occasional exclamations of "Snap!" and "Point!"

The staff turned down the ambient lamps, leaving only those suspended above the tables, so that the room was now a dozen pools of light amid general gloom. Seven or eight men sat at each table and servers were carrying decks of cards and racks of colored tokens from the bar.

When one of the staff had delivered her cargo to a nearby table, I waved her over. "Take a seat," I said, indicating the chair opposite.

She was a woman in her middle years, whom I had observed carrying out her duties with a brisk efficiency that must be born of long practice. Up close, she had an intelligent cast to her features.

"We're not supposed to sit," she said, her hands on the back of the chair.

"You know who I am?"

She nodded. "Reder told us."

"Then you can sit when I ask you to. This is about work."

She made an *if you say so* face, pulled out the chair, and sat.

I asked her how long she had worked on the *Swan* and she told me eight years, two in the kitchen and six "on the floor," as she put it.

"Who are the professional gamblers?" I said.

She didn't turn to look at them but answered that there were three. "Totun Bodmir is the one with the sequined jacket. Aflan Kretch is the one with an eyepatch. And the thin man who looks like a cadaver is Chay Verhessian."

"Verhessian is the name of the maître d'," I said.

"His brother," she told me, then lowered her voice to say, "They don't get along."

"None of them use their own cards."

She confirmed that was so. "The cards are given out by Basteen, the chief barkeeper."

I glanced along the bar and saw a man with a jowly face and a saturnine expression.

"He decides who gets what?" I said.

"I suppose," she said. "I've never thought about it."

"Don't think about it now," I said. "I'm just learning the way of things."

Brode Verhessian came bustling over, lips pursed and disapproval drawing down his well plucked brows. "Gratya," he said, "you have duties."

She started to rise but I stayed her with a gesture. "She is assisting me," I said. "She has been telling me how things work here."

The maître d' gave an audible sniff and said that if I needed any information it was his place to provide it. "I am in charge here."

"And I am the owner's representative, in all aspects relating to the security of the passengers. Tell me, does Ser Bernaglio know that your brother sits over there dealing cards with professional éclat?"

Verhessian looked from me to Gratya and almost turned toward the table where his brother sat. His mouth worked for a moment, then he recovered his hauteur. "I do not know what Ser Bernaglio knows or doesn't know. But my brother is a person of proven rectitude."

"As are you, no doubt," I said. "Thank you, Gratya."

She rose and went to the bar where Basteen indicated a tray full of drinks. I saw him look my way then ask her something, to which she replied very little. She took up the tray and carried it to a table.

Verhessian was saying something that started with, "I'll have you know, ser, that—"

"I'll know what I need to know," I said. "It might take me a little while, but be assured I *will* know."

I got up and brushed past him, and went to take a look at the play around the nearest table.

«»

Midway through the evening, I had a good sense of the state of play, and the quality of the players, around the different tables. The three professionals, as could be expected, were handling the shifting odds of brag with competence and skill. Each had an appreciable stack of tokens before him, but none was "sweeping the tiles," as the expression went. Some of the gentlemen were losing heavily, partly by luck but more by poor judgment. One or two players were having a very good night and, again, their success seemed to be owed more to temperament than to chance.

And then there was the fellow at the table where the one-eyed gambler presided. I did not learn his name; the staff said they did not recall his having traveled with them before. He was nondescript: slight of build, sandy-haired, without a single prominent feature to his face. In a crowd, an observer's eye would pass over him without a pause.

He played without excitement, no slapping down of cards or exaggerated gestures. He placed his cards down without fanfare and pulled the tokens he won toward him without chortling. And yet, standing behind him and observing his play, I saw no evidence of the guile and counterfeit that are an essential part of brag. The man just received good cards, not on every hand, but more — and far from marginally more — than the odds should have delivered to him. And he played them nearly perfectly.

I took a close interest in the hands of Aflan Kretch, the eyepatched professional at the table. He had an impassive face, its most distinguishing feature a scar that ran vertically through one eyebrow and down onto the cheek, which explained the patch that covered the eye. If he was manipulating the cards to feed the bland player, my two eyes were not capable of spotting the sleights. But it struck me that he might have been signaling by the way he rearranged the fan of cards in his hand, the way he touched his scarred eyebrow, the way he thumbed the little tuft of beard just below his lower lip.

Or it could have been my imagination leading me astray. I didn't know myself well enough to judge if I was that type.

I went over to the bar, where Basteen was pouring drinks for a waiting server. He gave me a sideways glance and his lip briefly curved in a sneer, but I noticed the hand that held the bottle shook a little.

"Do I make you nervous?" I said.

"No." He did not look in my direction but used a bar cloth to mop up some liquor that he had spilled.

"Where do you keep the cards and tokens when they're not in use?"

His eyes slid my way then back to his work. "Under the bar. There's a box."

It occurred to me that somewhere I must have learned the techniques of interrogation, because I knew that now — while he was nervous and expecting a follow up about the box — it was time to take a new tack.

"The man at Kretch's table," I said, "the one who's winning a lot, do you know him?"

"No," Basteen said.

"How do you know which one I mean? You didn't even look."

"One of the servers told me."

"Which one?"

"I don't remember."

"Give me a deck of cards," I said.

"Why?"

"Because I said so."

He reached under the counter and came up with a cardboard case containing a deck of sixty-four. Its seal was unbroken. I slit the cover with my thumbnail and shook out the cards. They were the kind with a geometric pattern on the back, alternating diamonds of red and black. I studied a few of the face cards, noting the colors and poses of the upper and lower arcana figures, miniature works of art in an archaic style.

I slid the cards back into their case and went over to the table where Aflan Kretch was just reassembling the deck for another deal. I reached down and took the cards from him.

"Use these," I said, offering him the new deck.

He said nothing but gave me a look that said my interference was not welcome.

One of the other men at the table, a double-chinned indentor with a modest supply of tokens in front of him, said, "What's going on?"

"New policy," I said. "The house switches decks randomly."

He didn't like it but I met his stare and let him see that my decision was final. He dropped his gaze and fell to rearranging his stacks of tokens. I put the cards in my pocket and walked away. I had noticed that the man who had been winning so much had said nothing and kept his gaze on his hands while I had been hovering over his table.

I returned to my seat at the end of the bar and fanned the cards out on the table. I saw nothing unusual about them: no marks on the diamond patterns, no nicks or bends on the edges, no stains or smudges. I could not have told them from the deck I had changed them for.

Magic? I wondered, but discounted the notion immediately. Among this many wealthy Exleyans there would surely be a few who carried the kind of telltale that Nulf Bernaglio had used on me when first we met. And what the wizards' Guild would do to a nonpractitioner caught using magic for nefarious ends didn't bear thinking about.

I wondered if Tolderman Ufretes might have equipment that could detect hidden markings. Probably, but that would not help me here and now.

I put the cards in my pocket and stood. The air in the saloon was becoming stifling. I crossed to a side door that led out to the deck for some fresh air. There was a wide promenade on this deck with a railing, faintly lit by lamplight from the refectory that filtered through the slats of the closed shutters. I leaned on it and looked down at the ten polemen of the starboard walkway as they completed their tireless journey forward and turned to go back to the starting point.

Then I lifted my head to look out at the dark shore of the river, a fair distance away from here. The lights of a village glowed downstream, but the stretch of river we were on now flowed past fields and forest, all black except for the faint gray of starlight.

I heard a slight sound behind me and the hairs on the back of my neck rose even before I had properly registered the noise. I straightened up and began to turn, but a brilliant flash of light — yellow, shot through with red — filled my field of vision. It took a moment for the initial shock to fade and for the pain to begin, and my knees had already struck the wood of the deck before I knew I had been hit hard on the back of my skull.

I reached for the railing to help myself rise. A second blow followed the first, but this one was more of a glancing strike. I shook my head and levered myself up. The pain was serious now and colored lights were still dancing in my field of vision.

Two figures were struggling before me. They both wore dark clothing and in the dimness of the poorly lit deck, and with the visual effects of the two blows hampering my vision, I could barely make them out. I heard a grunt and a gasp, then the two separated. Something heavy clattered on the deck. Then one of the combatants fell down, while the other sprinted toward the bow of the *Swan* and vaulted over the forward railing, landing with a thud on the roof of the wheelhouse which fronted the second deck.

A moment later, I heard a splash and shouts from the polemen, "Man overboard!"

The one who had gone down was rising. I reached into the rear pocket of my trousers for the slapjack I had bought before coming aboard and slipped its thong over my wrist. I was not in good shape to take on an assailant who was armed with a cudgel or iron bar, but the slapjack would help even the odds.

But the figure did not come at me. Instead, I heard a voice say, "Are you all right?"

"I will be," I said. "What happened?"

"You were hit on the head."

"That much I've worked out for myself. By whom? And who are you?"

New voices had joined the immediate soundscape. Captain Vosko had come out of the wheelhouse and was calling to the polemen, asking where was the man overboard. And Reder the mate was down on the walkway now, holding a lantern on a pole out over the water.

Then I heard her say, "Never mind. He's swimming for the shore."

"One of ours?" Vosko said.

"I don't think so."

"Do a head count of the passengers and check against the manifest," the captain said.

Reder gave him an "Aye, Captain," pulled in the light, and extinguished it. I heard Vosko swearing as he reentered the wheelhouse and slammed the door.

The person in front of me said, "We should see to your head. You might need stitches."

I reached and felt, found a painful bump but only a smear of blood. "It's not so bad. The second blow hardly touched me."

"Sorry I couldn't have stopped the first. He was fast. So am I, but I was not close enough."

My head was clearing a little, the ache receding. I said, "Did you get a good look at him?"

"Oh, yes."

"Was he the sandy-haired fellow playing at the table with the man with the eyepatch?"

There was enough light from between the slats of the shutters to see an expression of amusement. "No, he came aboard on a second-class ticket. Same as me."

"What's so funny?"

The face got serious again. "I think we should go down to your cabin and have a conversation where we're not likely to be overheard."

"By whom?" I said.

My rescuer's hand pointed down. I looked over the railing and saw Reder standing on the polemen's walkway, looking up. Her expression was that of a ship's officer far from pleased with how the business of managing the vessel was being run.

She called up to me, "Did you have anything to do with the man who jumped overboard?"

"Not me," I said. It was technically true, although he'd certainly had something to do with me.

"Huh," said Reder. The polemen were coming forward and she was in their way. She disappeared from view.

"Come on," I said, and headed for the companionway down to the second deck. There were more lights here, since some of the first-class cabins had their shutters open to let in the evening air. I made my way to my cabin and unlocked the door. The slapjack still dangling from my wrist rapped against the wood as I turned the key in the lock.

"You won't need that," my rescuer said.

I turned and got a good look at him in the lamplight of the corridor. Or was it a her? I saw a slight though well-knit person in shapeless clothing, with close-cropped hair and a face that gave away little information about what was going on behind it.

"Come on in," I said, opening the door. I slipped off the slapjack and put it back in my pocket.

He, or she, entered, closed the door, and took a quick look around the small space. There was a bunk and a table and chair the right size for one. I sat on the bunk and waved an invitation to take the chair.

"Who are you?" I said. "And who hit me on the head?"

"You don't need to know my name. I do contract work for Chadroyds."

"Ah," I said.

"Ser Ufretes called me after he met with you. It occurred to him that though you had lost sight of the man who recognized you, the... failing might not have been mutual. He assigned me to wait until you'd had your likeness taken then follow you."

"To see if anyone else did so," I said.

"Partly. Also, to see if the tale you'd told had been the truth. I was able to confirm that you are the security officer of this boat."

"Ser Ufretes did not take me at face value."

A shrug. "He'd be a poor inquiry agent if he did."

My estimation of Ufretes was rising. I said, "So who was it who attacked me?"

"We don't know, at least not yet. He was waiting across the street from Chadroyds and followed you down to the dock. He bought a second-class ticket, came aboard, then went up to wait for an opportunity."

"To kill me."

"Most likely. If he'd wanted to capture you, he would have attacked you down here, where he had a cabin to confine you in."

"Do you know which cabin?" I said.

"I do."

I got up. "Let's go."

It was in the same corridor as mine, a couple of doors down. I tried the handle and found it locked. "Reder will have a key," I said.

"Let's leave her out of this." The Chadroyds operative bent to the lock and did something I could not see. I heard a *click* and the door opened. We stepped inside and closed it.

The cabin was identical to my own. I looked in the small cupboard while my rescuer looked under the bunk.

"Nothing," I said.

"Same here."

We took the same positions as in my cabin. "What else do you know?" I said.

"Nothing, for certain. By reasonable conjecture, I would say the person had some skill in following people, at least those who do not suspect they are being followed."

I made a noise indicative of someone who realizes he has been careless.

"On the other hand," the operative said, "he was not part of a planned operation. I suspect he was the first person who could be put on the job and he didn't have time to equip himself with the right… tools."

"What did he hit me with?"

"A pry bar used to open crates. He picked it up from a locker on the lower deck."

I thought about it a moment, then said, "So whoever saw and recognized me sent this fellow to deal with me, but it was all on the fly. No time to organize a proper job."

"That's a reasonable assumption. It does argue for you facing some kind of organization, though. Most people don't have even one person they can send out to kill somebody on short notice."

"A criminal organization," I said.

"Or political," was the response. "Exley has factions among the powerful families. They sometimes settle their disputes in a direct and forceful manner. And then there are the more militant cults. They've been known to—"

The cabin door opened and Reder stood there, some papers on a clipboard in her hand. A couple of large crewmen were behind her in the corridor. She looked at the two of us. Her face went from surprise to anger.

"What the—" she said.

"It's all right," I said. "But I think it's time you and I had a talk."

The mate said nothing for a long pause and I could see I was being weighed up again. "What happened up above?" she said. "And I want the truth this time or you're going over the side."

"A man tried to kill me," I said. I bent and showed her the blood on my head. "This... person intervened. The attacker jumped overboard. This was his cabin."

Reder turned to study the Chadroyds operative, who returned a bland gaze. After a moment, she dismissed the two crewmen and stepped into the cabin. She closed the door.

"All right," she said, "let's have it."

«»

Some time later, we returned to the gambling room. The air smelled of sweat and liquor. Play at most of the tables had stopped so that the passengers could gather around Kretch's table, where the sandy-haired player had amassed a huge abundance of tokens. I saw wallets and purses on the table, indicating that the other players had had to resort to purchasing more tokens from Basteen the barkeeper to stay in the game.

I watched for a couple of hands, paying particular attention to the professional and the way his uncovered eye moved as he shuffled and dealt the cards. One of the other players won a small pot, then the bland-faced fellow won a big one. Kretch gathered the cards and fitted them together, then shuffled them several times.

As he was about to deal, I stepped behind him and slipped a finger under the cord that held his patch and lifted it off his head. I looked to Reder, who was standing opposite and observing. She nodded.

Kretch had dropped the cards and put his hand to his eye, but it was too late. I put the patch to my own eye and looked through it to the cards on the table. I saw patterns that had not been visible before. I supposed it was easy for the gambler to read the code and know each card's value.

I bent down and spoke softly in his ear. "You will come quietly with me. If you don't, I will reveal the fraud and let them beat you to death."

Silently, he stood. I beckoned to the sandy-haired man to follow us. I saw him look about as if he thought there might be some way to escape, then surrender to the reality of his situation as Reder put a hand on his shoulder.

I steered them both toward the door to the deck, leaving Reder to answer the growing chorus of exclamations and questions that rose as the other passengers got over the initial shock. The Chadroyds operative came with us.

We went down to Kretch's cabin, which was second-class but roomier than mine. I sat the captives down on the bunk. The Chadroyds agent and I stood so as to block the routes to the door and window. I took out the slapjack and slipped the loop over my wrist.

Kretch looked down at his hands. The sandy-haired man went pale and started to say something.

"Shut up," I said.

We waited in silence. After a while, the door opened and Basteen the barkeeper was thrust into the room by the two big crewmen who had attended Reder before. She came in after and shut the door.

I gestured with the slapjack for Basteen to join the two on the bunk. I looked at each of them in turn and said, "The one who talks first gets the least pain."

The bland-faced man said he didn't know anything except that Kretch had hired him to do a job. "I was going to get a tenth of what I won," he said. "That's all."

"Shut up," I said again.

Kretch continued to keep his gaze down. I turned to Basteen. "You know what I want to know," I said. "Tell me and you won't lose anything except your job."

"It wasn't my idea," he said.

"I know," I said. "But I want to hear you say it."

«»

Nulf Bernaglio received us in his office instead of his home. I made my report and he listened without comment until I had finished. Then he asked, "And where are they now?"

I told him we had handed Vosko and Kretch over to the wharfinger when the *Regal Swan* returned to Exley. We had let Basteen and the accomplice off at Vanderoy, but had informed the city's Watch as to what they had been up to. The offenses had taken place outside the Duke of Vanderoy's jurisdiction, but the Watch would make sure the pair did not remain in the city for any longer than it would take them to find a road out.

Bernaglio looked at Reder. "Can you captain her?" he said.

"I can."

"Then she's yours."

He turned back to me. "A man of resource and accomplishment," he said.

I smiled. "And with that compliment, I believe my employment ends."

"There will be a bonus," he said. "And I will be taking a caravan up to Ur Nazim in a couple of months. You can be in charge of the guards."

"I may take you up on that. If I'm still here."

His brows rose. "You have plans?"

"I'm going to see if I can find out who I am. It is probably necessary to prevent another attempt on my life."

"Chadroyds?"

"Yes. They seem to possess resource and accomplishment, too."

"Have them send the account to my steward," Bernaglio said.

"Good of you," I said.

"I see keeping you alive as a good investment."

I left him and Reder to discuss the terms of her new employment. My wallet contained a bank draft that would keep me solvent for months. When I stepped out onto the street, the Chadroyds agent was waiting for me.

I said, "If we're going to be working together, I'll need a name to call you by."

"You're going by Farouche, I hear."

"Uh-huh."

"Then I'll have to be Goladry." In the Farouche legend, Goladry had been the wanderer's guileless, innocent squire.

"So, I'll be referring to you as 'he' and 'him'?"

The wiry shoulders rose and fell. "Whatever you like," 'he' said. Then his tone turned business-like. "Mr. Ufretes wants to see you."

«»

Ufretes tapped a paper on his desk. "We have had some results from questioning those who attended the Institute twenty years ago."

I felt a slight shiver of anticipation. "What do they say?"

"That your surname is Minderlanz."

I waited for more, but nothing came. The name he had given was meaningless to me. It fell into the dark well of my memory without a sound, without a ripple. "And my first name?"

"That's where we have a wrinkle," he said. He picked up the paper, glanced at it and said, "It appears there were two of you, brothers — perhaps twins, even — as you are remembered as very much alike. The names were Etzel and Kain."

Again, the names were just sounds. They stirred no associations. I realized that Ufretes was watching me, looking for a response. I shook my head at him and said, "Nothing."

He made a wordless sound and continued to read from the paper, "You were both outstanding cadets. A fellow student who is now an instructor at the Institute said you were expected to have brilliant careers."

"And is there any indication we fulfilled that expectation?"

Now it was the agent's turn to shake his head. "You left the Institute at the time of the conflict known as the Clash of the Seven Cities. Do you remember that?"

"No."

"Interesting," he said and paused briefly to follow some thought he did not voice. Now he said, "It was a complex situation, a matter of shifting alliances, sudden reversals of allegiance, back stabbings and betrayals, even. Several Free Companies were involved, as well as civic militias. Lots of marching and countermarching, maneuvering on maps. You remember nothing of it?"

"Nothing."

"The Free Companies were recruiting busily. The instructor at the Institute thinks he remembers that Etzel and Kain Minderlanz signed on."

"Does he know which one?"

"No." He put down the paper, picked up another. "We have one other lead. The Minderlanzes lived in a rented house with a number of other students. Ownership of the property has changed hands since then. We are seeking to trace the person who rented the space, to see if they can tell us anything."

I nodded. "So," I said, "I appear to be either Etzel or Kain Minderlanz, a former mercenary with a talent for military science. It fits what I know about myself."

He said there was plenty more to look into. Most of the Free Companies had disbanded after the Peace of Illaran was signed. Officers and troopers found other employment: some in police work, some in what Ufretes called "the opposite of police work."

I thought about the reivers we had killed on the caravan road. It was conceivable I had once fought against some of them in a war of maneuvers. Or led them into battle.

"Do you think you might have been one of the darker sort?" Ufretes asked.

It was a fair question. I weighed it then said, "I don't think so. I seem to have a dislike for those who prey upon their fellows."

He looked at me again. I couldn't tell what he was thinking. He would be a good brag player. After a while, he said, "There is another avenue of approach. The direct route."

My face said I did not know what that route was but I would be willing to hear about it.

"We have ruled out magic as a cause of your amnesia," he said. "Also, you showed no evidence of head injury when you found yourself walking along the caravan road. That leaves open the possibility of some kind of traumatic psychic shock or the application of suggestion while under deep trance."

"Do you believe in trancing?" I said.

He rapped the wood of his desk and said, "As much as I believe in the existence of this object. That is because I have seen trancing work some quite remarkable effects." He was watching me again. "You are skeptical?" he said.

"Would that be a sign of something?"

"Well," he said, "if someone used the technique to remove your memories, it would be sensible of them to plant in you a strong disbelief in the process. That would keep you from seeking out a trancer to undo the effect."

"Hmm," I said. I thought about what I knew about the recondite art and found that it was not very much. "I don't seem to have any strong feelings on the matter, one way or the other."

"Good," he said, "then you won't mind visiting a practitioner."

"Not at all."

"I'll arrange it. Would tomorrow suit you?"

I said it would and we left it at that. Outside the Biswant Building, the person who called himself Goladry fell in beside me.

"Any lurkers?" I said.

"If there are, they're very good at it."

I had found lodgings not far from Chadroyds, in a boarding house Ufretes recommended. It had stout walls, iron shutters, and strong locks. The landlord was a former Town Watch commander who kept a practiced eye on the street outside.

Goladry walked me there. No one took exceptional notice of us. Along the way, I asked him if my assailant from the *Swan* had showed up.

"Not that we know," he said. "But, then, we didn't get a good look at him and the name he put on the passenger manifest was false."

"It would be useful to talk to him," I said.

"Very," he agreed, "but I doubt we'll have the opportunity."

He said he would return to accompany me to the trancer tomorrow and we parted. I went up to my room and lay on my bed. I tried again the names of Etzel and Kain Minderlanz, even introduced myself to the empty room using each variant, but doing so brought no sense of familiarity.

I thought of the Clash of the Seven Cities and how I knew nothing of it, although I knew about Exley and Vanderoy, and about caravans from Ur Nazim. It was clear that my memory loss was selective.

The landlord had a shelf of books in the downstairs parlor. I descended and found a history that touched upon the war and took it up to my room. Over the course of the afternoon, I learned the basics of the struggle, the names of the principal actors, the causes and the major battles. None of it lit a lamp in the darkened chambers of my mind.

If it was a psychic trauma, it was a big one, I thought. *And if it was the work of a trancer, he was good at his craft.*

I closed the book and reposed myself for a nap. Perhaps a dream would bring enlightenment.

I awoke some time later no more informed than before. But I was hungry and could smell dinner cooking. I went down to eat with my fellow boarders.

«»

The next day, Goladry came to escort me to the trancer. But I had been thinking about what such a session might entail — or more accurately, I had been *feeling* about the matter — and my feelings had become negative.

I told the operative, "I have the impression that rummaging around in people's minds can be dangerous. Demons can be called up — not real demons, you understand, but trancing can open doors that ought to be left closed."

His response was neutral. "Where do these convictions come from?" he said.

I didn't know. "I must have had some experience with the matter, I suppose."

"Well, you would have, if trancing was the cause of your memory loss. Indeed, if that were the case, there might have been implanted exactly such an aversion as you are now feeling."

I had to admit he was right. "And yet I do not think such a strong feeling should be ignored."

He smiled a little. "You think that? Or do you only *feel* it?"

We agreed that we would wait until other lines of inquiry had been exhausted. Trancing would be a last resort.

«»

Those "other lines of inquiry" were being pursued. Tolderman Ufretes maintained cordial and cooperative relationships with inquiries agents in other cities and counties. He had sent out letters to several of them asking for information about the Minderlanz brothers. While we waited for replies I met with Nulf Bernaglio to ask if there was something more I could be doing at his establishment.

"Not for the moment," he said, then I saw a thought occur. "Why don't you go down to the basilica and offer to train the Council's Watchmen bodyguards, the so-called Specials? They're not much better than Gashtun — simple brutes who lash out without science."

I took his advice and went down the street to the basilica where the Council of Oligarchs was headquartered and asked if they would be interested in giving me a contractual position to train elements of the Watch in unarmed combat.

A councillor by the name of Pavao Cornache was passing through the atrium of the basilica when I explained my proposition to the functionary who dealt with unsolicited proposals. He stopped and regarded me with the kind of smile the urban sophisticate assumes when confronted with the rustic simpleton.

"So, fellow," he said, "you think you have something to teach our Watchmen."

"Probably," I said.

Cornache beckoned to a large specimen wearing a Watchman sigil and with a truncheon at his belt, who stood ready to deny entry to any uninvited Exleyan who might seek to penetrate the inner sanctum. "Will he do?" the council man said.

"For a demonstration?"

Cornache gave an amused confirmation.

"Very well," I said. I turned to the Watchman and said, "Hit me with your truncheon."

The guardian looked to the councillor with a puzzled expression.

"Go ahead," said Cornache, "but try not to break anything."

The Watchman raised his lead-weighted club and swung a downward blow at my skull. A moment later, as he lay gasping on his back, staring up at the atrium ceiling, I reached down to help him rise.

"You'll get your breath again in a minute," I said. "Here's your truncheon back."

Cornache was now looking at me with a different expression. "Come into the office," he said.

«»

The contract was not to train the whole of the Watchman force, but to provide instruction to the special detail that guarded the members of the Council of Oligarchs and their senior staff. The Specials had been chosen more for size than natural aptitude but I did what I could with them, and all of them showed improvement.

With the permission of Cornache, whose duties included oversight of the Watch, I met with the force's mid-level leadership and from them developed a list of Watchmen who combined superior intelligence and superior physical fitness. I then included them in the training sessions for the bodyguard squad. Within a short time, I was able to put on a demonstration for the Inner Council, the new complement against the Specials. The result was a flurry of reassignments and promotions.

As it happened, a tax the Council had recently imposed on certain tradesmen — those who were not organized into guilds — led to civil unrest. A mob of artisans and their apprentices rioted outside the basilica and some of the more energetic protesters smashed a ground-floor window and stormed into the Council chamber, where the senior oligarchs were meeting to determine their strategy. The new guards I had trained dealt with the intruders efficiently and without causing deaths that might have exacerbated the public mood.

I was awarded a commendation and a bonus, with a contract to conduct refresher courses for the new Specials. By that time, Nulf Bernaglio was beginning to put together his northbound caravan, and I signed on to train and organize his guards. I was interviewing candidates at Bernaglio's warehouse when Goladry came into the office and said there was news. The day was well-advanced. I told him I would come as soon as I was finished my work.

«»

My subsequent interview with Ufretes was brief. He handed me a letter he had received from his counterparts in the Canton of Urzhendi. It was only a few paragraphs long and said that Etzel and Kain Minderlanz had been officers in separate battalions of a Free Company called the Golden Lions that had been raised in Exley, drawing mostly on artisans and laborers of the lower classes who faced a dearth of opportunities in the town's highly stratified social milieu. The Golden Lions comprised two regiments, each divided into two battalions. The outfit was organized by and commanded by Captain-General Tayton Ostralitz and, once the men had been trained, was hired by two of the polities allied together during the Clash of the Seven Cities.

The last paragraph said, *It is rumored that one of the brothers was a participant in the Drieff Massacre, though no official records of that lamentable incident have survived.*

I looked up from the paper and said, "What is the Drieff Massacre?"

Ufretes gazed back at me with a quizzical expression. "You don't know?"

"I have read a book that dealt with the war," I said, "but no massacre was mentioned."

"We really should get you to a trancer," he said. "If you were in Ostralitz's Golden Lions, you would not have easily forgotten the atrocity in Drieff."

I asked him to tell me about it and he showed me a look of distaste. He said, "I can give you only the barest account. It is not something decent people like to dwell upon. You would do better to consult your old classmate who now teaches at the Institute. He will know far more than I care to."

«»

Goladry accompanied me to the Institute. We arrived as classes were ending for the day and a porter told us we could find Preceptor Orce Shondiel in his lecture hall. We descended into a semi-circular space with tiers of seats to a dais where a spare and austere man of my own age was behind a podium, putting papers into a portfolio.

He glanced up at us, then his attention locked onto me as I stepped up onto the dais.

"Minderlanz?" he said.

"So it seems."

He peered at me. "It's been twenty years and more, but you could be a Minderlanz. But which one?"

"I don't know. You don't remember any scars or markings?" I showed him the scar on the web of flesh between thumb and forefinger.

He said, "Some of the Golden Lions had a lion's head tattooed there. After the massacre and the disbanding, they obliterated the mark with acid. But I don't remember whether you or your brother had one. You could both have had the tattoo."

I told him about the letter from Urzhendi. At the mention of the massacre his face grew still. "I had not heard you were involved in that," he said. He went back to packing away his papers and I sensed a chill in his attitude.

"My involvement has the status of rumor. I know nothing about the subject," I said. "I was hoping you could enlighten me."

He laughed a cold laugh and kept his gaze on what he was doing. "Enlighten? More like darken your soul. It was an evil thing, a monstrous, evil thing."

"And yet it seems to be part of the mystery in which I find myself wrapped."

He looked at me now and I saw indecision evolve into a choice made. "'Involved' can have a variety of meanings," he said. "You might have been with one of the other battalions." He finished his packing and tucked the portfolio under one arm. "Come to my office. I have something that would help."

He led us out of the lecture hall and across the green and leafy campus toward a building that housed offices. Along the way, I reflexively studied my surroundings to see if anything triggered a memory. Nothing did, although I had an odd sense that I could find my way around the Institute's campus without difficulty. Perhaps the kind of memories that beasts have about their territories remained with me, beneath human levels of understanding.

In his book-lined study, Shondiel ran a finger over the spines and drew forth a slim volume bound in simple cloth without gilding. When he handed it to me, I saw that the title was *The Shame and the Horror: The Drieff Massacre*. The author was F. Ardulon Baz.

"The initial stands for 'Frater,'" the preceptor told me. "Baz was a soldier in the Golden Lions. After the massacre, he resigned his commission and became a monast of the Elyomosnyiast Brethren."

As was becoming my habit, I held the small book and consulted my feelings about opening it. I found that I had none. Still, I did not open it.

"May I take this with me?" I asked Shondiel.

"You can keep it," he said, with the same expression of distaste Ufretes had shown. "I've learned from it all that I could expect to. And more than I would have wished to know about my fellow man."

I put the book in my pocket and thanked him for his help. When I extended my hand, he hesitated for a moment before clasping it. I did not take offense.

«»

Goladry walked with me back to the boarding house. Among the crowds of Exleyans following the custom of the pre-prandial promenade, we saw nothing along the route to cause alarm. We stopped at one point in a small park where a band was playing rousing tunes while men and women wearing ribbons of green and white handed out pamphlets supporting a slate of candidates in the ratherings. No one took an interest in me.

"It's been a while," I said, as we reached the front steps of my lodgings, "and no one has made another attempt on my life."

His mouth quirked in a way that said there could be different explanations, and he said, "True, but the first was a hurried operation, staged without time for forethought. We cannot assume that the motive for the attack, whatever it was, has evaporated. Perhaps your enemies are preparing something more organized."

It was my turn to say, "True. I will remain alert."

"It may well be," he said, "that your movements have been studied. An assault while you were surrounded by Specials was risky. But soon you will depart for the wilderness."

"Where I will be surrounded by a complement of guards I have trained to be effective."

"Indeed," Goladry said, "which is why, if I were hiring your assassin, I would be hiring one of those guards." He thought again. "Or somebody you wouldn't notice."

With that, he touched his hairline and went away.

«»

Nulf Bernaglio's compound was necessarily a secure facility, with locks and guards and some discreet magical wards. Only persons wearing talismans provided by Bernaglio could enter and leave the complex of buildings where the merchants' goods — and that of other consigners — were stored ready for transshipment to Ur Nazim and points beyond, in the northern wastes.

The goods included wines and candied fruits from farther south, dried and smoked fish from the shores of the Sundering Sea, intricate mechanical devices from Vanderoy, books from Exley's expert binderies, semi-precious stones from the mines of Platzurum, and many more. As the warehouses began to fill, the guards I had chosen and was still training moved into barracks in the compound, as did I.

Not long after I took up residence, a gate guard sent a boy to tell me that someone was asking for admission. When I went out to see, I found red-bearded Gashtun sweating in the noonday sun, his ditty bag at his feet. At my appearance, he stood to attention and announced he was reporting for duty.

"Really?" I said.

He looked surprised at my skepticism. "I have served Ser Bernaglio for many years," he said, "and my family has served his family for three generations."

I looked a question at the guard — one of those I remembered from the trip south — and he replied, "It is so. His father and mine served the Old Man before the present Ser took charge of House Bernaglio."

I asked Gashtun, "And will you be content serving under me?"

He looked me in the eye. "You cleaned up the *Swan* and sent the treacherous Vosko to walk a treadmill at the Incarcery. That stands well in my eye. I'm hoping that we can put other things behind us."

I considered him a moment, then said, "Fair enough." I sent a boy to bring a talisman and chain from the chest in my quarters and when Gashtun was admitted, I told him to get squared away then join the guards in the training arena.

Before I left the gate, I advised the guard there to be watchful for anyone who seemed to be taking an undue interest in the premises.

"I already do," he said, a tinge of resentment in his tone.

«»

Most of the new hires had done well in the training program I established for House Bernaglio. I had to discharge only two who failed to master the basics of unarmed combat. The program expanded to include not only the caravan guards but others of the establishment whose skills Nulf Bernaglio wanted enhanced. I also gave classes in spearmanship and the shooting of bolt-throwers, about which I discovered I knew some useful skills.

The day before departure, I organized a small tournament between six of my best students and a similar number of the Council of Oligarchs' Specials. The competitions were watched by a select audience of Council members and my present employer. I was glad to see my guards hold their own against the Specials in both the individual bouts and the final melee.

When the prizes had been awarded and the visitors had gone home, Nulf Bernaglio lingered and came to where I was putting the practice weaponry in the storage room. "Have you learned anything more about your past?" he asked me.

I told him about having attended the Institute and apparently serving with the Golden Lions in the Clash of the

Seven Cities. His brows rose then condensed as he took in the implications of what I was saying.

"So, you might have been in Drieff for the atrocity," he said.

I confirmed it was so. I saw something like pain cloud his expression. "I had family in Drieff," he said. "The House had a depot there."

I did not know what to say. After a moment, I said, "I am sorry."

He gazed at me for a long pause, then he said, "I'll see you tomorrow," and left.

I put the last of the soft-tipped spears back in their rack and returned to my quarters. Baz's history of the massacre was in a footlocker at the bottom of my bunk. I picked it up, carried it to the table and chair that were the room's only other furnishings, and sat down.

I held the small volume in my hand and waited to see if anything came to me out of the blankness at the back of my mind. When nothing did, I opened the book and began to read.

«»

The caravan's wagons had started being loaded at dawn. Before noon, the drivers had the mule teams hitched up. Nulf Bernaglio came down from his mansion, spoke briefly to the head teamster, nodded to me, then climbed aboard his riding horse. It was traditional for the master of House Bernaglio to lead his caravan through the city and out onto the North Road, and my employer was a staunch traditionalist.

I climbed aboard a wagon midway along the train. As we rolled through the gates, Goladry was waiting at the curb. He lightly sprang up onto the bench beside me and said, "I thought I'd come along."

"My budget for guards is all allocated," I said.

"Think of me as a supernumerary," he said. "Chadroyds is paying my salary and Ser Bernaglio is paying Chadroyds. It all comes out the same."

"Fine by me," I said. "You can be my administrative aide." He made a face at that, and I said, "There is always work for manure shovelers in the mule lines."

That drew an even sourer expression. "I would prefer to wield a pen."

"Then a pen it is."

So on we rolled through Exley's industrial area, then the suburbs, and on into the croplands. On the hills ahead, the road wound up into the forest.

"Can you shoot?" I said at some point.

"Oh, yes."

«»

Frater Baz had a colorful writing style. His descriptions of the massacre were graphic and intense in their use of detail and deliberate appeals to sentiment. I found them disturbing, as any civilized person would. As I read the account, images of horror appeared on the inner screen of my consciousness, but I could not tell if they were conjured by the monast's florid prose or by real memories seeping through the barrier that kept my past from me.

It was as that thought occurred to me that I realized I had known all along that there was a blockage of some kind in my mind. My memories were not erased; instead, they were sequestered. I was a mansion of many rooms, but living only in the barest and smallest of them, like a mad relative confined to the attic.

I returned to the Baz book. The Elyomosniast Brother provided few real details as to who had done what, and almost no names at all. The Golden Lions had definitely played a part, though the details that would have shown them to be monsters or deliverers were missing. It was all vague, except for the scenes of slaughter.

There was frequent mention of a pernicious cult who called themselves the Justified Celebrants, none of whom had survived the massacre. There were rumors and third-hand reports, all dutifully gathered by Frater Baz, but he made no attempt to sort them into categories like "reliable," "doubtful," or "ludicrous."

But he was a master of evocative imagery. Now, as Nulf Bernaglio's caravan made its way from one fortified caravanserai to another, the monstrous scenes he conjured up replayed themselves whenever my mind was not occupied in my duties. I began to regret having decided not to consult the trancer in Exley.

It was one thing not to know who I was; not knowing whether I was a monster with hands permanently stained with the blood of innocents, that was another thing altogether.

«»

"Are you ill?" Nulf Bernaglio said.

It was his daily practice to ride a saddle horse up and down the caravan for a personal inspection of the rolling stock, the draft beasts, and the personnel who tended and guarded them. I was riding on the bench seat of the wagon in which I and Goladry slept, and which carried a small arsenal of weapons and armor.

"I have not been sleeping well," I told him. I had been having nightmares that evaporated upon awakening, leaving me with vague images of horror and a persistent feeling of dread.

"I will have the orderly provide a draft," he said. "We are coming up to the more dangerous part of the passage and I need you at your full capacity."

My first instinct was to decline the offer, but I realized before I spoke that it was, in fact, an order. I was finding that I automatically deferred to Nulf Bernaglio. The habit of a soldier, trained to follow orders without hesitation, perhaps.

"Very well," I said. I could receive the medication and neglect to take it.

He did not move on, but regarded me with a questioning air. "Who is the... person who shares your wagon?" he said.

I could not avoid the question. "My bodyguard. From Chadroyds."

His brows climbed and made a series of furrows beneath his receding hairline. Then they contracted. He said, "It is becoming clear to me that there are matters concerning you that I am not aware of, even though I belatedly discover that I am paying for a bodyguard. This is to do with your amnesia?"

"It is."

"I will finish my inspection. Then you will come and see me. I want to know everything."

I nodded.

"And bring the bodyguard."

I said I would.

"Is it a him or a her?" he asked.

At that I could only shrug.

"See me," he said. He kicked his heels into the horse's flanks and rode off up the column.

«»

I had an uncomfortable interview with my employer. When I had told him what I had learned from Ufretes, Shondiel, and the Baz account of the Drieff Massacre, he was silent for a long time, though his hard stare eloquently expressed his response.

Finally, he said, "You did not think I ought to know about these things?"

I confessed the truth. "I had not — still have not — grasped the reality of it all. It seems like a dream. Or like some tale I've heard that has nothing to do with me."

He partially conceded that it might turn out to be a false lead. "You may not be the brother who presided over the atrocity," he said. "Indeed, you may not be one of the Minderlanzes at all. You may just resemble them. No one knows who you really are. Perhaps you should put it out of your mind and concentrate on the here and now."

I had been operating on the assumption that I was a Minderlanz and might have been a monster. The possibility that I was neither came to me like a small beam of light breaking into a dark and somber space. My relief must have shown in my face because Bernaglio looked satisfied. He ended our discussion by saying, "Return to your duties. I will have the orderly prepare a sleeping draft. Tomorrow, you will be right as Rudderford. And just in time for us to enter the danger zone."

I left him and went back to work. I was still tired, but it felt as if a cloud had lifted from my view of the world. The sky was bright again. I visited each of the pairs of guards in their various stations along the length of the caravan, and paid particular attention to the four who rode at the tail end.

The men were sober and their weapons and gear were in good order, their mounts well looked after. Still, I reminded them to keep their eyes open and watch for anything out of the ordinary. The stretch beyond the next caravanserai was notorious for reiver attacks — indeed, the ambush I had countered had taken place there — but some smarter than usual bandit leader might reason that an attempt where it was less expected could have a better chance of yielding loot. Some of the goods we carried were easily sold in places where buyers did not ask too many questions about origins.

Throughout all of this Goladry rode beside or sometimes behind me. He carried a loaded bolt thrower and I knew he was good with it. On our first caravanserai stop he had fastened a piece of wood no bigger than a hand against one of the stockade walls and proceeded to put three darts into it in rapid succession.

"You don't appear to aim," I said.

"Practice," he said. "Or, if you prefer a more original explanation, I become the missile and it goes where I wish to go."

"Seriously?" I said.

"If you wish. Just be assured that if I need to shoot, I will hit what I'm shooting at."

«»

That night, secure behind the gates of a caravanserai, Goladry and I ate with the guards who were scheduled for sentry duty later in the night. I was still getting to know the men as individuals. Though I had selected and trained them, I knew that a man can be one kind of person within the security of town walls, but something else when he goes out where the darts may fly at any moment.

Another indication I have been a soldier, it occurred to me. But then I thought, *There are plenty of soldiers who aren't Etzel or Kain Minderlanz.*

In a better mood than I had known lately, I climbed into my trailer, Goladry on my heels. Our two bunks were on either side of the vehicle, with a small table between them on which sat a lit oil lamp. Beside it was a glass tumbler covered with a white cloth: the sleeping draft.

I picked it up and put it to my lips but hadn't taken more than a sip before the glass was knocked from my hand. It fell to the wooden floor and broke, the brown liquid it had contained spraying beneath the table.

"What the—" I began, but stopped as I felt a numbness in my lips and tongue. I gathered spit and expectorated, then gestured to my mouth and said to Goladry, "Wadda!"

He brought me the waterskin hanging on the wall and I rinsed and spat, rinsed and spat, until the strange taste in my mouth was mostly gone.

My speaking apparatus was still affected but I told him, "I dink um ollrite."

He encouraged me to take more water and opened my eyes, holding up the lamp to see my pupils. They must have contracted in the light because he nodded and said, "A close one."

"Yaz," I said. Apparently, someone thought I was a monstrous Minderlanz and was determined to do something about it.

«»

We went looking for the orderly. He was not in the camp, though no one had seen him leave. On the other hand, the guards were watching for surreptitious approaches, not departures, and he could have slipped out during shift change.

Bernaglio said the man was not his regular medical aide. The man he usually employed had not turned up on recruiting day, but the man he hired had good credentials and answered the test questions perfectly.

"He certainly knew about poisons," Goladry said.

The merchant turned a hard eye his way, while gesturing toward me. "I did not know then what I know now," he said.

Goladry shrugged. "Life is about learning," he said, then offered a mollifying wave and departed before Bernaglio could take full umbrage.

«»

The caravan passed through the forest and climbed up to the high plateau without suffering any attacks from reiver bands.

"Perhaps the surprise we gave them last time discouraged them," I suggested to Nulf Bernaglio.

His mouth twisted in a doubtful way. "More likely the goods we are carrying up to Ur Nazim constitute less of an incentive. Illustrated books and mechanical toys are sellable but do not bring high prices, especially when the sellers have to discount them for being stolen. On the other hand, Ur Nazim's swords and daggers command high prices and prompt few questions."

We were riding side by side on the merchant's horses. He had once been in his wagon going up the incline when something had broken, separating the vehicle from its team and sending it careering backwards. Fortunately, it had crashed into the earthen bank and come to a stop instead of going the other direction and tipping over the road's edge. Ever since then, Bernaglio got into a saddle for the transition between forest and plain.

Waiting for us at the top of the winding road were thirty or so mounted riders on the shaggy, short-legged ponies that were standard transportation on the plateau. Their conical fur hats, fringed leggings, and long, supple lances identified them as members of the Azarine nation, a fiercely independent people who lived a nomadic life centered on their herds of a long-necked species of camel that gave them meat, milk, leather, and wool. For everything else they needed, they hired out as caravan guards and were paid in coin or, occasionally, a wagon that would become home to an Azarine family.

Bernaglio greeted the leader, a bandy-legged man of mature years who affected the heavily waxed and curlicued moustaches of upper class Azarines. They exchanged a complicated series of handshakes and arm grips, the Azarine standing in his stirrups while the merchant leaned down from his higher perch.

Then Bernaglio gestured for me to come forward and introduced me to Ragnath, as the man was known. Whether that was his name or title, I could not tell.

"This man joined my company when we came south from Ur Nazim," Bernaglio said, then proceeded to describe the strange circumstances of our meeting.

"He has lost his memory and does not know how he came to be on the road a day's walk from here," he continued. "I am wondering if you saw anyone in that vicinity."

Ragnath tossed his head and made a *tch* sound of teeth and tongue. Bernaglio informed me that it was the Azarine way of signaling a negative.

"But we did not go straight back up the road after seeing you to the end of the plain," Ragnath said. "We went east to visit my cousins. There was a wedding."

"Ah," said Bernaglio. "Still, I had to ask."

But the Azarine was thinking. "Some people from my wife's family were also coming to that wedding," he said. "They may have seen something. This year they are grazing their herd near Ur Nazim. When we get up there, I could send to ask."

"I would be in your debt," I said.

Ragnath shook a finger at me. "Don't say that to an Azarine. Our concepts of debt and obligation are more stringent than among you town-dwellers."

He was smiling as he said it, but I caught the seriousness behind the smile.

"Thank you for telling me that," I said.

He looked thoughtful again. "Most people who cross our plains know about our customs and take pains to avoid giving offense. We expect good manners from sojourners. Some of us can be quite harsh if our sensibilities are offended. And such offense can come all too easily."

I saw what he was getting at. "If I had encountered your troop, there might have been trouble."

"For you, yes. Some of my men are sticklers for protocol."

"I probably would have asked for water and directions."

"Probably not in the correct way," Ragnath said. "There are certain forms and procedures."

"Perhaps that was the idea behind putting me where I was put."

"Then you have an enemy."

"Of that I'm sure," I said.

He stood in the stirrups again to give me a congratulatory slap on the upper arm. "Good for you," he said. "An enemy gives shape to a life."

The first of the wagons now came up onto the plateau. We moved out of the way.

«»

The journey to Ur Nazim proved uneventful. The Azarines did not tolerate the presence on their territory of criminals, nor most other categories of intruders. The lands where Azarine law was paramount encompassed the entire high plateau from the southern forest to the Stained Desert that began a long day's ride to the north of Ur Nazim, and from Olliphract on the west to the Hills of Old Whorley to the east. Ur Nazim was tolerated as a necessary exception.

The plains were not without their dangers, however. They were the haunts of the sinewy, needle-toothed fand and the heavy-jawed woolyclaw which, though more likely to take a mule or horse for their prey, were not averse to feeding on a human corpse — nor to creating the corpse in the first instance. So, each night, the wagons were drawn into a circle and the livestock tethered to lines inside the laager. Torches were lit and kept lit, and guards armed with spears and bolt-throwers stood watch.

But the only incident came when one of the Azarine lancers spotted a pelgrane circling high in the offing, away to the northeast. We kept an eye on it, in case it diverted toward us, but after a while it showed us the bottoms of its black leather wings as it heeled over and glided out of view.

At Ur Nazim, House Bernaglio maintained a compound where, as in Exley, the wagons were unloaded, the livestock put in paddocks to rest, and the wagons were repaired and made ready for the return journey. Unlike at Exley, however, Nulf Bernaglio lived on the premises rather than in one of the grand houses on the banks of the brown river that flowed through the town.

"I will stay with the goods. Ur Nazimites have a flexible view of property," he explained to me. "Anyone who does not guard his possessions adequately is assumed to have no proper regard for them. On the other hand, an Ur Nazimite who covets another's goods can easily convince himself that a transfer of ownership is right and just."

I made sure that the guards under my command carried out their duties meticulously and we had no serious shrinkage of inventory, what Bernaglio referred to as pilferage. His House had longstanding relationships with the merchants of the town and it did not take him long to dispose of his goods at prices that satisfied him. He then began the somewhat longer process of finding merchandise to take south and dickering for the most advantageous terms. Accompanying him on some of these expeditions into the souks and markets of Ur Nazim, I sensed that he enjoyed the process immensely.

He had paid off the Azarines as soon as we entered the compound. Each lancer received a purse of silver coins. In addition each man was given a gift, above and beyond his pay. For some, it was a tasseled sash, for others an embroidered shirt or a pair of fur-lined gloves. Ragnath received a pair of thigh-high riding boots, reinforced with steel at the toes and where they would meet the stirrups of his mount.

He immediately shed his worn footgear and pulled the boots on over his leggings, then stomped around to sit them thoroughly. When he climbed into the saddle and stood, thrusting here and there with his lance, he grinned and pronounced the present as much to his liking.

He led his men out of the compound's gates and toward the marketplace where they would spend their pay on useful items and little luxuries for their wives and children. But Ragnath was back in a couple of days, calling for Bernaglio and me to come out.

"I have talked to my wife's people," he said, "about what they may have seen when your Farouche was on the road. They saw no traffic, but Midgeran swears he saw a flying contraption heading west."

"Could it have been a pelgrane?" I said.

"I do not take offense," Ragnath said, "because you could not know that Midgeran has exceptionally keen eyes. Also, he is only a cousin of a cousin of my wife, and his honor is his own affair. Even so, because you are not a bad fellow for a *shamaz*, I will not mention the matter to him."

"Thank you," I said. "Are flying contraptions common sights in these parts?"

"No. We discourage them. They frighten our animals and cause the milk to curdle."

I thanked him and asked if a gift would be appropriate for his trouble in making the inquiry and coming to tell me the news. He said it would not, and I feared I had once again trespassed on the complex views the Azarine had about themselves and the world.

But he smiled and said, "One day I may ask you for a favor."

"It would be my honor to deliver it," I said, at which he clapped me on the arm and said that I had "the makings of a fine human being."

When he had ridden off, I asked Bernaglio what a *shamaz* was. He said it was a kind of dry-country toad known for storing copious amounts of fetid liquid it would squirt when handled. "It is also the Azarine term for outlander."

«»

Later, in his office, Goladry, Bernaglio, and I discussed the import of what Ragnath's wife's cousin's cousin had reported.

"Flying," Bernaglio said, "involves magic. And not the magic of a hedge-sorcerer or some marketplace runes caster. A flying platform requires the conscription of a demon or a pair of imps. And the power to create such bondage is the province of a powerful thaumaturge."

I told him that did not come as news to me, and he agreed that it was common knowledge among educated persons. Then he reminded me that when we first met he had used a talisman that detected the presence of magic. It had indicated that I had been at least in the presence of magic.

"So that would appear to be how I came to be on the road," I said.

"And close enough to the edge of the plateau to lessen your chance of encountering feral beasts or Azarines," Goladry said.

I brought up the fact that the platform had been seen heading west. "It might be logical to assume it had come from that direction when it brought me."

Bernaglio disputed the point. But when Goladry pressed the point, the merchant went to a cupboard and brought out a map, which he unrolled onto the table where he counted coins and worked on his ledgers. Goladry put a finger on the spot where we figured I had started to follow the caravan. Then he moved that finger some distance west and tapped a representation of a walled city among some triangles that represented mountains.

"Olliphract," Bernaglio conceded. "I imagine one could find a wizard or two there."

I told him the name was a mere sound to me.

Goladry said, "That might be significant. No one who has been to Olliphract soon forgets it."

"Then perhaps I should go there," I said. Bernaglio looked at me sharply and I added, "Once we are safe back in Exley. I'll need something to keep me busy."

"Olliphract will certainly do that," Goladry said.

«»

When we set out south from Ur Nazim, a different troop of Azarine accompanied us down to the southern end of the high plateau. Ragnath's people hired out only when they needed coin, and Bernaglio's payment would keep them in salt for their meat and sugar for their tea until next year. As we descended into the forest and made our way from one fortified caravanserai to another, we kept a sharp eye on the woods. Occasionally, we saw shadows and flickers of movement, and I considered staging another invitation to assault the last pair of wagons.

But Bernaglio said it would not be necessary on this trip. He paid for intelligence regarding the shifting bands of reivers who haunted the woods and had heard that a crew had lately scored a success against a competitor's goods. The other bandit gangs now pressed in upon their newly wealthy brethren, there being no honor among their kind.

And so we came down to Exley unscathed. Bernaglio dismissed the muleteers and most of the guards, but asked me to remain in charge of the smaller number that would guard his compound until he had disposed of the wares he had brought from Ur Nazim. Having nothing more pressing to do, I accepted the extension.

My duties were light and my guards well trained. I could afford to leave the compound and go about the town on purely recreational forays. One afternoon, I returned to Holfman Brothers fiduciary pool in Varderon Square to see how my funds were coming along. I had been there on two occasions before the last caravan to the north, to deposit excess funds and advise that my address was no longer the *Regal Swan*. On neither of those visits had I seen Amalthea.

But when I passed through the doors this time, she was at her station, making notes in a ledger. She looked up as I approached and her smile brightened the room.

"How are you going?" she said.

"Well enough." I said that I had missed seeing her on my previous visits and she let me know she had been temporarily seconded to the subterranean counting room, after one of the regular tallymen had suffered an apoplexy.

"I'm glad to see you back in daylight," I said.

She gave me a direct look and said, "You should see me in evening light."

The women of Exley were known for their forthright expression of affections and their opposites. I returned her gaze and said I would be pleased to escort her to dinner and whatever entertainments Exley offered that she would enjoy.

She mentioned a restaurant across the square. It was near to a theater that was showing a play about which she had heard good reports. We quickly worked out the details as to time — she would go home after work and change into something less utilitarian — and she made clear that she would pay her own way, that being the Exleyan custom.

I agreed and handed over some funds to deposit. When that was done I said I looked forward to seeing her in a less utilitarian mode.

Goladry was waiting outside, his eyes taking in all movements about the square. I told him I had an engagement for the evening and suggested he find somewhere else to be.

He smiled and said, "How about if I just make myself less visible? I'm good at that."

"You're not going to leave me alone?"

"You are not my employer. To be rid of me you must dismiss Chadroyds."

I was not prepared to do that. I was even leaning slightly toward consulting the trancer Tolderman Ufretes had recommended. Baz's history of the Drieff Massacre had stirred a motivation in me.

"Very well," I said, "but be unobtrusive."

He lifted a hand in a gesture that suggested effortless ability.

From across the square came a blare of music as a band struck up a tune played on brass instruments and hand-held racks of silver bells. The air drew the attention of passersby to the hustings that was still standing. Exley's ratherings were nearing their climax.

It was a long and complicated process and, although it had been explained to me by several Exleyans, I had never quite grasped the intricacies. There was a Council of Oligarchs, all of them wealthy, all of them engaged in business. Aristocrats could be oligarchs, but they had to show themselves at work to drive the town's economy. Mere inherited wealth did not constitute adequate qualification.

But the Council did not appoint itself. Instead, every few years — or sooner, in the event of an emergency that created public dissatisfaction — a group known as the Electors was chosen by some method I had not ever understood.

The Electors were supposed to be anonymous, although rumors as to the identity of this one or that circulated through the populace. Then there was something called the "casting of the lots," which took place in a black pavilion erected outside the basilica, its entrance closely guarded.

When the time for the "Tenting" arrived, Exleyans assembled in the great square that surrounded the tent. Virtually every adult of the town came, some carried on their sickbeds. They engaged in a curious form of massed vocalization, a humming and rasping deep in their throats that sounded like one vast animal breathing in its sleep.

The "Sonoring," as it was known, might continue for hours, during which the Electors, who had come to the Tenting in masks and wearing long, dark robes and cowls, made their deliberations. Finally, they would emerge, and one of them would hold up a slate chalked with the names of the chosen Councilors. They would circulate among the Sonoring crowd until every Exleyan had seen the nominees.

At that point, the sound would stop. A great silence would fall upon the square. Then a new humming would arise from the throng, three notes repeated over and over. If the triplet ascended in tone, the nominees were accepted. If it descended, the Elector must return to the pavilion and deliberate again.

It seemed to me a peculiar method of establishing governance. Goladry had told me, "The triplet is always right. The proof: look at how well they are governed."

I countered with the business of the taxed artisans and the riot that my Specials had to deal with.

He waved a dismissive hand. "These things come and go. I did not say they are perfectly governed. Just well."

And I had to admit there were few disruptions in the town's daily life. People were busy at their occupations, public drunkenness was not rife, and murders were rare.

But I had noticed my bodyguard had said "they," not "we." That raised an issue that had not previously occurred to me. I said, "I'm apparently a product of Old Almery. I do not know where you hail from."

"No," he said, "you do not."

«»

My evening with Amalthea was a success. The play was a revival of a classic from an earlier artistic vogue, but the costumes and staging were contemporary. What might have caused dissonance instead prompted a consideration of how things might change yet remain the same. Also, it had some moments of ribald humor.

We had dined earlier and the meal had sat well. After the performance, we went to a drinking establishment that used high prices to winnow its clientele. The place was quiet except for some musicians softly stroking stringed instruments and a low buzz of conversation.

Amalthea and I continued a conversation that had begun over dinner, in which I told her of my odd circumstances. But I did not mention Drieff.

"It does not trouble you, not having a past?" she said, her glass poised halfway to her lips. "You may have family who are worried for you. Children, even, wondering when their father will come home."

That possibility hadn't occurred to me and she saw the realization in my face. And I could see that her perception of me was now changing.

She asked me, "Are you self-involved? Do you limit your concerns to yourself alone?"

"I don't think so. I believe in giving full measure for what I receive. I think I am honest. Recently, I came across a situation where I found that some people were using unethical means to enrich themselves. I could have profited by extorting a share of the proceeds. Instead, I handed them over to the authorities and received no more than my pay."

"Did you think about extorting them?" she said, studying my face for a response before I spoke. "Did you weigh up the gives and takes before acting?"

"No," I said. "Indeed, the possibility didn't occur to me until just now."

"Hmm," she said and took a thoughtful sip of her drink. After a moment, she said, "What are you doing to resolve the questions?"

I told her about Tolderman Ufretes and the inquiries he was making and how I was beginning to lean towards consulting a trancer. "Also," I said, "I may go to Olliphract to make inquiries."

"Olliphract?" I heard a distinct note of alarm. "That place?"

I realized I still had not the slightest impression of the city in the mountains, although people seemed to react strongly to its mention. I asked Amalthea, "Everyone appears to have a strong view of Olliphract."

"And you don't?" When I shook my head, her brows contracted and she said, "I've never known anyone who doesn't have a 'strong view' of that place. It's a den of wizards and spellcasters who care only for themselves. They are said to use people in ill ways, even to grow them in vats."

I thought about it. "I knew about Exley before I came here, and had a good idea what Ur Nazim was like. Vanderoy was not unfamiliar to me. And when I hear the names of other cities I have a sense of what they are like. But not Olliphract."

"Which everybody knows about," she said.

"Meaning whoever edited my memories put that one in the waste bin."

She was looking at me with concern again. "I think I should go home now," she said.

"I will escort you."

She agreed to that but made clear that our evening would end at her door. "You have given me a lot to think about."

"Me, too," I said. I planned to search the bookshelves at my lodgings for information on this thaumaturge-haunted city that caused the hairs on people's necks to prickle up.

We were silent for a while, each of us immersed in our thoughts. Then she said to me, "Something has been done to you, yet you do not seem offended. Are you the kind of person who takes maltreatment and philosophizes it away?"

I thought about my first encounter with Gashtun and about the fellow who attacked me on the boat. My response then had been to fight. "No," I said, "I'm not."

"Yet you are going on, day by day, not making any strong effort to find out who has done this to you and why."

The point struck home. "Perhaps whoever interfered with my memories also interfered with my will to do something about it," I said.

"If it were me," she said, clenching her fist in front of her, "I would resent that. And I would fight it."

I made up my mind. "I will consult the trancer."

She patted my arm. "Good."

Another silence ensued, but this one was more comfortable. On her doorstep, I said good night to Amalthea and received a smile and a conflicted look before she closed her door.

«»

When I opened the door to my room there were two people waiting for me. One was Goladry, bound and gagged and tied to a chair. A bruise on one temple showed a deep purple. The other was a man of indeterminate age dressed in nondescript garments, sat on my bed. If I'd had to describe him, the words "precision" and "tidy" might have come to mind.

"I mean you no harm," he said, looking up at me. I decided that "placid" might also fit his description.

"All right," I said, closing the door behind me. "What do you intend?"

"To talk."

"About what?"

He straightened a crease in his trousers. "Actually, it's about a whom."

"All right, then," I said. "Who is this whom?"

"Radovatch Komaire."

The name meant nothing to me. He saw that, which meant I would have to add "observant" or, even stronger, "perspicacious" to the list.

"You don't know who Radovatch Komaire is?" he said.

I didn't, but from the way Goladry was shifting against his bonds and making sounds behind the gag, I saw that he did. The neat man moved a finger in my bodyguard's direction and I loosened the length of fabric that held a wadded ball of cloth in Goladry's mouth.

While I was doing that, the man on the bed said, "He's very good, by the way." Addressing Goladry directly, he said, "If you ever consider applying to the Guild, I would support your candidacy. The androgyny would work in your favor."

"What Guild?" I said.

Goladry spoke. "The Terrible and Tenacious Guild of Vindicators."

"The assassins' Guild?" I said. "They don't have a chapter in Exley."

The trim and tidy man turned out the inside of his collar, to show a small button of gold with an enameled design of a blue hand holding a dagger. At the same time, he said, "True. I came from the city of Wal."

"Sent for, I presume, by this Rado-something?"

"Radovatch Komaire," said the assassin.

"I still don't know anything about him," I said.

Goladry cleared his throat. "He's one of the Electors for this year's rathering."

I was still no clearer. I used my hands to convey my ignorance. The vindicator studied me for a moment. Then he said, "Komaire is convinced that you know him. More, he believes you know something about his past that would cause his plans to be overturned."

I shook my head. "I have no memory of him or his past. Nor of my own."

The assassin's brow clouded. Again, Goladry chimed in. "It is true. He has amnesia. Chadroyds is working to try to discover how his memories were erased."

The vindicator made a small sound of understanding. "My client," he said, "will have to be informed. He has already made two attempts, lamentably amateurish, to silence you. Finally, he realized that it was a job for a professional."

"And yet, here we are talking," I said.

The man's lips formed an indulgent smile. "We charge less for intimidation."

"You can tell your client he has nothing to fear from me. I could not tell him from his Uncle Flapp."

The assassin stood. "Because you do not remember him," he said. "But you have engaged Chadroyds, presumably for help in recovering your past."

"True."

"In which Radovatch Komaire appears to have figured."

"So he says."

The tidy man straightened a cuff. "I think we can assume he is not just speculating. Intimidation costs less than final resolution — that's the Guild's term — but it still isn't cheap."

I saw his point. "I have been intending to consult a trancer," I said. "Also, to visit Olliphract, which seems to have figured in my amnesia."

The assassin's expression was that of a man coming to an obvious conclusion. "If you did so, and if either course of action resulted in your regaining your memories, then we would likely meet again."

"And there's no telling how that would go," I said.

Now his face said he was too polite to differ on that point. "I am sure you will think about it," he said.

He stepped past me and opened the door. A moment later it was closed and he was gone. I noticed that his footwear made no sound on the floorboards, nor did I hear the creak that always sounded when I stepped out onto the landing.

I untied Goladry. He rubbed his wrists and ankles. "Sorry about..." he said, with a gesture that indicated the circumstances in which I'd found him.

"We can only do what we can," I said. I sat on the bed and blew out my cheeks. "Radovatch Komaire," I said, then shrugged.

"Wait a moment," Goladry said. He went out and came back a few moments later. I heard the landing floorboard squeak each time. He unfolded a wide square of paper and held it so I could see it.

"Here are the biographies and pictures of the candidates for electorship," he said, then pointed to one of the illustrations. "And that is Komaire."

I took the broadsheet and studied the image. It was the man I had seen in Varderon Square who had fled when I tried to pursue him.

"Well," I said, "that closes one mystery."

Goladry took back the paper and refolded it. "And opens another," he said.

«»

"I am undecided as to what to do now," I told Tolderman Ufretes when next we met.

He leaned back in his chair and steepled his fingers beneath his chin. "If Komaire is unfit to be an Elector of Exley because of some past sin," he said, "as a good citizen of the town it is your duty to make that known."

"But I am not a citizen of Exley, merely a sojourner."

Goladry chimed in. "He used the expression, 'I wouldn't know him from his Uncle Flapp.' That is a colloquialism of Old Almery. Along with the traces of accent, I think we can safely assume that is where he hails from."

"That is not helpful to the question before us," his employer said. "In fact, now that we know Komaire is unfit, it is *our* civic duty to uncover the truth."

"We have only the word of an assassin," Goladry argued.

Ufretes's hands came apart and he pointed a conclusive finger at his employee. "Who had no reason to lie."

I said, "We are not here to discuss your civic duty, but my best course of action. I am again inclined to forgo the encounter with the trancer."

"And do what?" Ufretes said.

"Two possible courses present themselves. One, I could waylay Radovatch Komaire and induce him to tell me what he knows of me."

"Chances are," the detective said, "it is what we already surmise: that you participated in the Drieff Massacre. And so did Komaire."

Goladry said, "And once he had told you, he would have no choice but to sic his vindicator on you."

"We could not protect you from the Guild," Ufretes said. "No one could." He leaned forward and peered at me. "What is your second option?"

"To go to Olliphract and learn what I can."

Ufretes drew back his head as if something of sharp odor had been thrust under his nose. "You will almost certainly learn it is dangerous to ask questions in Olliphract. Lethal even."

I conceded his point. I had been reading about the place. Its reputation was lurid and furtive. A city of dark corners and lonely streets, haunted by thaumaturges who fought each other for prestige and to wrest items of lore and power from one another. They also hired out for nefarious projects.

The conversation continued without me. I was coming to a decision. I interrupted them to ask, "Where do I find Radovatch Komaire?"

Ufretes frowned, but Goladry said, "This time of day, he will be in Varderon, for the showing."

"What showing?" I said.

Ufretes answered, "It is part of the process by which someone becomes an Elector."

I had not paid much attention to this "process" since I did not consider myself an Exleyan, but just a man passing through their polity. Nor did it seem to be much discussed in the local periodicals, which assumed that everyone knew the ins and outs of the system.

I stood up. "I will go and speak with him."

"You may be signing your death warrant," Ufretes said.

Goladry got up as well. "I will go with him."

His employer showed concern. "I would not like to lose you to a vindicator," he said, then looked at me. "We now know it was Komaire who tried to kill you and his vindicator will have told him that you are no threat to his aims. I don't see why you need our protection."

"I would like to go anyway," Goladry said. "Consider me to be on my own time."

"Madness," said Ufretes, though without much fervor. He waved a hand and said, "Go."

«»

As we walked to Varderon Square, Goladry tried to explain the Exleyan system of government. It was based upon the notion of *sympathos*, that he could only describe as a sense of fellow-feeling among the portion of the populace that possessed the franchise. The members of the Council of Oligarchs, all of them extremely wealthy persons, were chosen by the College of Electors.

"And the Electors meet in a big tent and cast lots," I said. "I know that much. But how are the electors chosen?"

"By *sympathos*."

"But that doesn't tell me how."

He said it was difficult to explain to an outlander. When the time for the ratherings neared, persons who felt that they might be qualified to be Electors donned a distinctive garment known as the stoa. They went out into the public squares and presented themselves to the citizenry.

"Do they declaim?" I said, "or offer proposals and policies?"

"No, no. Policies are the province of the Councilors." His features congealed for a moment as he sought for words. "They walk about. They pause so that people can get a good look at them. They sit on the hustings. They are seen."

"But they don't interact with the citizens?"

"Of course they do. Presenting themselves is a form of interaction."

I couldn't grasp the subtlety — or was it absurdity — of his meaning. "How do they cast the lots?" I said.

"That is a mystery," he said, "that only Electors know. They meet, they confer, eventually they name the Councillors."

"And the crowd says yes or no by the way they sing the troad?" That much I had grasped.

"There you have it," Goladry said.

"And do they always sing their approval of the Electors' choice?"

"Yes, because the Electors have *sympathos*. Their choices are infallible." He stopped walking and spread his hands in a gesture that said it was all obvious. "If they didn't have *sympathos*, the people would not choose them as Electors. It's quite simple."

"But what about when the Council's policies go against the will of the people? As when they taxed those artisans?"

Goladry made the sound that Exleyans make when they scoff at nonsense. "Those metics? They don't matter. They don't share in *sympathos*, thus they are nobodies."

«»

We approached the hustings in Varderon Square at a little before midmorning. Several men and women were seated on a bench up on the platform beneath the bunting. They were all of middle age or older and each wore a one-piece garment of white fabric that covered their bodies from neck to ankles, with a purple sash diagonally draped from one shoulder to the waist. On every face was what I could only call an expression of serene dignity. They appeared to ignore the crowd, instead fixing their gazes on what I assumed was a vision of the future.

Seated on the left side of the bench was the man who had seen me and showed alarm on my first visit to the square. His was an unremarkable face and it sounded no resonance within me. As I neared the hustings, I saw him glance down and take me in. The muscles at the hinges of his jaw showed themselves as hard knots and he returned his gaze to the ineffable. I could see cords standing out in his neck.

Abruptly, he rose and made his way to the steps that led down from the hustings near his end of the bench. His motions were stiff and formal — somewhere, I had seen actors on a stage move with such studied technique, though of course I could not recall where — and he descended the steps with precise dignity.

I moved to intercept him but he turned at the bottom of the stairs and moved away like a tall ship that has caught a following breeze. I pursued him, Goladry at my heels.

"Wait!" I called out. "Komaire, I must have a word!"

My shout created a stir in the crowd. Faces turned toward me, full of surprise and turning immediately to censure. Goladry took hold of my arm and said, "You can't do that while he wears the stoa. Let him go and we will follow."

To the crowd, he said, "He is an outlander and his business is urgent. Please forgive."

We hustled out of the square in Komaire's wake. He was not hard to follow because, unlike on our first encounter in Varderon, his civic role required him to move at a solemn gait. We settled in about ten paces behind our quarry and ambled along after him.

After a short while, along a street where the pedestrians were few, he stepped into an alley. We increased speed and arrived at its mouth as Radovatch Komaire was pulling the stoa over his head. The purple sash was on the ground at his feet.

As the garment came off he saw me and his face paled. "You can't do this to me!" he said. "I have expiated all my past wrongs and have mastered right thought! Efferion is my rock! His light infuses me! He has enlarged my *ka*! I will achieve *sympathos*!"

I raised my palms in a gesture of peace. "I mean you no harm," I said. "I want only to know who I am."

He stared at me, his mouth open. Then he swallowed and said in a hoarse voice, "It's true? You don't remember?"

"I have no idea who you are, nor who I am, nor how we once knew each other. I swear it is so."

He continued to goggle at me and I could see that he was swept by inner emotions.

Goladry spoke. "For what it is worth, I vouch for what he says."

"I will go further," I said. "If you will tell me what you know of me, I promise you that I will depart Exley as soon as I can. I mean to go to Olliphract and make inquiries there."

Komaire blinked. "Olliphract?" he said. I saw emotion yield to cogitation. After a moment, his brow cleared. He looked at Goladry. "Swear to me," he said, "as an Exleyan, that he is not lying to me."

"I swear it," said Goladry. "He means to go to Olliphract. He may never return to Exley. In fact, it's highly doubtful. I mean..." — he spread his hands — "Olliphract."

"That's for sure," Komaire said. He looked at me. "Come to my house," he said. "I will try to relieve you of your ignorance." He bundled his sash and stoa under one arm, then turned and headed down the alley. What he said next I think was meant only for himself.

It was, "Though you will curse me for it."

«»

Komaire's home was a simple cube of unpainted stone blocks at the end of a short street. A piece of polished black stone was fastened to the jamb and he touched fingertips to it and said something under his breath before inserting a key in the lock and opening the way. He beckoned me in after him but said to Goladry, "This is between him and me, only."

My erstwhile bodyguard opened his mouth to argue, but Komaire raised a hand. "You," he said, "are not departing for Olliphract."

I said, "I will be all right. Besides, if there are terrible things to be learned about me, it is better that knowledge is withheld from you."

Goladry shrugged and leaned against the house wall, his arms folded. I went inside and shut the door.

I was in a room as plain as the house's exterior, without even furniture except for some woven mats on the floor and some backrests for those who would sit cross-legged. A table only a hand high stood against a wall, with some simple crockery and an incense burner. Above it was a scroll adorned with complex calligraphy in a script I could not read.

Komaire stood and regarded me. I saw mixed emotions pass across his face before he settled on resignation. He said,

"The tenets of my faith obligate me to offer you refreshment. I hope you will relieve me of that duty."

"I want only information."

"Then hear it," he said. He took a moment to order his thoughts then said that Radovatch Komaire was a name he had assumed after he left Tayton Ostralitz's mercenary force. He would not divulge how he had previously been known.

"That person died when I was reborn in Efferion," he said.

"Fair enough," I said. "What of me?"

"You are Kain Minderlanz. You held the rank of Field Captain and were second in command of the First Battalion of the Golden Lions. We were named such after our cap badge. I was a senior fugleman with twenty troopers under me."

"What happened at Drieff?" I said. He focused his eyes on the air between us and began to tell me.

The Clash of the Seven Cities brought disruption and dislocations beyond the seven polities that were active belligerents, he said. The entire Greshland Peninsula and its extensive hinterland felt the effects as trade ceased and whole populations relocated to places where they felt safer, or where they might regain some semblance of a normal life.

The conflict also gave rise to novel social and religious movements. One of the latter, the Covenant of Justified Celebrants, rose in the farmlands surrounding the market town of Drieff, on the Great Northern Trunk Road. The Celebrants were a militant sect, led by a prophet who had renamed himself the Anointed after experiencing a series of visions. A compelling orator, the Anointed drew to himself a fanatical band of men and women who practiced sexual abstinence and followed a rigorous dietary code.

As more and more converts were attracted to the cult, the Celebrants outgrew the modest farm that had been the Anointed's home. They descended upon Drieff and occupied a disused temple near the marketplace. Not long after, the town's elders came to complain that the noise and brouhaha attendant upon the Celebrants' exercise of their faith, which involved consuming a dried weed that provoked holy exuberance, loud shouts, and paroxysms of ecstasy, was affecting the wool trade on which Drieff depended.

The Anointed, standing on the steps of the temple with his adherents clustered about him, was seized by a new revelation. He fell upon the elder who had voiced the complaints, knocking the old man down and kicking him, then jumping up and down on the poor fellow's rib cage until he expired. The other Celebrants copied their prophet's example and none of the elders escaped.

The cultists, numbering more than a hundred, now took control of the town, closing the gates and instituting a policy of forced conversion that required all the inhabitants to swear fealty to the Anointed. Those who refused were executed in ways that horrified the townspeople, who were herded into the marketplace and forced to watch.

A reign of terror now ensued, with roving gangs of Celebrants stopping people at random to quiz them on the faith's catechism. Those who could not answer correctly, or who were suspected of consuming forbidden foods, of which there were many kinds, were beaten with iron rods or had their thumbs twisted off by a hand-held mechanism.

"It was into this monstrous chaos that our battalion came marching up the Great Northern Trunk Road, on our way to reinforce a brigade of allied mercenaries who were being menaced by the forces of the Tolton-Cadawal Alliance.

"Our battalion commander, Lance-Major Gallifray Vashonne, knew nothing of the situation at Drieff. None of us did. We only learned about the Celebrants after we had… done what we did."

He paused for a moment, cleared his throat, then resumed. "Lance-Major Vashonne was anxious to reach the threatened brigade. We had force-marched without a baggage train, expecting to purchase rations at the town's market.

"When he found the gates closed against him and received no answers to his hails, he concluded that Drieff had switched its allegiance to the Tolton-Cadawal Alliance. He detailed my squad to scale the mudbrick wall using daggers as pitons. We opened the gates and the battalion poured into Drieff. We were expecting resistance but found the streets empty. The Celebrants had ordered a curfew."

The commander led them toward the central square. There they found a group of Celebrant enforcers. Words were exchanged but there was a drastic failure of communication. A cultist under the influence of katch struck down the Lance-Major with an iron bar, splitting his head.

"We were shocked and outraged," Komaire said. "We fell upon them with spears and swords, and slaughtered them."

But the screams and shouts drew other gangs of enforcers who, energized by their sacramental intoxicant, did not weigh the odds against them. With shrieks and wild swings of their crude weapons, they threw themselves at the Golden Lions. The troopers cut them down and speared them.

"And then it got out of hand," Komaire said. His face took on a look of pleading.

"You must understand, the Celebrants wore no distinctive clothing, no emblems. They were indistinguishable from the Drieffers. And we were simple, unworldly men. When we saw the commander's brains spilt upon the cobblestones, we began to rampage through the town, killing and burning. Our rage fed upon itself. Men, women, and children — even infants — we butchered them without mercy. It was revenge."

When their bloodlust was spent, no more than a dozen Drieffers had survived by hiding in places the searching troopers had missed. Of the Celebrants, not one was left alive. The Anointed one was assumed to lie anonymous among the corpses.

The Golden Lions placed Gallifray Vashonne in the largest tomb in the town's cemetery, having dispossessed and scattered the bones of its legitimate occupants. Then they marched on up the road, under the command of Field Captain Kain Minderlanz.

A day later, a trio of the massacre's survivors traveled south to Captain-General Ostralitz's main camp to beg for help in burying the bodies. It was then that the full story became known. Tayton Ostralitz sent a commission of inquiry. They found the evidence at Drieff to be overwhelming. They pressed on to where Kain Minderlanz's battalion was camped and placed him under arrest.

"When we heard the truth about what had happened... what we had done, we were ashamed. Immediately, out of fear, some of our men deserted. Others argued that we were victims of unusual circumstances, but some of us volunteered to be punished so that the stain could be cleansed from our honor."

But the situation in the Greshland Peninsula was precarious. If word of the battalion's role in the massacre got out, alliances would shift. The outcome would be disastrous for the cities that had hired the Golden Lions.

Tayton Ostralitz concocted a face-saving story. The Drieffers had been killed by the Justified Celebrants, driven mad by religious fervor and chewing katch. The battalion had arrived too late to stop the massacre but had inflicted appropriate punishment on the Anointed and his acolytes. Lance-Major Vashonne had perished in the fighting.

A couple of the surviving citizens of Drieff refuted this tale. They disappeared. The remaining few said nothing. They had hidden in cellars and cocklofts, and had only heard the screams and cries for mercy. As an inducement, Ostralitz paid them handsomely for the supplies he needed, without asking too many questions as to who rightfully owned the goods he was paying for.

"And so, it was all put behind us," said Komaire. "We went on up to Aberschamp and for once there was an actual battle. Ostralitz threw our battalion into the thick of it, and a lot of us didn't come out the other side. A few weeks later came the Peace of Velsac and most of us mustered out.

"But I was ruined for a soldier after Drieff. I wandered for a while, even thought about becoming a reiver — once you think you're lost, well, you are — but then I met a traveling brother who showed me the truth of my god, the Divine Efferion.

"Efferion saw my pain and showed me a way to be free of it. I became Radovatch Komaire and traveled down to Exley, where my family had come from, to do what good I could."

"And Kain Minderlanz," I said. "What became of him?"

Komaire shrugged. "No one knew. Ostralitz had locked you up, but one day your cell was empty." He looked at me, making up his mind whether or not to say his next words:

"We thought Ostralitz had had your throat cut and buried you without a marker."

"Apparently not," I said. "So, it seems I am Kain Minderlanz, mass murderer." Saying it did not make it more real. Then I said, "Unless I am the other Minderlanz?"

Komaire sought for an answer, then I saw it come to him. "Etzel," he said.

"That is his name."

"Was," Komaire said. "I remember now. He was with the Fourth Battalion of the Lions. They were on the left of the line at Aberschamp when the Iron Fist attacked. Heavy cavalry, with those awful long lances. The Fourth tried to stand but they were overrun and died to a man. If Etzel was there, he is dead."

"If?" I said.

"I did not see the body, only heard the reports."

The news of a twin brother's death should have moved me, but did not. I asked Komaire, "Did I ever say anything about family, where I came from?"

"You were second in command of the battalion, three ranks above me," he answered. "We did not converse beyond orders and reports."

I showed him the scar on my right hand. He showed me a similar scar on his own hand, and sighed. "I wish I could obliterate the memory as thoroughly," he said. "But Efferion has helped."

So now I knew what had happened at Drieff. But I was no closer to resolving my part, if any, in the mass murder. I sighed and asked Komaire, "Is there anything more you can tell me?"

Again he shook his head, but then I saw a thought strike him.

"What?" I said.

He pointed at me, his finger moving in rhythm with his words. "You had a batman," he said. He looked up at the ceiling. "What was his name? Vedder? No, Vedler, Arsengio Vedler."

"What happened to him?" I said. "Where is he now?"

He looked blank for a moment then said, "He was one of the deserters, before the thing was all hushed up."

"Ah," I said, "well." I uttered a frustrated profanity and prepared to say goodbye.

Komaire was rooting around in his memory. Finally, he said, "I believe I heard he became a spoliator."

«»

"It seems I no longer have need of you," I told Goladry as we walked back to Varderon Square.

"True, but I am caught up now in your mystery," he said. "I am of the kind who cannot get up and leave a play before the last scene."

"I am not a character in a play," I said.

"Or we all are, and fool ourselves otherwise," he replied. He smiled to take the sting out of it.

We walked on in silence, going nowhere in particular, skirting the groups of people who stood about in the square. Some of them regarded the figures on the hustings, and there was a small buzz of conversation as Radovatch Komaire returned to his seat. Others merely stood and gazed into the middle distance, their expressions as empty as those of the prospective Electors.

I was thinking about what I would have to do. Goladry seemed to read my thoughts because he said, "If you are planning to seek out this Vedler, I will accompany you."

I stopped and looked at him. "Ufretes will not pay you," I said.

He shrugged. "I have funds and my wants are small. Besides, I might despoil a spoliator or two. Efferion's devotees say one should seek a balance that is inherent in how the cosmos is arranged, if one can but see it."

"Are you a follower of that view?" I said.

"Not as such," he said, "but I like the idea of equanimity at the root of phenomenality."

He was quiet for a while, then he looked toward the offices of Holfman Brothers and said, "You will have to tell the young woman."

"Yes," I said, "I will."

«»

She was at her usual place. Business seemed to be slow, despite the large numbers of people in the square outside.

As I approached her counter she gave me a tentative smile. I greeted her in the subdued Exleyan manner — I had been relearning what I must have known as a cadet — and she gave me a gesture of approval.

I wrote a request to withdraw funds on a piece of paper. It was a substantial amount and brought a question to her face. I said, "I have to leave town for a while. I have heard of a man who may be able to identify me for certain and tell me… things I need to know."

She began counting out scrip. "Is he far from here?" she said.

"Not far. Somewhere in the Weftruin Forest."

She stopped counting. "There is no one in the forest but murderers and thieves," she said.

"He is one such."

"It is a dangerous place."

I sought to reassure her. "Not for me. So long as I keep my wits about me."

She returned to counting the pieces of paper, finished, then added some silver and brass coins. Her face had grown very still, though her lower lip fought a tremble.

"I will return," I said. "And then, perhaps…"

She looked at me in that direct way I was still getting used to. "You ask a lot of a woman. Is the past so much more important than the present?"

I spoke gently. "You said yourself that I should fight what has been done to me."

"Yes," she said, "I did, didn't I?" She stopped the tremor of her lip by taking it between her front teeth.

"I will come back," I said. "It is a promise."

"And how do you know," she said, trying for a light tone, "you're a man who keeps his promises?"

"I don't," I said, "but I promise you I will find out."

That brought a half-smile, then a sigh. I gathered up my funds, touched her hand, and said goodbye.

«»

Goladry following, I went to my lodgings, paid in advance and asked the proprietress to keep my room against my return. I dressed in wool and leather, donned a pair of stout boots I had acquired in Ur Nazim, and took from the closet the sword and spear Bernaglio had given me. Goladry had gone home while I'd been at Holfman Brothers but was waiting for me on the porch when I came out the door of the boarding house. He was dressed for rough travel, with a dagger in his belt and a strong staff with an iron ferrule at each end.

"How well do you know the forest?" I asked him.

"A little," he said, "at least the nearer stretches."

"Any idea how to find a reivers' camp?"

"Oh," he said, laying his staff across one shoulder, "I should think they'll find us."

We stopped near the north gate at a place that sold traveler's supplies and got roadbread and hard cheese, filled wineskins, and some twists of dried meat. When we went out through the gate the sentries stopped us briefly, but once I was recognized as the trainer of the Specials they sent us on our way with an invocation to have care.

It was too far to the first caravanserai to make it there before nightfall. At sundown, we left the road and stopped at the edge of the trees, where a spring bubbled out of a rockface. We made a fireless camp, though it was doubtful we would encounter any serious danger this close to Exley. But that meant that if we did meet reivers, they were likely to be the truly desperate, even insane, who were driven out of spoliator gangs after indulging in behavior that was too much even for hardened wrongdoers.

In the morning, we shook the dew from our sleeping cloaks and prowled the border of the forest, looking for paths that led inward. We found a number, but none of them showed any recent human footprints, only the tracks of wild beasts. My plan, such as it was, was to follow any signs that might lead us to a bandit encampment and, if it did not look too rowdy, try to insinuate ourselves into its complement.

A fall-back strategy would be to come upon a single forest-dweller, seize him, and squeeze what information we could about who was who and what was what in this part of the forest. "Elementary intelligence-gathering," I told Goladry.

He gave me an indulgent nod and said, "The persons we are likely to encounter here will fit the description. Their intelligence will be elementary."

We planned to describe ourselves as Exleyans who had fallen afoul of the ruling power structure. We had chosen self-exile over imprisonment in the town's incarcery. A submotive would be to exact revenge on the oligarchy by robbing the merchants who sustained the elite in their high places.

By noon, we had investigated eight or nine tracks, and found no signs of recent human presence. What footprints we found were faded or half-filled in by weather or the split-hooved signs of browsers.

Goladry said, "We are perhaps out of season. If no caravans are expected, the reivers probably withdraw to more remote regions. If they built their permanent camps near the road, they would invite punishment expeditions from the town."

"Could be," I said. "Do we go deeper into the woods, or do we wait nearer the road until someone comes?"

We talked about it and decided we would rather find bandits than be found by them. When next we came upon a trail that led toward the forested ridges we could see if we climbed a tree and looked east, we began to follow it. It led in time to a stream that came down from the higher country and, from then on, we used that as our guide.

The stream we were following ended at another rockface near a spring that bubbled out of a crack in the limestone. But we climbed the slope beside the jut of rock and saw that the forest went on, ridge after ridge. More to the point, we could see a smudge of smoke over a distant hill.

"More than one fire," I said, "but not a forest burning."

Goladry agreed. "Somebody lives there."

We kept going, down the reverse slope of that ridge, across a narrow valley and up the next incline. The forest here was more evergreen than broad-leafed, the trees growing close together. Even when we found a trail that went the right way, it was slow going. By the time we reached the top of the second slope, the day was fading. We ate bread and cheese washed down with sour wine, and slept under our cloaks on heaps of gathered bracken.

By noon the next day we were within sight of the source of the smoke. We crested a ridge that overtopped another steep valley choked with dense growths of evergreens. But directly eastward the next elevation was cleared of trees. I saw a wall of earth and logs, with wooden towers every fifty paces and a strong set of gates. Below the walls was a deep ditch and although it was hard to see clearly at this distance, the ditch looked to be full of sharp stakes.

"Somebody knows how to build a stronghold," I said to Goladry.

He shaded his eyes against the sun and said, "I count at least thirty smokes. That's a substantial settlement, not a camp."

"We need to get somewhere where we can observe," I said. "I don't want to walk in there without some idea of what we're getting into."

But whoever had designed the fortification hadn't wanted anyone to be able to watch the place unseen. When we finally arrived near the top of the cleared ridge, after angling south, crossing the valley, and climbing up through the trees, we found we could only see the southern wall of the fortification. To see the interior we would have to climb a tall tree, but all the trees up here were no more than three or four times my height.

It was getting dark. I said, "Let's hole up and get some sleep. Then we'll creep up and see if we can scale the wall, get a better look."

That would have been a good plan except for the part we didn't know. At sundown, the inhabitants let loose a pack of dogs to forage for rabbits or whatever they could find in the cleared zone or the surrounding forest.

Of course, they found us.

The howling woke us. We had barely time to snatch up spear and staff, wrap our cloaks around our arms, and put ourselves back to back. Goladry did something with the shaft of his staff and out of the iron-tipped end sprang a single-edged blade. We fended off the snarling, snapping, lunging pack of mongrels, some of them big enough to be lethal if they got a bite in the right place.

But they didn't try all that hard, and soon we realized that, mongrels or not, they were well-trained. They made a lot of noise and soon we saw the glare of torches coming across the cleared space and into the trees.

"Here we go," I said. "Better let me do the talking."

Goladry discouraged a half-sized cur that was taking a run at his ankles. "Be my guest," he said.

«»

"We're not spies," I told the wall-eyed man in the big log building at the center of the town where they'd taken us, after seizing our weapons and tying our hands behind us. At least they'd driven off the dogs when we surrendered, so we didn't have the pain and indignity of bites and torn garments.

"You're spies," he said. "Nobody comes into these woods except runaways and those who come looking for them. You can call yourselves bounty hunters or thief-takers or regulators, it don't matter to us. We call you spies and we make short work of you."

His words drew a chorus of grunts and muttered threats from the forty or so men who surrounded us, many of them summoned from their beds to arrive with weapons in their hands. I saw that things could go badly, and very quickly, if I couldn't head the situation in another direction. The first thing was to be calm. The aphorism *nothing calms like calmness* came into my head, something I must have learned at the Institute.

"I'm looking for a man I used to know," I said. "We were soldiers together and I heard he'd taken up the life of… you folks."

More growls and ominous shifting of bodies came from behind me, but the wall-eyed man held up a hand. He must have possessed some real authority because the noise and motion stopped.

"Who is this man?" he said.

"When I knew him, his name was Arsengio Vedler."

I heard a snort of mockery from nearby. Somebody said, "Everybody knows Shortshanks Vedler. He's picked a name we'll all recognize and while we're waiting to hear if Shortshanks can vouch for these two, they'll be looking over our defenses and counting our spears."

Wall-eye quieted them down again. "And what's your name?" he asked me.

"That's a tricky one. Somebody has stolen my memories—"

That brought mocking laughter and somebody jabbed something hard, probably a spear butt, into my shoulder.

I kept my calm. "It's why I need to find Vedler, to find out if I am who they say I am."

"And who's that?" said Wall-eye.

"Kain Minderlanz."

The man in front of me blinked. "Kain Minderlanz," he said. It was not a question.

I heard a stir of movement behind me, then a man pushed his way to the front of the crowd and took a good, close look at my face. I didn't know him from his Uncle Flapp but he clearly knew me.

"That's him, all right, Cherko," he said to the wall-eyed man. "Field-Captain Minderlanz, when I knew him. Second-in-command, first battalion of the Golden Lions." He straightened up so I could get a good look at him "You remember me? Undersergeant Blass, headquarters company."

"No," I said, "I don't remember any of it. I'm trying to get my memories back."

Blass stared at me and I saw his face change as he let the past come up in him. "You shouldn't," he said. "You're better off not knowing. You'll sleep better."

"Maybe," I said, "but I need to know."

The mood in the hall had shifted. People were talking behind me. I heard the words "Drieff" and "murdering," and whisperings I didn't catch.

"Enough," said Cherko, and the room quieted again. "So, you're Minderlanz the Butcher. What are we supposed to do with you? Or your little friend?"

"Let us go find Vedler," I said. "That's all we're here for."

Cherko turned his attention to Goladry. "What's your story?"

"I'm with him," my bodyguard said.

"Why? Somebody steal your memories, too?"

"No. I just need to know."

"Oh, you do, do you?" Cherko said.

Goladry shrugged. "It's my major character flaw."

The room was silent as Cherko stared at my companion. Then he burst out laughing. He slapped his leg and said, "This one's got balls!" Then he peered at Goladry with one eye, then the other, and said, "At least, I think so."

Cherko's mirth didn't last long. He signaled to a few of the others to join him a little distance away. They stood in a corner and talked in quiet tones. After a while they called Blass over and questioned him. I couldn't hear what they were saying but the former undersergeant's hand gestures and head movements were emphatic. Finally, the wall-eyed man dismissed the group and came back to me and Goladry.

"All right," he said, "you're not spies. Maybe I even buy the memory loss thing. But you're not staying. And we're not setting you loose to wander around in our territory."

"What does that leave?" I said.

"There's a couple of wagons going down to the Sunter Valley in a couple of days. You go with them, and you don't come back. We see you again, we kill you. Got it?"

We got it. In the meantime, he said, we would "go in the hole," which turned out to be a literal description of the settlement's jail: a log-lined square hole in the ground with a roof of squared, heavy timbers. It was where they put members of the gang who got out of hand, they said.

There was no ladder. They cut our bonds and gave us a choice of jumping down or being pushed. At least, they let us have a couple of stools to sit on and a bucket to relieve ourselves in. They also threw down our food bag and wineskins, then they lowered the roof in place. I'd seen a couple of hefty boulders beside the hole and now I heard grunts as they were rolled onto the timbers. Through the gaps between some of the square baulks, a little light came from torches set around the prison hole.

"Could have been worse," Goladry said, taking one of the stools and rummaging around in the bag for a cob of hardbread.

I shrugged and sat down. The interview with Cherko and Blass had given me plenty to think about. Apparently, I really was a mass murderer — Minderlanz the Butcher, no less — and the kind of man not even a gang of spoliators wanted around.

I stilled my mind and closed my eyes, fell into a style of slow and steady breathing that came naturally to me. I let my awareness of my surroundings fade, which wasn't difficult in a nearly lightless hole in the ground. I let come whatever might rise from the darkness of my mind.

Drieff, I said to myself and waited. But all that came were the images that had presented themselves to me when I'd read Frater Baz's account of the massacre. They had no shock value, no immediacy: they were generic images of the dead and dying, without the detail of the corpses I'd searched for valuables after the attack on the Ur Nazimite wagon.

I made a noise of frustration.

"What?" Goladry said, around a mouthful of bread.

"It's not enough," I said. "They can tell me I'm Kain Minderlanz, but they might as well tell me I'm Farouche."

"Or Uncle Flapp," he said.

"It's not funny," I said.

"No," he said, then moistened the mouthful with some wine and swallowed. "You want my advice?"

"If it's practical. I'm up a blind alley."

He leaned forward on the stool. "Sunter Valley's up a tributary of the river. We get a boat and go back to Exley." He emphasized his next words with a double-handed gesture. "And you finally see the trancer."

It was a logical step, yet something in me still resisted. Goladry saw that in my face, even in the dim light, and he said, "Suppose this was done to you by a trancer. What one trancer has done another can undo. So the bad trancer makes you stay away from the good 'un."

If that was so, I ought to resent it, as Amalthea had said. Yet, I didn't. When I considered the matter, I felt nothing either way. But the young woman had been right: I was not the kind of man who would take such interference without resenting it. And doing something about it.

"I'll do it," I told Goladry. Then, recognizing my own lack of spirit behind the declaration, I added, "Make sure that I do."

⟨⟨⟩⟩

It was only a day's paddle down from Sunter Valley to Exley. I bought a scullboat with scrip from the belt I'd worn around my middle under two shirts when we'd been captured by the reivers. They had taken the silver and brass in my purse but didn't find the paper money.

I told the wharfinger we had no further use for the boat and said he could do with it what he liked. He grumbled, but when he saw it was a decently built and maintained craft, he cheered up.

I set off for my lodgings. Goladry said he would accompany me partway, then divert to visit the trancer and make an appointment. We parted in Varderon Square, where the process of the ratherings was reaching some kind of cusp. I stood for a while and watched as a crowd moved around the hustings, where the would-be Electors sat and stared into space. I noticed that many of the citizens had the same far-look expression on their faces, as if they were caught up in some mystical exercise.

I really must have someone explain this to me, I thought. But then I faced the fact that I had more important things on my agenda. I turned to go the several blocks to my lodgings, then stopped and changed course toward Holfman Brothers.

Amalthea was at her station. I approached and she saw me. The expression of happiness that illuminated her face raised my spirits, even though the news I had to tell her was the kind of intelligence that would make most people, let alone a possible romantic partner, turn away in horror.

"You're back," she said, "and so soon."

"Things did not go as expected," I said, "but I learned something."

"Tell me."

"Not here. Will you meet me for dinner?"

She would, and we arranged for me to be waiting for her when she finished work. I turned to go and became aware of a rising humming sound from outside in the square. I looked back to Amalthea and she waved a dismissive hand. "Just the ratherings," she said.

I gave a wave of my own and went outside. Several hundred people were now moving in peculiar ways in the square: they had formed a column three or four individuals wide, most of them men of the merchant and indentor class, as well as some artisans of the more respectable guilds. There were women too, of the same social rank, altogether perhaps a thousand of them, each with one hand on the shoulder of the person in front. But though I called it a column, there was nothing of a military cast to their movement. Instead, they moved like a large, sluggish snake, winding their way around the square in a sinuous motion.

But, unlike a snake, they were not silent. From the thousand throats issued the humming sound I had heard in the fiduciary pool, now become a deep thrumming of three notes, the first one up, the second one down, the third in between the two. Over the sound, the only noise was the shuffle of their feet against the flagstones.

I realized the hairs on the back of my neck had risen. A shiver went through the muscles of my back. I saw there were other people in the square, of lesser social rank, and they watched the movement of the snake with various expressions. I saw one man, in a worker's smock, spit and turn away. A gaggle of street urchins capered along behind the tail of the snake, until a woman from one of the food stalls swiped at them with a ladle and they scattered, laughing.

Nothing to do with me, I said. I was about to take the street out of the square that led to my lodgings when it occurred to me to visit Chadroyds and ask if they had received any more replies to Tolderman Ufretes's requests for information. I crossed the square, skirting the snake, and turned up Idderlond Wynd.

As I came up to the temple of Efferion, I saw a curtained litter waiting near the entrance, along with four burly bearers. I knew that, in some cities, being a litter carrier was regarded as a lowly occupation, consigned to the illiterate and unteachable. But in Exley, it was considered as dignified a labor as any other and its practitioners took pride in the ability to carry their passengers smoothly and rapidly from one destination to another. Indeed, there were occasionally competitive races involving litters in which rode full glasses of colored liquids. The teams that ran the course in the best times with the least spillage were feted and won prizes.

I was passing the litter and offering a polite salute to the bearers when the temple door opened and out from it stepped Philaria, the wife of Nulf Bernaglio. She saw me, blinked three times, and raised a tentative hand in greeting. I realized that she had taken my courtesy to the bearers as being meant for her, so now we both had to stop and engage in the small talk that was considered good manners in Exley.

I asked after her health and she after mine. When our soundness had been mutually established I made the same inquiry as to her husband and learned that he too was hale and hearty. The conversation then lapsed and, for lack of any other topics, I said that I had not known she was a devotee of Efferion.

Her well-tended brows knitted a little. "For a very long time," she said. "I have found the spiritual exercises of the faith to be of great benefit. Indeed, though we do not proselytize, I recommend them to anyone who has not ease of mind."

I had no interest in such matters, but politeness required me to say that I might consider learning more about Efferion's system at some point when I had the leisure.

At that, she put a hand on my arm and said, "Never put off the work of the spirit. One does not know when the *parosha* may arrive."

"*Parosha*?" I said. "I am not familiar with the term."

"Ah," she said. She looked left and right before returning her gaze to me and saying, "That would take a deal of explaining, and one has to be… prepared before the true meaning of the revelation… reveals itself."

"I'm sure," I said, wishing now to end this conversation. It seemed I was the kind of person who finds religious enthusiasm somewhat wearing. "Perhaps someday you might be so kind…" I made a circular motion of the hand that indicated an event set in an indefinite future.

Her brows drew down again, and I reminded myself that it was her brother whom I had driven from his employment and sent off into exile. I said, "It has been a great pleasure to see you again. Your playing of the Farouche aria still resonates in my mind."

She accepted the compliment and assumed the attitude of one who has places to go and not much time to get there. We parted with the usual courtesies after I assisted her into the litter. She drew the golden curtain and the bearers carried her swiftly and silently away.

I looked at the temple of Efferion and, for a moment only, considered entering and relieving my mild curiosity as to what went on within its cloister. But I already had my own mystery to work on, and Ufretes might be able to shed more light on my condition than some god I had scarcely heard of.

I set off again up Idderlond Wynd toward the Biswant Building.

«»

"I've had a reply from our associates' office in Fetteck," Ufretes said. He fished through several folders on his desk and found what he was looking for. "It says that Kain Minderlanz was seen wearing the livery of a thaumaturge named Malbroch the Omnifacient." He paused and allowed a look of bemusement to steal across his features. "What extraordinary sobriquets these wizards award themselves."

"So, I was a wizard's henchman?"

The detective made a noncommittal gesture. "If you are indeed Kain and not his twin brother Etzel."

"I'm fairly sure Etzel is dead," I said.

He was rummaging around in his desk drawer, saying, "I have an instrument that will tell us whether or not you have been in contact with fluxions."

"What are fluxions?" I said.

Ufretes continued his rooting. "Channels of arcane force that crisscross the world. Thaumaturges tend to establish themselves where particularly strong fluxions cross each other. That leaves a permanent signature on their persons. Also, their close retainers. Ah, here it is!"

He produced an object I found familiar: a round-surfaced green gem set in a gold armature.

"Nulf Bernaglio has a similar device," I said. "He used it on me when first we met and it showed nothing much."

"Really?" said Ufretes. He rose from behind his desk and came around to where I was seated in the client's chair. He held the object a finger's breadth from my breastbone, then examined it. The green cabochon turned a bright red.

"That's the same thing Bernaglio's did when he applied it to me," I said.

Ufretes showed mild surprise. "This red?" he said. "And he said what?"

"That the contact was negligible."

The detective's face remained impassive, but he blinked several times. "It's hard to conclude that Ser Bernaglio did not know what bright red means. You're sure he said 'negligible'?"

"The very word. What are you thinking?"

"That something is amiss."

We were both silent for a moment, consulting our thoughts. Then Ufretes said, "There may be some moral hazard here. You are my client, but Ser Bernaglio pays the account."

"Why would he not want me to know that I had been in contact with magic?" I said.

"A most pertinent question. You could ask him, of course. But if he lied to you the first time, he may lie to you again."

"Why would he lie?"

"Again, you could ask him. But, as I say, once someone has been found in a lie, anything else he says must be suspect."

I had to agree. "So, if I don't ask Bernaglio, where does that leave me? Are there any practitioners of magic in Exley I could consult?"

The question won me a look of consternation from Ufretes, followed by a head-shake and a short laugh. Finally, he said, "No, there are not."

He saw the confusion his reaction to a simple question had sparked in me. He said, "I keep forgetting your condition.

You present as an intelligent and worldly individual, with a capacity for keen logic and cogent analysis. Then you reveal that you don't know what any child knows."

"What does any child know about wizards in Exley?"

"That there are none," he said, "and have been none since generations ago. The Council of Oligarchs banned them and called upon the civic pantheon to enforce their edict."

"Civic pantheon? You mean gods?"

"I do, indeed. Particularly the deities Arbrachs, Ganfoche, Hillip, and Po. The priests and laity of all four cults combined in an arduous common effort of prayer, sacrifice, and mantra chanting to evoke the gods and ask them to drive the thaumaturges out."

He peered at me. "You really did not know this?"

I assured him I had not an inkling.

He steepled his fingers and stared at nothing for a while, his well-calibrated mind chasing down the implications. After a while he folded his hands across his middle and said, "It would seem the trancer will most likely prove to be a waste of time."

I raised my eyebrows in a query and he went on. "You know your way around Exley but do not know one of the most signature aspects of civic life. The cabochon glows a bright red. That argues, to me, that the cause of your amnesia is magical. Someone has put a spell on you, or possibly you have had an interaction with a demon. A corollary of that spell or contact is a disinclination to seek out a remedy."

It was true. I was not strongly motivated to recover my memories. I told him so.

"Yet if I slapped you across the face," he said, "I expect you would respond with anger."

"I would."

"Then I think we have found another corollary."

Yes," I said, "a young woman I know made the same observation. Yet still I did not follow up on her suggestion."

He cocked his head in a way that gave emphasis to my conclusion. "So what will you do?" he said.

"It would be better to have more information before confronting Nulf Bernaglio," I said.

"Will you confront him?"

"I think I must. But this time I would have the facts, or at least more facts than I have now."

He said, "There are several reputable thaumaturges downriver at Vanderoy. Red and Blue Schoolers, even a couple of Purples."

"Can you recommend one?"

He thought briefly then said, "Several years ago, we dealt with a fellow named Audelanz, Blue School. He was competent, although, like all of his kind, he was temperamental. I will give you a note of recommendation."

«»

The *Regal Swan* was leaving a few hours after sundown. I met Amalthea as she came out of Holfman Brothers and before I could tell her my plan she said, "You're wearing traveling clothes."

I explained as we walked, arm in arm, across Varderon Square. When I reached the part about having been ensorcelled, she detached her arm from mine and stood still. I saw a mix of expressions cross her face, none of them positive. She gave a little shudder.

"I am sorry," I said. "I did not ask to be as I am."

"Are you sure?" she said.

"Who would ask to have his past magicked away?" I said. "And to what purpose?"

Even as I asked it, an answer came to me. It was not a pleasant one.

«»

Gashtun was back at his old place at the bottom of the gangplank, scrutinizing passengers' papers as they came aboard. He did not glance at mine but stood to attention and rendered a passable salute. I returned the gesture then made reference to a welt on the side of his neck.

"There were two of them," he said, "and I had enough drink in me to make them think they could have my purse. But those moves you showed us? I've been practicing. I laid them both out proper. Bare hands against cudgels, too."

"Well done," I said. The praise made him swell a bit.

"Will you be going north with us again?" he asked, then added a ser.

"I don't know. I may have to go somewhere else to solve my little mystery."

"The memory thing?" he said. "Might be better off as you are. I know I've more than enough stupidities I wouldn't mind forgetting."

I conceded the point, slapped him on the shoulder, and went aboard. Reder was on the second deck. She regarded me with a stern expression as I stepped off the gangplank. I threw her a wave that she didn't return. Instead she said, "Did Himself send you?"

"No, I'm just taking passage to Vanderoy. On business of my own."

She grunted and some of the wrinkles went out of her brow, though it would never be unmarked. Now she sketched a wave and went forward to the wheelhouse.

A little while later, relaxing in my cabin, I heard the polemen come aboard with a clatter of poles. They began their pacing chant and the boat pulled away from the dock.

«»

I'd lain down on my bunk to take a rest and must have just dozed off when I was awakened by a pounding on the door. I opened it to find Reder, brow lines now deeply etched, looking up at me with an expression that said I was trouble. Gashtun was behind her, looking sheepish.

"What is it?" I said.

"You tell me," she said, and signaled I should follow her. We went out on deck and over to the boat's port side. The polemen were digging their long shafts into the river bottom, holding the *Swan* motionless against the push of the current. Below them was another craft: a water taxi of the kind used to ferry travelers across the river or out to boats moored away from the docks. Four heavy-shouldered men rested on their oars, looking at nothing, while on the rear seat sat Izmah, Nulf Bernaglio's majordomo. His worried face brightened now as he saw me.

Reder said, "He brought a message from the owner. You're to go back with him."

"I've got business in Vanderoy," I said.

She shook her head. "There was a second part to the message. If you don't go with Izmah, I'm to turn the boat around and go back to the dock until you disembark."

My face showed my lack of understanding. She held up her hands to show that she had no more comprehension than I.

I said, "I'll get my bag."

Not long after, I was watching the packet boat continue on downriver while the oarsmen turned the taxi around and bent their backs to the struggle against the current. I'd already asked Izmah what the meaning of his message was, but he gave me the same gesture as Reder. "You must ask the master," he said.

I would have, but after we'd pulled all the way back to where Bernaglio's carriage waited at the dock, then been carried through the town to the merchant's manse, we found a footman waiting to tell the majordomo that Bernaglio had been called away on some urgent matter. I was to be made comfortable against his return.

"And when will that be?" I said. But for the third time that evening I saw two palms raised and spread.

"I will show you to your chamber," Izmah said. "Would you like some refreshment?"

"I would like some information," I said.

"I'm afraid that commodity is in short supply," he said.

«»

Bernaglio did not return. Izmah came to apologize, bringing along the footman with a tray of savory cakes and a flagon of pale yellow wine. I put down my frustration and sat at a small table overlooking the garden, redolent with the heady scents of its blossoms. I didn't remember being a soldier, but I was sure I had spent many an hour in waiting, and doubtless in less comfortable quarters. The wine and cakes were excellent. And I owed Nulf Bernaglio a great deal, although I knew I ought to be concerned about his apparent lie about the red-glowing jewel.

Eventually, when my host and benefactor did not return by the time the evening had worn on into full night, I went to bed.

He was still not back when I rose, washed, and went down to breakfast. His wife, Philaria, met me in the morning room and encouraged me to fill my plate from the several chafing dishes on a long refectory table, while a serving girl poured a mug of rich-smelling punge and set it at my place at a small table set for two on the patio.

It was a beautiful morning, the air fresh and vibrant. From a distance, I could hear a rhythmic drumming and a hum like that of a vast hive of deep-chested bees.

"What is that sound?" I asked my hostess, when she came to sit opposite.

"The crescendo of the ratherings," she said without concern, spreading preserves on a white muffin. "Today they choose the Electors."

"Ah," I said, though her words explained nothing.

"You've lived in Exley before?" she said.

"I was a cadet at the Institute, or so everyone says."

A small vee appeared above the bridge of her nose. "And yet you don't know about the ratherings?"

"I suppose I've had other things to think about," I said.

She chewed reflectively then said. "Well, it's not as if people would thrust information upon you."

That puzzled me. "Why not?"

And that puzzled her. She cast about for the right words, finally settling on, "Everyone knows, but no one speaks of it. It has to do with the... shameful thing that was done in our great-grandparents' time, the thing that left us... peculiar."

She said nothing more but went on eating her muffin, her thoughts clearly turned inward. After a while, I could not help but ask, "How peculiar?"

She blinked and came back to me. Then she blushed and kept her eyes on her plate while she stirred some fragments of deviled egg with her fork. After a moment, she said, "Would you mind turning your chair and looking at the garden while I speak?"

"I have embarrassed you," I said. "I am sorry."

"No," she said, "it is just not something we talk about easily. But if you're to be part of my husband's affairs, you ought to know. Please, oblige me."

I inclined my head in submission, then rose and made my chair face the garden. I waited as a silence grew and lengthened, then she began to speak.

In her grandfather's time, Philaria said, there had been wizards in Exley, including three of note: Effretz, Hoshikkan, and Voz. As is usual with thaumaturges, they contested with each other for prestige and precedence. Eventually, one of them — it was probably Hoshikkan, considered the most bumptious of the three — proposed a contest of skill and power.

Such tournaments were not unusual among high-ranking practitioners of thaumaturgy, but Hoshikkan's proposal had a unique feature: instead of taking place on one of the Planes accessible to wizards, it would be sited in the universe of dreams, otherwise known as the collective unconscious of mortal human beings.

The noösphere was difficult to access, even for wizards. Entering and functioning in that symbol-drenched realm normally required long years of study and practice before mastery of the necessary recondite techniques could be achieved. There was, however, a shortcut: the territory of archetypes could be entered at will by demons of the Seventh Plane, amoral creatures of supernal power that sometimes amused themselves by haunting the dreams of humankind, spreading terror and despair — emotions on which the fiends apparently dined.

Now, Philaria went on, taming a demon and bending it to a thaumaturge's will was a task fraught with peril. But Hoshikkan proposed that the three wizards pool their powers and bind the chosen fiend securely. After long and contentious negotiations, they agreed on a plan that relieved the trio of the danger that one of their number might use the demon against the others — when wizards cooperate, there is always the chance of treachery.

Once frightful oaths and binding pledges of reciprocal retaliation had been sworn, a demon was targeted and ensnared. It was coerced into creating the dreamscape in which the thaumaturges would hold their contest.

At this point, Philaria paused to take a sip of punge. It took her a few moments to gain the equanimity required to go on with the story. Finally, she said, "To form the arena in which the wizards would contend, the demon — Xaddathoth by name — caused the entire population of Exley, man, woman, and child, to fall into a deep sleep.

"It then linked all of their minds together and imposed upon them a single dream. When that common reverie was established, it folded Effretz, Hoshikkan, and Voz into the dreamscape. They then set about their various trials and struggles, with Xaddathoth keeping score and adjudicating protests and penalties."

As she told the tale, her face had grown pale and her voice had hoarsened. She took another restorative sip of the steaming brew and plunged into the rest of the telling.

"When they had finished their sport, they bade the demon revive the town. All of Exley woke up at once. But, while under the rule of the fiend, many of the people had gone mad in their sleep. Others were cast down into a pit of despair from which they could not lift themselves. It was worst for the children, some of whom never grew up right. Indeed, many killed themselves rather than face the risk of another night's sleep taking them back to the horrors they had experienced."

The people revolted. They demanded of the oligarchs that they drive the thaumaturges from the town and never again allow a wizard, or anyone who had truck with thaumaturgy, to set foot in the town again. And so it had been for all the years since.

But there was a curious after-effect, she said. At some profound level, the surviving people of Exley remained connected. They often shared dreams. Strangers felt at ease with each other. But the connection was most useful when it came to the process by which the town's governance was decided.

Before the great coalescence, as the demon-driven mass dreaming was called, the selection of the Electors was occasioned by raucous debates and night-long shivarees, the buying of drinks and the doing of favors, some of them intimately personal. After, it became a more sedate process. The prospective Electors put themselves forward and stilled their minds. The people engaged in rhythmic movements — mass dancing to hypnotic drumming — that calmed their own mentation. In time, a consensus emerged: the people knew whom they wanted, and those who were not wanted felt the disconnection. They stepped down from the hustings and left the job of choosing the Council of Oligarchs to those who had the people's confidence.

"The business was called the ratherings," Philaria said, "and my husband was not part of it, he having relocated to Exley long after the coalescence. Today will see its culmination. The town will gather en masse in Varderon Square for dancing and drumming, and the selections will be made."

She cocked her head and put a hand to one ear. "If you listen, you should be able to hear the first drums."

I did as she said. I could hear a pulsing beat from the heart of the town.

The Electors would soon convene and choose the members of the Council, she said, their choices ratified by the populace, who would gather and chant their triads of notes together.

"It's all rather tiresome," she said, then made a comic face to acknowledge the unintended wordplay.

The drumming somehow appealed. I felt strangely drawn to the rhythm and wanted to be where it was happening. I got up from the table and said I believed I would go down to Varderon Square and observe the proceedings. "If Ser Bernaglio returns, he can send a servant to find me there."

«»

The plaza was thronged with Exleyans of all ages and categories, the crowd thickest over where the prospective Electors sat upon the hustings. A sound of drumming came from that direction, deep throbbing strokes upon what must have been a large drum indeed. Then, near to where I stood near the offices of Holfman Brothers, a lean man with a gold pendant dangling from one ear lobe began to strike a tambour slung on a cord around his neck. His rhythm wove itself into that of the unseen drum as he moved into the crowd, which parted for him. In moments, he was out of view but the sound continued.

The Exleyans were swaying, nodding, twisting this way and that to match the insistent beat of the two drums. And now a third drummer struck up somewhere I couldn't see and a collective sigh went up from all over the square. The doors of the restaurants and offices that surrounded the open space opened, and out came a heterogeny of people, cooks, clerks, servers, indentors, intercessors, and officers of the fiduciary pools. They flowed toward the crowd, found places, then stood still and joined in the rhythmic movements.

Amalthea stepped past me, unseeing. I put out a hand to make her aware of my presence, then thought better of it. I could not see her face but I could tell from the way she moved that her expression would be the same as the look all the Exleyans wore: rapt, yet vacant; lost in their common waking dream.

Suddenly, I felt myself a complete stranger, almost embarrassed, as if I had turned a corner and unexpectedly come across a moment of intimacy. I decided to go.

But when I made to turn away, I found I could not move.

I wondered if the drumming had had an effect on me. Perhaps I truly needed to consult a trancer. But now I gathered my powers of will and instructed my feet to take me from there. They would not.

I could turn my head, I found, even twist from the waist. I just could not take a step. Now I was genuinely embarrassed. I thought about asking some passerby for help, even calling out to Amalthea, then put the idea out of my mind. Because, beneath my mortification, a new emotion was rising in me: a sense that something important was about to happen and where I was at that impending moment was exactly where I was supposed to be.

By now, more drums had joined the original three. Varderon Square throbbed with a complexity of rhythms, anchored by the deep bass of the first drum and overlayed with cohering and syncopating cadences. The crowd swayed like a field of ripe grain under a wind, and from their throats rose a humming, a single note that never paused, because whenever some stopped to take a new breath, others carried on the communal sound.

I saw a motion from the corner of my eye and turned in that direction. Nulf Bernaglio had made his way through the fringes of the crowd and now stood a few paces away, his gaze intent on me. But his usually controlled expression was gone; in its place was the aspect of a predator about to bite down hard on its prey. His eyes gleamed with appetite.

I opened my mouth to speak to him, to tell him I couldn't move and to ask his help. But the words did not come. Instead, from deep within me came a wordless sound, an octave deeper than the note thrummed by the Exleyan throng. It filled my head, then seemed to spread like a miasma from where I stood to the back of the crowd. And as it touched the people and rolled over them, the timbre of their own humming changed to match mine.

And as my deeper note reached out to change theirs, its strength increased. Now there was no longer a hum, but a raw, croaking sound that arose from their throats. And they did not sway, but stood and shook with heavy vibrations. I saw some sink to the ground, their knees giving out, yet still they lay upon the cobbles and from their open mouths rose that thick, coarse rasp of sound.

I could not control what came out of me. But my gaze went back to Bernaglio and the anticipatory gleam of predation was now gone from his visage. Instead, I saw a grin of triumphant glee and he clapped his hands together and danced a step or two.

I wanted to shout to him, *What is going on?* But my voice was separated from the words that rang in my mind; I could not bring the two together, hard though I tried. And then I realized the question ought to be: *What have you done to me?*

Because there was no doubt in my mind. Of all the people gathered in Varderon Square, only one knew the answer to both questions.

Bernaglio ceased to regard me and turned instead to look over the heads of the crowd to the hustings. The men and women who had been seated there were now standing up, and they shook and vibrated like the swarm who filled the vast space before them. Some of them, pale and trembling, weakly grasping the railings, made their way down and disappeared into the crowd. Three others, clad in their celebratory robes, stood quivering, their gazes blank.

And now they raised their hands to the sky. The sound coming from me, though I couldn't believe it, swelled louder. It was matched by the noise of the crowd, which became a full-blown roar, the voice of one huge animal.

I looked again to Nulf Bernaglio and saw his fist strike the air in a gesture of victory. He regarded the crowd for a moment, seemed satisfied with what he saw, then turned and walked toward me, weaving through the scattered people between us.

As he approached, the sound that had been pouring out of me ceased abruptly. At the same moment, the crowd fell silent. They stood, many of them still trembling. Some lowered themselves to the cobblestones and sat there, like fever victims whose strength had ebbed away.

As for me, I felt my jaw ache as I closed my mouth. When I swallowed, it was as if my throat had been seared by fire. I coughed and agony shot through my windpipe. My knees shook and a cold chill rippled my back muscles and quaked my diaphragm.

The crowd began to disperse. I found I could move again. I saw Amalthea coming toward me. I raised a hand to catch her eye, tried to speak and found I could only make hoarse creaking sounds. But I doubt she would have heard me. Her eyes were blank, staring ahead without focus. She reached me and passed me by without notice.

And now Bernaglio was in front of me, a look of sly triumph on his face. I gathered spit in my dry mouth, swallowed, and formed a question to ask him.

But he raised a hand and spoke a word I did not hear.

«»

Again, as on the road across the plateau, it was as if I awakened from a dream. I was sitting at a table in the grand salon of the *Regal Swan*, my hand around a glass of liquor half raised to my mouth. Captain Reder was sitting across from me, her face wearing an expression in which concern competed with suspicion.

"Are you hearing me?" she said.

I blinked. "Yes," I said. I looked around. "How did I get here?"

"Like any other passenger," she said. "You showed Gashtun a ticket and climbed the gangplank."

I looked at the glass in my hand, slowly set it down on the table. "Am I drunk?" I said.

The question took her aback. "Don't think so. That's your first drink here and you walked straight when you came aboard." Her brows drew down. "But you were not yourself. You ask me, you looked like you were sleepwalking."

I was having trouble putting it together. I remembered the events in Varderon Square, though they seemed dreamlike to me now. I remembered Amalthea walking past then Bernaglio speaking to me, though I could not recall what he had said. After that, there was… nothing.

"Did I have luggage?" I said.

"Your ditty bag. It's in your cabin."

That made me think and I felt my shirt over my waist. My money belt was there, and well stocked.

"Something has happened to me," I said. I looked out the salon windows, saw darkness. "I have lost several hours."

She stood up. "I've got a ship to run. Look after yourself, and don't drink too much of that stuff. If you're having blackouts…"

She finished the thought with a face and a gesture that encouraged me to be sensible, then left the salon. I pushed the drink away and sat staring at the table top. I felt inert. I might have said "curiously inert," except that I clearly lacked much curiosity.

But something had changed in me since the events of Varderon Square. A part of me, a coldly rational part, appeared to have woken up. That newly alert part of me thought I ought to be seeking an explanation for my lassitude. I remembered my conversation with Amalthea. Something had been done to me and I ought to resent it. And now it dawned on me as it should have some time ago: the one who was behind it was Nulf Bernaglio.

It had been no accident that it was his caravan I found myself following, all those months ago. He had not been my benefactor. He had had a scheme. The scheme was something to do with the ratherings of Exley. I was a part of that scheme. I had been Bernaglio's mule. I had carried something into the town that was not welcome there.

And I knew what was most unwelcome in Exley.

Magic. And creatures of other Planes.

And, letting the rational part of me work on the problem, I thought I knew what Bernaglio had wanted: to subvert the singularly peculiar empathic process by which Exleyans chose their governors.

I supposed that one of the new members of the Council of Oligarchs would be Bernaglio. There might be others in league with him. Their motives? Unknown. Perhaps to enrich themselves further. Perhaps merely for the pleasure of holding power and exercising it.

Or perhaps for some darker purpose.

Either way, I now realized one more truth: my role in the plot was finished. I was being sent downriver. I tried an experiment: imagining myself returning to Exley, to confront Bernaglio and undo his scheme.

No sooner did I entertain the thought than I experienced a profound sense of dread. If I went to Exley, I would surely die.

My skin cooled and my heart beat faster. My breath came and went in gasps.

The rational part of me examined this fear. I found I could not specify the fatal threat, although I recognized that, as an Oligarch, Bernaglio would now be guarded by a cadre of highly competent Specials — the very same skilled combatants that I had recruited and trained.

I tried again, visualizing myself stepping off the *Swan* and striding toward Bernaglio's manse. The fear came charging back, along with a rising nausea. My hands shook and my skin erupted in bumps. I put the thought aside and the sensations faded then disappeared.

This is part of what has been done to me, the cool part of my mind said. *I need to find a way to deal with it.*

There were thaumaturges in Vanderoy, and probably trancers, too. I had funds and nothing else to do.

But the rational part of me continued to evaluate my situation. It said that if I was being sent to Vanderoy, then Vanderoy was not where I would find answers.

And then a name popped into my consciousness, like a bubble of foul gas bursting out of a swamp.

Olliphract.

Whatever had been done to me, it had been done in demon-haunted Olliphract — done by the wizard whose flying platform had delivered me to the plateau road where the dust of Bernaglio's caravan had scarcely settled.

If I wanted answers, Olliphract was where I would find them.

I would go there. Indeed, I wanted to go there. The more I thought about it, the stronger grew the inclination. The cool, rational part of me picked at this determination to travel to the place where I had been ensorcelled and abused. I could find no good reason behind the urge.

But I was going to Olliphract.

Part 2

Goladry speaks

He was almost certainly Kain Minderlanz, the Butcher of Drieff, who later served the wizard Malbroch the Omnifacient. I had gotten used to calling him Farouche, for all that he was probably the least romantic fellow ever to bear that storied name. And I was content to be addressed as Goladry, though I was far from innocent of our ancient world's sins and iniquities. And not anyone's definition of young, to boot, though I had been born fully grown.

When he came down the *Regal Swan*'s gangplank, his ditty bag over his shoulder, I was watching from the upper deck. When he looked about and chose a bearing, I hurried down the companionway and took up my usual station, several paces behind. By habit and the result of long training, I kept a partial eye on his progress toward one of the gates that pierced the river wall of the city of Vanderoy, but paid more attention to the people he passed. None of them took any unusual interest in Farouche's passage and no one began to follow him.

The gate guards knew him from the time he'd brought them a pair of criminals who'd been part of a fleecing ring operating on the packet boat. They let him pass without comment and took no more than a cursory appraisal of me. I was prepared to show my credentials as a Chadroyds operative — the firm had accreditation with the Vanderoy City Watch — but I was judged as harmless and waved through the gate.

Past the river wall and the warehouses just within its precincts, the streets trended upward. Farouche chose a wide thoroughfare and began to climb. A few intersections on, he turned onto Fitcherence Parade, a street of tall houses, his gaze watching for placards on porches or in windows. He saw one that caused him to halt and stood on the boardwalk taking a long, evaluating look at the place. Then he climbed the front steps and pulled on the bell rope.

A woman of mature years, almost as wide as she was short, answered. They exchanged a few words then Farouche stepped inside. I loitered not far away, sitting on a low fence that separated the front yard of a house across the way from the boardwalk. Not long after, the door of the boarding house opened and my charge came down the steps. He saw me at once and crossed the street.

"I don't need a bodyguard," he said, "and I doubt Bernaglio will pay your employer's fee anymore."

I showed him that the matter did not bother me and said, "I have left Chadroyds. I have adequate funds for a spell of unemployment. I thought I might continue to pursue my interest in your case on a voluntary basis."

"You have an interest in my 'case,' do you?" He cocked his head and studied me. "And what would that be?"

I shrugged again. "I can't abide mysteries. I have to solve them. As you may recall, it's my major character flaw."

He made a neutral sound in his throat, then it was his turn to shrug. "I take no responsibility for you. I will pursue my own concerns, but I have no objection to your company."

"Most people don't," I said. "There are some, though, who take exception to my existence."

His brow wrinkled. "Why is that?"

"I've never bothered to inquire." I looked up the street and changed the subject. "Would I be correct in assuming you are bound for the wizards' Guildhall?"

"You would," he said.

"Do you know where it is?"

"I had planned to ask the first Watchman I saw."

"No need." I slipped off the fence. "I happen to know the way."

«»

The Guildhall was a small and nondescript building on a street that otherwise housed the offices of one-person firms of intercessors and mortgage brokers, identified only by a plaque whose lettering was too small to be read except at arm's length.

"This is it," I said. "Do you mind if I go in with you? I've never seen the interior."

He did not mind. He stepped up to the portal, seized the iron knocker — it was in the shape of a hand — and rapped twice. In response, the door swung slowly and silently inward, revealing a dark space beyond. He looked at me as if for a comment, but I had none, and only extended my hand in a way that invited him to lead the way.

We entered and found ourselves in a dim and shadowy atrium, scarcely lit by a dome of glass set in the ceiling, its surface half-covered by twisted vines and dead leaves. The walls and floors were unadorned.

"What do you seek?" said a sepulchral voice. It took us a moment to locate the speaker, who turned out to be a lean-visaged man whose face and hair were almost as gray as the apprentice's gown he wore. I was reminded that apprenticing to wizards could be a lengthy process, and one that could wear down the body's resources. He was seated at a small table on the far side of the atrium, next to the only other exit from the room.

We crossed the floor until Farouche stood over the man, who was looking up at him with an expression of complete indifference.

"Knowledge," Farouche said, "and probably assistance."

The receptionist made no reply. He looked at me. "And you?"

"I have no need of your Guild's services," I said.

He looked me up and down. "Are you sure of that?"

"Make no mistake about it," I said.

He turned back to Farouche, while drawing a sheet of paper and a stylus toward him on the table top. "Your name?"

"It's a long story," Farouche said.

When nothing more was coming, the guildsman said, "Your complaint?"

"I have been put under a spell. It has cost me my memory and involved me in a situation I still do not understand."

The stylus scratched across the paper, the receptionist's handwriting resembling interlocking spider legs. "Define the situation."

"It has to do with the ratherings of Exley."

"Exley?" said the guildsman, and now his attention was fully engaged. He pulled open a drawer and brought out a hand-sized badge of dull metal that enclosed a gem with a rounded, polished surface. He stood and came around the table, then held the object a finger's breadth from Farouche's chest. The gem changed color: from emerald green to a soft pink.

The man studied the color for a long moment, then put the thing down on the table. Returning to the drawer, he reached deep into its recesses and came out with a slim tube of pale material; bone or ivory, I would have guessed. Crystals enclosed both ends.

He put the tube to one eye and regarded Farouche from several angles. He made a sound that indicated concern, and his brows congealed. Then he reversed the instrument and studied Farouche again, this time emitting a noise that was half hum, half sigh.

Finally, he turned toward me and gave me a once-over through the scryer.

I put up a hand to block his view and said, "No need for that."

He lowered the instrument and cocked an eyebrow. "No," he said, "I suppose not."

He turned back to Farouche, took a brief survey again through the tube then sat down at the desk, took up the stylus, and made more spider-leg scratchings.

"Well?" said my companion.

The guildsman continued writing. At last, he set down the stylus and looked up again, his mask of uninterest restored. "You are not under a spell," he said, "though you have definitely been interfered with, and quite recently."

Farouche's voice grew sharp. "If I'm not bespelled, where are my memories?"

The tone would have worried most men. The wizards' functionary was unmoved. "I would suggest you consult a trancer. Your… channels show blockage, but not the kind that indicates they have been the focus of fluxions."

"I don't understand," Farouche said.

"Of course not." The guildsman put away the gem and the tube, and closed the drawer. He interlaced his fingers and rested his hands on the table top, and gave the appearance of a man who is considering what to say.

After a moment, he said, "You have been, for some time, in contact — close contact — with an interplanar force. The scryer indicates contamination by gists of the Seventh Plane. You are free of it now, but there remain… traces. In time, they will fade and disappear. There is nothing a practitioner can do for you."

Farouche put his hands on the table top, moved them to grip its edges, his scarred knuckles showing white. "I still don't understand," he said. "Gist, interplanar force, the Seventh Plane. What are you telling me? Put it in words I can make sense of."

Anyone else would have been wanting to put distance between himself and the looming anger. The wizards' man sat unperturbed. Finally, his shoulders gave a slight movement and he said, "In layman's terms, you have until recently been possessed. By a demon."

Farouche let go of the table and straightened up. He blinked and stared at nothing for a moment. Then he took in a breath and let it out.

"What do I owe you?" he said, reaching for his purse.

"Nothing," said the receptionist. "We do not charge to tell you we cannot help you."

"All right," said Farouche, and I saw him putting himself back together in the way he did. "Any advice?"

"See a trancer. There's one with offices on Shosun Square. Although, given what the traces show, you might prefer to forgo recovering your memories. Most people who have truck with demons — even thaumaturges of rank — would give anything not to recall the experience."

«»

We walked aimlessly for a while. Farouche seemed a little dazed. Eventually, I spotted a tavern with tables and chairs outside on which were seated patrons who did not look the type to over imbibe and start brawling. I touched Farouche's elbow and suggested we sit, and let the news he had received sink in.

Vanderoy is known for good vintages so I ordered us a glass each of a pale and peppery wine made from flowers most people consider weeds. It came chilled with beads of moisture on the stemware. I sipped and found it pleasantly refreshing. Farouche drank half of his without any sign of a reaction.

"Demons," he said, after a while. He was gazing at the people passing by, though I doubted he saw them. "Who has 'truck with demons'?"

"'Thaumaturges of rank', according to that fellow at the wizards' Guild," I said.

He came partly back from wherever he had been. "What do I do?"

"Drink the wine," I said, "and let's talk about it."

But he just shook his head. I was not used to seeing him like this. My impression of him to this point had been of a man who laid out plans and implemented them with sustained vigor. Now he appeared to have come adrift.

Perhaps that was not such a bad thing. After all, I had goals I wished to accomplish. Perhaps I would set the agenda for a while. I took another sip while I composed my thoughts, then began.

"What happened in Exley to send you here?" I said.

He blinked. "I don't know. It was like when I woke up walking on the road behind Bernaglio's caravan. One minute I was in Varderon Square, the next I was on the *Swan*. I don't remember what happened in between."

"What do you remember from the square?"

His face clouded in concentration. "The ratherings. The Electors came out of the black tent. The crowd started to hum. I couldn't move, but I opened my mouth and..."

He looked down and to the side, hunting for a memory. Then he looked at me and I saw confusion. "I think I made some kind of sound. Bernaglio was there. He said something to me and then I… roared."

"Actually, it was more like a croak," I said. "The kind a giant frog would make."

"You were there?"

"I was keeping an eye on you."

"Then you tell me what happened," he said. He reached for his glass and drained the rest of the wine.

I told him what I had seen and heard, how Bernaglio had approached him and spoken.

"What did he say?"

"I was too far away to hear, especially with the crowd noise. It seemed like only a single word. And then you made that strange noise, which the crowd took up."

"Then what?"

I told him how the creaking-croaking noise went on for a long while. I was amazed he had that much breath in him. Then he stopped and the crowd fell silent. Bernaglio, with an air of triumph, spoke another word. Immediately, Farouche turned on his heel and walked away.

"I followed you. You went to your lodgings, came out with your bag, and went down to the dock. You bought a ticket, then sat on a bench until they started loading passengers. I bought a ticket and followed. You went into your cabin and stayed there for a while, then you came out and went to the first-class salon and ordered a drink."

"Reder," he said. "She was there."

"I spoke to her. I was concerned for you. You appeared to be sleepwalking."

He blinked at that. "Maybe I was. And maybe I finally woke up when she spoke to me." He looked down and to the side again. "I was different after that. I'm not sure how to describe it except to say that my thoughts seemed… clearer somehow."

He was quiet for a bit, trying out his new, clearer mentation, I supposed. I ordered us another two glasses of the weed-flower wine and waited. Eventually he looked at me again and asked the question I was expecting.

"When the crowd fell silent, did you hear what Bernaglio said to me?"

"Yes."

"What was it?"

"You don't know?"

He sought for the memory. "I can see him open his mouth and speak, but I cannot remember hearing what he said."

That confirmed what I had suspected. I told him I didn't think I should say it. It was a single word, not of any language I recognized.

"I think it is what trancers call a 'prompt'," I said. "That's a word that tells a person who is under a trancer's influence to do something particular, something that has been planted in his mind but hidden from his consciousness."

"Like pack and leave town, and never come back," he said.

I nodded, finished my first glass and turned to the second. Farouche continued to consult his thoughts, then his face became more grim than usual.

"Bernaglio," he said, in a tone that reminded me of a magistrate passing sentence.

"Yes," I said. "It would appear that your initial encounter with him was no happenstance."

"He put me on the road. He brought me to Exley. He kept me within his circle until... whatever happened during the ratherings."

"Based on what the wizards' man told us, he also had you infected with a demon."

"Why?"

"Obviously to affect the ratherings. Presumably, to overwhelm the collective under-consciousness of the Exleyans in a way that would see Bernaglio ascend to power. By now he has probably been invested as one of the ruling oligarchs."

Farouche's face went pale and the muscles of his jaw grew hard as knuckles. I imagined that face was the last sight some people had ever seen. Then I saw the anger abruptly disappear behind an expression I wouldn't have expected to see on this man.

"What frightens you?" I said.

He looked without seeing at the passing traffic. "I thought about returning to Exley and serving Nulf Bernaglio his just deserts."

"And that terrified you." I handed him his second glass. "Drink," I said, "and think of something else."

He did as I asked. Some color returned to his face. I waited until he was settled then said, "As the Guildsman said, you have been interfered with, almost certainly by a trancer. Someone has planted an order to keep away from them, which is why you always slide away from the notion.

"And once Bernaglio said that foreign word, you not only left Exley but discovered you had a deep fear of returning there."

"It's true," he said. "It makes no sense, but it terrifies me just to think of it."

"Then there's only one thing to do," I said.

"What?" He seemed sincerely mystified.

"There's a trancer in Shosun Square. We go there, now, and get you fixed." I saw the reluctance that instantly rose in him. "Tell me," I said, "what do you have against the idea?"

He frowned. "I don't know," he said. "It just seems like a bad idea."

"And that's why we have to do it," I said. "Drink up. Shoshun is only a little way from here."

«»

The trancer was in a three-story building on the edge of a small plaza with a few shade-throwing trees and a fountain at its center. Down a marble-floored corridor on the second story, a plaque on a door with a pebbled glass window in it said her name was Thybalda Hache and that she was available by appointment only.

Farouche was wearing a hang-dog expression that didn't suit him. I'd had to take his arm and coax him up the stairs, and the sight of the trancer's name and instructions made him turn away. But I caught him and brought him back.

"Look," I said, "just accept that your reluctance has been forced upon you. It's not from you, it's from someone else who has no business being inside your head. Find your anger and use it."

He gritted his teeth and looked down at his feet, but he stood there as I knocked on the door then opened it. I took his arm again and guided him in, then shut the door before he could get out. That seemed to bolster his determination to overcome whatever was urging him to depart.

We were in a waiting room that had a few wooden chairs and a plush settee set around a braided rug of good quality. A small desk stood to one side, untenanted at the moment. An inner door — solid wood, no window — presumably led to the space where the trancer did what she did. Keeping a hand on Farouche, I led him across to it, knocked, and opened.

A woman past her middle years looked up from her lunch, a forkful of noodles halfway to her mouth. Her face was youthful, but the mop of indifferently tended white hair above it gave her a grandmotherly aspect — at this moment, the look of a grandmother whose grandchildren were misbehaving. She set the fork down in the bowl and said, "You need to have made an appointment. My assistant will return shortly and you can make an arrangement with him."

"This is an emergency," I said. "My companion has been placed under some compulsions, one of which is to avoid practitioners of your art. I can't guarantee I'll be able to get him back here."

She stared at me for a moment then switched her gaze to Farouche and frowned at his aspect. "Can you speak?" she asked him.

He twice had to clear his throat, but finally managed a yes. She got up and came around the desk and her frown deepened when she saw him look away. Then her expression changed and she wore the look of a professional who accepts that sometimes the standard procedures have to be abrogated.

She touched Farouche gently on the arm. "Please," she said, "come and sit here."

She led him to a comfortable chair that folded back to allow him to recline with his feet supported. He looked deeply uncomfortable in what should have been a restful position. She stood and examined him for a long moment, pulling down one his eyelids to focus on his eye, then went to a cupboard that stood against one wall and brought out several items.

One was a shallow stone bowl that she set on the desk, into which she shook out some white powder from a stoppered glass vial. Then she took up a steel needle and approached my companion. "Let me have your hand," she said.

Again, I saw him overcome an impulse to refuse. I was impressed by the strength of his will. He held out his calloused hand and did not look away, as many would have done, when she poked the steel into a finger tip then squeezed out a droplet of blood.

She reached for the bowl and positioned it under his hand as she turned his finger over and squeezed again. The size of the droplet increased and it fell into the powder. She stirred the mixture with the needle, and her frown deepened again at what she saw.

"Who did this to you?" she said.

I answered for Farouche. "He doesn't know. His memories have been taken from him."

Now I saw genuine anger in her matronly face. "Reprehensible," she said. "Deeply reprehensible."

She stood in thought while the room filled with silence. Then she nodded decisively and addressed Farouche. "You have been administered a substance that is banned by the trancers' Guild as unethical and dangerous to the recipient. Its effect is to intensify the power of suggestions made while you are in trance."

"Is there an antidote?"

She shook her head. "No, but the effects diminish with time. How long have you been in this condition?"

He calculated the number of weeks since he had come to find himself walking the caravan road and told her. The information only caused the lines around her mouth to grow still deeper.

"That suggests that someone has renewed the dosage at least once and more likely twice or even three times, depending on how much you have been given."

"Could it have been slipped into his food?" I asked.

"It is tasteless and odorless, and its potency is not affected by cooking. So, yes."

"Bernaglio," I said. "You have dined with him a number of times."

Farouche nodded grimly. "He set a very good table."

I addressed Thybalda Hache. "Can you undo the suggestions?"

She gave her mouth a thinker's twist. "Possibly. I should at least be able to weaken their power, so that he can push back against them." She looked at Farouche. "The question is, will you help me to do that?"

His face went pale again and I saw him take in a long breath and let it out. "I will do my best," he said.

A young man put his head through the doorway saying, "I heard voices. Who are—"

"It's all right, Audair," the trancer said. "Cancel my appointments for the next two hours. And bring us a pot of punge."

«»

It was a good hour before she said to me, "He's now in a light trance. We'll see what we can do to delineate the interference."

She had begun by administering what she called a mild soporific via the punge she got my companion to drink. It acted, she said, to suppress the secretions of glands that responded to intimations of danger. "The danger is, of course, illusory but the glands don't know that. They react and that reinforces the sense of peril and fear."

Remembering our trip to the spoliators camp, I told her I found it hard to imagine Farouche as fear struck. "He faces death-dealing bandits with a calm aspect."

"That's why the criminal who altered him had to use the chemical enhancer." She shook her head and softly spoke a curseword. "If you discover his name, let me know it. My Guild takes a dim view. We may decide to send a vindicator."

"Chances are," I said, "that the perpetrator is a wizard of Olliphract, using both chemical and magical means to alter my companion's mentation."

A wash of pallor came over her grandmotherly face. "A wizard of Olliphract? They are despicable."

"Indeed," I said. "However, I believe that, should he be freed from his constraints and compulsions, my companion will not hesitate to take revenge. He has a history of it."

"Fair enough," she said. She studied the man in the relaxation chair. His breathing was regular and even now, his eyes closed, his hands loose in his lap.

"I think we're ready," she said. She pulled a stool closer to the chair and sat. Before she began, she looked up at me and requested that I step back and remain silent.

I will not relate the entirety of what happened. My layman's impression was that she was metaphorically picking apart an object that had been constructed in layers, each one of which had to be peeled gently back to expose the next layer beneath.

Much of the technique had to do with soothing the subject and convincing him that he was in no danger, and that he could entrust the person behind the voice he heard not to lead him into peril. As the process continued, I saw Farouche become more relaxed, until I would have thought him sound asleep if he had not spoken clearly and appropriately whenever she asked him a question.

When he was well settled, she told him he could safely look back to the moment when his memories began. I had quietly told her what I knew.

"All right," he said.

"Describe where you are and what you are doing."

He told her he was walking along the road on the high plateau toward some dust clouds on the horizon.

"Now," she said. "Imagine you have stopped at that moment and all the world has stopped with you. Can you do so?"

"Yes."

"Now, you are perfectly safe. The whole world is stopped and still and nothing can harm you. Do you feel that way?"

"Yes."

"Then turn and look about you in all directions. What do you see behind you?"

"The road, empty."

"Off to your left?"

"Some distant hills."

"To your right?"

"The plain, empty."

"Now, again, you are perfectly safe and nothing can harm you."

"Safe," he said.

"Look up."

I saw him tense and draw in his breath. His fingers contracted into claws.

"Nothing to fear," the trancer said. "All is frozen and cannot hurt you."

He let out the breath and his hands opened again.

"What do you see?"

"The platform. Flying away."

He started to breathe rapidly and she spent some time soothing him. Then she said, "Describe the platform."

It was rectangular, he said, with a balustrade around its circumference. It had chairs to sit in and an awning over them to protect from sun and rain. Beneath were two pods of metallic mesh that housed the imps whose powers lifted and drove the platform.

All of this he got out without much distress. She spent a little more time soothing him then put a new question.

"Was there any sort of heraldic device visible?"

Again, he drew into himself, like a hunted creature backing into its den. But under her coaxing, his mind's eye roved over the image of the flying platform and found an answer.

"Two snakes, their tails curled around an egg, their heads confronting each other."

His breath came fast again and his cheeks moved from the grinding of his teeth beneath them. Thybalda Hache calmed him again then told him he had done very well and now could fall into a deep and restful natural sleep. In moments, his breathing indicated that he had gone under.

"Well," she said to me, "I think that's enough for a start. You wanted me to ask about the heraldic device. Did his answer mean anything to you?"

"Not yet," I said, "but it will."

I asked her the amount of her fee and she named a figure. "I am abrogating the common practice of Vanderoy of setting a number twice what I expect," she said. "This matter is too serious for such foofaraw."

I thanked her and paid her in silver. She gave me some of the soporific, in separate twists of paper, and said I should get Farouche to take a dose before sleeping, and again in the morning.

"Then bring him back here in the first hour after the midday meal."

I said I would. She looked down at him sleeping and said, "It is a crime, what has been done to him. I am required to notify my Guild."

The matter gave me pause. Many Guilds are riven by factions, with masters vying for ascendancy. Any issue can become a weapon on their battlefield.

"Must you do so immediately?" I said.

I saw her weighing her obligations. "How long will you remain in Vanderoy?"

"No longer than this business takes, I think. There are answers to be got in Exley. And, I'm afraid, in Olliphract."

Her eyes grew large. "Olliphract?" She thought for a moment then said, as if to herself, "The snakes and the egg. Of course."

"Indeed," I said. "So perhaps best not to bring this matter to the attention of your Guild's masters until we are gone from Vanderoy."

"Yes," she said. "And in the meantime, keep a sharp eye around you at all times."

"And overhead, as well," I said.

«»

"You need to rest and relax," I told Farouche the next morning, handing him the second twist of the soporific. I had taken a room down the hall from his in the boarding house on Fitcherence Parade. We were the last of the residents sitting at the long table while the landlady, Sera Finnhoddle, bustled about in a manner that said she would prefer us to be out of her way.

Nonetheless, I saw my companion pour the powder into his punge and drink some of it. He had taken a similar draft after dinner last night and, when I inquired, told me that he had slept through the hours of darkness without dreams.

"Good," I said and poured a little punge for myself. Our hostess did not buy the finest grade, and I suspected her pot was encrusted with old grounds, but I had drunk worse in times gone by. Much worse.

"Tell me," I said, when I saw the soporific having an effect, "What do you remember from yesterday's session with Thybalda Hache?"

"Not a great deal," he said. "I think I fell asleep."

"How do you feel about going back again?"

I saw a small ripple of discomfort affect his mouth but then his expression cleared and he said, "I suppose I should. Do you think she'll be able to help?"

"She already has."

That caused him to draw down his brows. "How so?"

"We'll talk about it later," I said. "I have to run an errand. I'll be back to accompany you to your appointment."

"What appointment?"

"Never mind. Finish your punge then rest in your room."

When he was settled upstairs, snoring on the bed, I locked the door and went out. A brisk walk took me down to the wizards' Guildhall. I knocked and the door theatrically opened itself as it had the day before. I entered and found a different apprentice at the reception desk, this one much younger and apparently in need of practice to deepening his voice if he wanted to make as convincing an impression of gravitas as yesterday's receptionist had.

"What do you seek?" he said, the last word split into two syllables as his tone went up an involuntary octave.

"Information," I said. I described the arms Farouche had seen on the flying platform: "An egg gripped in the tails of two serpents that face each other, their mouths open."

"It's not the device of any member of the Guild in Vanderoy," said the squeaker.

"That much I knew," I said. "Do you not have a compendium of thaumaturges' heraldry?"

"In the library," he said.

"And will you consult it?"

"For a fee."

"Then do so."

I paid over the sum he mentioned. It was not an onerous amount. He told me to wait then stood and waved a hand at the inner door, said a word I could not hear, and it opened. There were no chairs in the atrium, wizards not being known to be solicitous of others' comfort. I folded my arms and leaned against a wall.

Time passed, more of it than I would have thought needed for the apprentice to go to another room, find a book, and consult its pages. I waited, my eye on the door he had left by, but I was growing concerned that much more delay would encroach upon the time required to return to the boarding house and get Farouche to his appointment with Thybalda Hache.

The inner door did not open. Instead, a curious thing happened. A kind of dimness — I lack the words to describe it properly — affected the air in the middle of the atrium, creating a tall oval of gloomy dullness. This thickened until it resolved into an ombrous vista, as if I was looking down a twilight road into a landscape draped in shadows. As soon as the image gelled in my vision, I saw two figures striding along the road toward me. They grew rapidly in size until they stepped through the oval into the atrium, at which the view into the shadowy land winked out of existence.

I recognized one of the arrivals: the gray-robed apprentice who had gone off to the library. The other was a tall man in a robe of purple marked by arcane symbols of shimmering gold. His features were aquiline, his thin lips set in a frown, and his eyes were hidden behind spectacles of deepest jet. Under his arm he carried a heavy tome bound in red leather.

He looked at me and I felt a chill. The black spectacles were, I intuitively knew, a kind of weapon, and I had just been targeted by them. He set the book down upon the receptionist's table, then opened it to a page marked by a strip of leather that matched the cover. He pointed to a colored illustration and said, "Is this the device you were asking about?"

I looked and saw an image of egg and serpents that matched the description Farouche had given while entranced. I said, "I believe it is. I have not seen it myself but heard it described."

"Described by whom?" said the thaumaturge, who I had decided must be one of Vanderoy's two practitioners of the

Purple School, almost certainly the one named Radegonde the Ineffable, the other being a recluse.

"My companion. We came yesterday and your apprentice told him he had recently been possessed by a demon of the Seventh Plane."

This was not the information the wizard had been expecting. His expression hardened even further and he strode around the desk, the squeaker apprentice scuttling out of his path. The wizard opened the drawer and brought out a sheaf of papers. He sorted through these impatiently until his attention was caught by one. He dropped the other pages onto the floor, causing the apprentice to kneel and gather them up, while the Purple Schooler studied what was written on the sheet he held. When it bent a little, I recognized the spidery hand in which it was written.

A look of thunder appeared on Radegonde's already grim face as he set the page down and looked at me. "Are you from Exley?" he said.

"Not originally, but I have lived there recently," I said.

"Were you involved in the… manifestation that occurred there a few days ago?"

"I was not, but my companion was." I hastened to add, "His participation was involuntary. He appears to have been used, criminally perhaps."

"What is his name?"

I explained about the memory loss, but that we now believed he was Kain Minderlanz. The thaumaturge's expression ameliorated somewhat, though I doubt he was capable of displaying warmth or empathy.

"Where is he now?"

"At a boarding house."

Radegonde was silent for a moment, his attention focused on his own concerns. Then he looked at me again, removing the jet spectacles to reveal eyes of an unnatural violet. He said, "I am going to give you some advice."

"I would welcome it if it is helpful."

"Return to your companion and depart Vanderoy at your earliest opportunity," he said.

"We are engaged with a trancer to recover his memories. The procedure may take several sessions."

Radegond waved the matter away. "Go. I can tell you that His Grace, Duke Auerbrache, is deeply offended by what happened in Exley. His special constables, the Eyes and Ears of the Duke, have been assigned to discover the details of the events. Their methods of investigation are… let us say, unbridled."

"How do Exley's affairs concern the Duke of Vanderoy? They are an oligarchy and he is a hereditary autocrat."

I saw impatience grip the thaumaturge, but it was brief. He reached somewhere within him for a rarely used patience and said, "Each polity has its own ways of handing power from its old wielders to the new. But some ways cannot be tolerated. The use of demonic powers is high on that list."

"I see," I said. "Then I will be going—"

"Good," the thaumaturge said, dismissing me and turning to the apprentice. "Who was in your place yesterday?" he said.

The squeaker opened his mouth to reply, but now it was my turn to interrupt, as I completed my truncated sentence. "Just as soon as you tell me the name of the wizard whose device is the egg and serpents."

The Purple Schooler returned his gaze to me and this time he made no attempt to disguise his irritation. I was tempted to step away and depart, but instead I said, "I have paid for the information."

"I will give you more good advice," the thaumaturge said. "Take your money back and forget you ever saw these arms." He indicated the open book then slammed it closed.

"I need to know," I said. "So does my associate."

A new expression came over Radegonde. He studied me as if seeing me for the first time, then reached into his robe and drew out a tube similar to the one yesterday's apprentice had used to examine Farouche. But the wizard's was larger, and a line of symbols were etched into the side of the scryer.

He touched one of these characters and it briefly glowed. Then he set the instrument to his eye and regarded me for a moment.

He said, "Ah, I see," then put the tube away. "Your kind are generally not well received in Vanderoy."

"I cannot help my origins," I said.

The purple-clad shoulders rose and fell. "Suit yourself," he said. "My advice still stands."

"As does my need, and my companion's."

The hard face briefly displayed the expression of a man who has done his best to prevent foolish behavior, then he said, "They are the arms of a thaumaturge named Fatezh, who styles himself 'the Force.' You would be wise to forget you ever heard that name, and certainly to avoid speaking it often, or better yet at all."

"Of what school is he?" I said.

The answer was a snort of derision. "No school. He is of that detestable ilk who disdain the rigors of schools and guilds."

I knew what he meant. "And he would be found in Olliphract," I said.

"He would," said Radegonde, "and whoever found him would surely regret it, probably for a long and horrifically painful period."

I made a courteous gesture and turned to depart. The thaumaturge called me back. "I will advise you further," he said, "because it is the interests of my Guild to do so."

I waited to see what would come. He composed a thought and said, "The Duke of Vanderoy is unhappy with my Guild at present. You have no need to know why. He is also unhappy that some kind of wizardry has been employed to alter the governance of Exley. The thought that some such might be employed here in Vanderoy, while the succession to the ducal throne remains undecided, makes him extremely unhappy.

"The Duke is prone to take short, sharp decisions. If his Eyes and Ears discover you in his city, the consequences will be quick and decisive. Am I being clear enough?"

"You are," I said. "You recommend that we find somewhere else to continue our investigations."

"Forthwith," said Radegonde, "to borrow one of the Duke's frequently used terms."

«»

I hurried back to our lodgings. As I turned onto Fitcherence Parade, I saw a familiar figure descending the front steps of the boarding house next to ours. As I came within hailing distance, he was climbing to Sera Finnhoddle's porch.

"Gashtun!" I called. "Are you looking for Farouche?"

He turned and regarded me with surprise, then recognized me. "You're the bodyguard," he said. "Do you know where I can find him?"

"You have," I said. "He's inside. What do you want with him?"

It turned out that Captain Reder had received a messenger from Ser Ufretes of Chadroyds, asking if she knew the whereabouts of my companion. When she said she could probably locate him in Vanderoy, the man had handed her a sealed envelope. When the packet boat docked this morning, she had given it to Gashtun and told him to try at all the boarding establishments near to the docks.

"Smart," I said. "Come up and we'll see him."

Farouche was in his room. The morning's draft of calming powder was beginning to wear off, and he was restlessly pacing the floor when I entered with the guard from the *Swan*.

I should have knocked, because his back was turned to the door. He turned with a quick motion and for a moment I saw the face of one who has killed often and without hesitation. His gaze went from me to Gashtun and murder turned to puzzlement.

I told him about the missive from Chadroyds. He took it from Gashtun's proffered hand and examined it as if he had never seen an envelope before.

"Chadroyds are known to be thorough," I said. "They tie up loose ends, even after an investigation is terminated."

He said something I did not catch and used his thumb to break the wax seal, then extracted a folded sheet of paper. He scanned it and said, "Do you remember that Ufretes was sending to his associates in other cities, to inquire about my identity?"

"There's an answer?"

He looked at the paper again. "The fellow student who rented the accommodation where my brother and I stayed while we were at the Institute. His name is Harul Bok and he lives in the city of Wal. He is some sort of civic functionary." His finger touched a line of the text. "Here is his address."

"We should go there immediately," I said.

"What, and not continue with the trancer?"

I told him what Radegond the Ineffable had said. The worry that had been lurking in his face fled.

"It is not something to be glad of," I said. "Auerbrache's Eyes and Ears are notorious for their interrogation routines. If we lived, we would never be right again."

"True," he said, already turning to begin packing his possessions, "but the trancer made me uncomfortable. Perhaps I can learn what I need to know from this Bok fellow."

There was no point arguing. He was right, if perhaps for the wrong reasons. "All right," I said, "I'll get my things together."

Throughout our exchange, Gashtun had been hovering by the door. Now he said, "I'd like to come with you, if I may."

Farouche stopped and looked at him. "You have a secure position with House Bernaglio. We cannot afford to pay you what they do. And, ultimately, our journey may take us to Olliphract."

When that registered with the man, I saw him swallow, but he stood to attention and said, "Things are not what they were at House Bernaglio. There may be no more caravans, now that he is an oligarch of the Council."

He lowered his eyes then raised them again. "Besides, you treated me square after I thumped you when you weren't looking. I'm a better man for what you showed me."

I think Farouche was affected by the sentiment behind Gashtun's declaration, but forbore to show it. Instead, he came to the man and shook his hand, saying, "It will be an honor to serve with you."

"Serve whom?" I said, but they ignored me.

«»

Wal was two days' travel distant, but along good roads. An omnibus departed twice a day from Vanderoy, and we were in time to catch the afternoon coach. We bought our tickets an hour before the scheduled departure and spent the intervening time in a nearby tavern, reasoning that we were less likely to come under the gaze of the Eyes and Ears if we were three anonymous drinkers huddled in a back corner, rather than three out-of-towners in the omnibus line's waiting room.

As it was, we boarded without incident, Farouche and I in one of the rear seats of the covered charabanc and Gashtun riding on the roof. He said he didn't mind since the weather was fair and the ticket was half the price for insiders.

"Besides, I'm not one for padded seats," he said, giving his rump a hard swat. "Might lose my callouses. And then where would I be?"

«»

We rode the coach to Breem, the vehicle pausing only to change teams of horses every four hours, giving the passengers barely enough time to stretch their legs, relieve themselves, and drink a bowl of lukewarm soup at the station stops.

"At least the bread's not stale," said Gashtun as we finished up the hurried meal and headed back to the omnibus. "Last few days of a caravan, you're lucky if the bread's not moldy or crawling with weevils."

They slept through the next stop, full darkness having fallen, then awoke as the coach was pulling into the Breem depot at dawn, with a layover until the Wal-bound carriage left at noon.

I'd been thinking during the night and while we breakfasted on eggs and bacon — both unfortunately boiled, the depot's cook being woefully unskilled — I unburdened myself of my thoughts to Farouche, itemizing them on my fingers.

"You accept," I said, "that you have been tranced, the procedure augmented by a drug."

"I do," he said.

"And you accept that whoever did this implanted in you a dread of trancers."

He nodded, his mouth full of limp, chewy meat.

I bent down a third finger. "Since it seems you came by flying platform from Olliphract, it makes sense that there was where you were interfered with."

He swallowed and reached for his mug of punge. "It makes sense," he said, then washed down the bacon.

Now I held a finger up in interrogation. "Then why is it, when every sensible person feels a chill frisson of fear at the thought of going to a place where half-mad wizards cultivate hideous demons, that the prospect is as unintimidating, to you, as a stroll in a garden?"

He put down the mug and blinked at me. "All right," he said, "tell me why."

I meshed my fingers together and leaned over the table. "Because," I said, "the same someone who wants you to avoid trancers wants you to come to Olliphract."

He thought for a moment, then said, "That does make sense."

"More sense than why *I* am going to Olliphract," I said.

"So, why are you?"

"I'm still working on that," I said.

«»

The noon coach to Wal was better sprung than the vehicle we had traveled in overnight. The roads were smoother, too, making for a more restful journey. Farouche wedged himself into a corner and fell asleep. I managed a half-doze for at least an hour but was awakened when Gashtun leaned down from his place on the roof and appeared upside-down in the window.

"Did you see that?" he said.

"What?" I said, coming fully awake and looking about. The other passengers in the coach, an intercessor from Wal and his teenage son, did the same.

"The shadow," Gashtun said.

"What shadow?" I said. I looked to the intercessor, who raised and settled his shoulders in a show of ignorance, but the boy said, "I saw it. I thought it was a cloud but when I looked out the window, the sky was clear."

Gashtun said, "I was half asleep when suddenly it got dark. Then the sun was back. It took me a moment to think, 'That was odd,' and then I opened my eyes, thinking it might have been a pelgrane looking at me as a possible meal, but there was nothing."

He thought for a moment — I'd noticed that when he did that, it took some time — and said, "There might have been something, high up, right in line with the sun. But I couldn't be sure. Anyway, I thought you should know, since I heard you talking about flying platforms."

I craned my neck to look out the window he was not obscuring. The sun was bright and not that far past the zenith. If there was anything lurking in its glare, I couldn't see it.

"Thanks," I said to Gashtun. "Maybe keep an eye out."

The boy was looking at me with speculative interest. "Flying platforms?" he said.

"Forget about it," said his father. "Wizard-stuff."

Gashtun pulled himself back to where he rode. Farouche slept on.

«»

We rolled into Wal in late evening and went to a nearby inn the station's ostler recommended as, "reasonably clean for the price, and the food won't kill you." Supper was bread and sausages, with ale that was not too cloudy, and we took a room that contained three beds, although the beds contained creatures left behind by previous travelers.

We shook out the covers, but I suspected all that did was transfer the parasites onto the reed mats that partly covered the splintery floorboards, from where they surely jumped back onto us as we slept. Itching and scratching, we rose in the morning, ate another meal of bread and sausages — this time washed down with bitter punge — and made our way to the city hall, where the fuglemen of Wal exercised civic governance.

"We're looking for Harul Bok," I said to the person behind the grilled wicket, after waiting in line for our turn. The man, skeleton thin with a bump in the front of his throat that suggested he had half-swallowed the egg of a large species of bird, clearly did not like our request.

"Ser Bok is a busy man," he said. "You will have to make an appointment."

"We will not take much of his time," I said. As I spoke, I leaned forward to emphasize the importance of our request. Unfortunately, one of the creatures I had acquired as passengers during the night decided that the thin man offered a tastier meal. It leapt from my person onto his hand that held a stylus and began to draw some blood.

The functionary looked down, aghast, and used thumb and forefinger to squeeze the offending insect. But when he opened his grip to inspect the damage, the mite was unaffected. It got its legs under it and leapt into the space between his limp collar and his neck, and disappeared.

"I'm sorry," I said, although I was not responsible for the flea's choices, but my apology was not accepted. Indeed, the fellow had ceased to pay any attention to me at all, being busy pulling out his shirt tails and unbuttoning the front in a frantic search for his new resident.

"He must be one of those finicky citified types," Gashtun said. "Wouldn't last too long on the trail."

Farouche, meanwhile, had drifted over to a notice board that listed the various departments of the Wal government and the numbers and floors where their offices were located in the building. Beneath a listing for "Revenue Services" was a name and title — H. Bok, Steward — and a number that appeared to be one flight up.

"Here," he called to me and Gashtun, indicating a nearby flight of stairs. A sign said, "Official Business Only," but he ignored that and began to climb. Gashtun and I followed.

Bok's office was not hard to find nor, upon entry, did we find it to be a hive of activity. We were in a large room, high-ceilinged, full of desks — some of them requiring high stools for their occupants — and the only sound was of the scratching of styluses upon the pages of large ledgers. In a corner, a man seated at a table was counting silver and brass coins, and placing them in orderly heaps.

No one paid particular notice of our entry. When we were not approached, I said to the room in general, "We are here to see Ser Bok."

A clerk at one of the high perches stopped his work, used a blotter to remove excess ink, and gestured with a thumb to an inner door. When I approached it, I saw the same legend that had adorned the notice board in the lobby. I knocked twice, turned the knob, and opened the door.

Harul Bok was a thin-haired man past his middle years, wearing an eyeshade and a pair of half-spectacles as he pored over a ledger spread wide on his desk. He glanced up with a bemused look that turned to irritation as he saw faces he did not recognize. He opened his mouth in what was surely going to be an order for us to depart, but then Farouche stepped into clearer view.

Bok's eyes widened and I saw understanding come into his face. "Minderlanz?" he said.

"Apparently," said my companion.

That caused a look of mild confusion. I stepped forward, identified myself as a Chadroyds operative — true, if one didn't quibble over dates — and reminded Bok that he had been contacted by one of the firm's associates.

"Yes," he said, removing the spectacles and polishing them on a cloth in what had the appearance of a habitual action. "Though they didn't say why. You're not a hunted criminal, are you?"

"Not that I know of," said Farouche. He explained succinctly, without mentioning demons or thaumaturges, that he had lost his memory and was in search of it. "I've come to understand that I am probably Kain Minderlanz. I'm hoping you might be able to shed some light on the matter."

"And you've come all this way from..." Bok repositioned the lenses and moved his hand in a way that said he was trying to remember.

"Vanderoy," I said. I was coming to understand that a connection with Exley might not be a recommendation.

"Vanderoy," Bok said. "So that's where you ended up. I thought I remembered something about a Free Company."

"It's a long story," said Farouche, "and not worth the telling. But can you tell me anything that might help me know for sure that I am Kain and not Etzel?"

Bok put out his lower lip as he peered back into the past. After a while, he said, "Hohsin buns."

Farouche and I waited for more. I didn't think Gashtun was much engaged by the conversation.

Bok fixed his gaze on Farouche. "You were twins, as alike as two pins in a cushion. But one of you liked hohsin buns, couldn't get enough of them."

Farouche shook his head. The reference did not land on him.

I said, "Hohsin buns are those confections made of soft and fluffy dough, around a nugget of meat that was soaked in a marinade. They are fiery hot, burn your sinuses like a squirt of lava. No one can eat one without reaching for a jug of liquid."

"Etzel Minderlanz," said Bok, "could eat two without needing a guzzle. Three if he could find someone who didn't know him and bet he couldn't."

I looked at my companion. "Turn up any memories?"

He shook his head.

"Perhaps," I said, "if we fed you one. Taste is, like smell, a deep-planted memory."

Farouche said to Bok, "You are sure it was Etzel, not Kain?"

"Completely. 'Hotsy' was his nickname. Nobody ever called Kain anything but Kain." Remembering, he added, "Or ser."

"Can you find hohsin buns in Wal?" I said.

Bok nodded. "Oh, yes. There's a stall in the market by the southern gate. Make sure you buy a stoup of ale before you taste the bun. Before, it's two groats a mug; after, it's four."

«»

Farouche took a good bite of the white bun and chewed contemplatively. Then his eyes bulged in his head and he spat the wad of dough and peppered meat onto the cobblestones and reached for the leather tankard of ale. His throat worked as he poured the drink down his throat, then he took another mouthful and swashed it around before spitting it out. The stallholder who had sold him the bun and ale was doing his best not to laugh. Comical as the performance was, my companion had the look of a man who was capable of meeting mockery with forthright action.

"Did it bring up any pleasant memories?" I said, when he had rinsed and spat again.

"I've tasted it before," he said. "I'm sure I never liked it."

He looked at the white orb in his hand, with the bright red knuckle of flesh at its center. He offered it back to the vendor but the man showed his palms in refusal. Gashtun, who had been standing to one side during the performance, reached and took the hohsin bun, regarded it for a moment, then took a bite. He chewed and swallowed, asked for the stoup of ale, and washed away the taste.

"They're hotter in Exley," he said. "We used to eat them on a dare."

Farouche spat again. "So, I'm Kain Minderlanz," he said. "Kain, the Butcher of Drieff."

"So it would seem," I said. "Now that you know, is there still any point in going to Olliphract?"

He thought about it. "Revenge, I suppose," he said, after a long consultation with himself. "I don't feel a burning need, but the rational part of me says I ought to, and the only reason I don't is that I've been blocked from my own feelings. I ought to resent that, too."

"The rational part of you?" I said. "This is the first I'm hearing of it."

He looked for words for a moment, then sighed and said, "After the business in Varderon Square, it was as if something left me, and the space it had occupied was filled with… cold thought."

He nodded to himself, then went on, "I think whoever did this to me, rooted around in my mind and restacked my memories and motivations to make room for whatever was planted in here," — he tapped his head — "didn't do a perfect job. The hole had to be filled after the whatever-it-was departed, so the thinking part of my mind moved into the empty space."

"Interesting," I said. "Do you have any strong feelings? About other things, I mean."

"Not really," he said. "I liked Amalthea, still do. I was proud of the work I did with the *Swan* and training the guards and Specials, but I wasn't swept away by emotion. I would have to call myself… lukewarm."

Again, I said that was interesting. And that the name Farouche was becoming less and less appropriate. "But," I added, "I recommend you keep using it. Bernaglio can't be the only person who had family at Drieff."

Gashtun had finished the bun and the ale while we spoke. Now he wiped his red-whiskered mouth on his sleeve and said, "What do we do now?"

Farouche held up a hand to tell us both to wait. A new thought had occurred to him. "Can Bernaglio be the cause of all this?" he said, after a moment. "Yes, he's rich, and he married into a powerful family, but wealth and political influence don't butter many beans with wizards."

I shrugged. My impression of the merchant was of a subtle mind and a taste for refined living, but that didn't argue for any connections to thaumaturges. Yet, it was becoming manifestly clear that such connections existed.

The answer to the puzzle came from an unexpected source. "I think I know something," Gashtun said.

We both looked at him. "What do you think you know?" Farouche said.

Whenever the caravan went up to Ur Nazim, the guard said, Nulf Bernaglio would spend a day touring the shops in the city's Street of Sorcerers, buying talismans and charms and odd items of magical paraphernalia.

"He'd have me and a couple of the boys along to keep him safe, and to carry the goods back to the camp," Gashtun said. "Some of that stuff was weird."

"He didn't go to the Street of Sorcerers when I was in Ur Nazim," Farouche said.

"No, he didn't," Gashtun said. "That was funny, because he always did, the other trips. He particularly liked little old gods. You know, ones that nobody worships anymore. I once heard him talking to Mashem the 'purveyor of gently used deities' — that was what he called himself — and the boss said that some of them still had powers and would do stuff for you if you knew their true names and could recover the forgotten rituals."

Farouche was staring at the red-bearded man but his gaze was turned inward on whatever the revived rational part of him was chewing at. Then he said, "Let's go sit somewhere. I need to think."

"There's a tavern over—" Gashtun started to say.

"No. Somewhere quiet."

We'd passed a park on the way to the city hall and now we found our way back to it. There was a pond with ducks and benches under shade trees. Gashtun went to look at the birds on the water, while Farouche and I sat near where a pair of old men were hunched over a table playing a board game with colored counters and a pair of dice.

Farouche was quiet. I could see from his eyes that he was chasing thoughts along the alleys of his mind. Finally, he let out an audible breath and said, "How does this sound? Bernaglio wants revenge on the Exleyans for what the Golden Lions did at Drieff. But he needs a demon to overwhelm the group mind and seize control of the government. For that he needs a wizard of power. But wizards don't care much for worldly goods — they can whiffle up anything they want by saying the right words and waving the wand."

He pointed a finger at me. "But suppose you come across a little old god whose still got powers if you know how to coax them out of him. Would a thaumaturge be interested?"

"I could see that," I said.

"So he sends a message to Olliphract, to the one the purple mage mentioned, Fatezh the Force..."

I nodded. "And the boulder begins to roll. Yes. But where do you come into it?"

"That I don't know," he said. "Not yet."

"Are you motivated to find out?"

He consulted himself. "It's strange," he said, eventually. "I know I ought to be angry. The thinking part of me tells me that. But the feeling part, it's neutral, disengaged."

Having pushed him to address the situation, I wanted him to continue. I said, "Leaving aside all that we know or suspect about trancers and drugs, demons and wizards, what is it you want to do more than anything else?"

He sat and stared at Gashtun and the ducks for a while, then said, "Go to Olliphract."

"Why?"

He shrugged. "I don't know why. I just do."

"That is probably the worst reason I have ever heard for going to that awful place," I said.

Another lifting and settling of his shoulders. Then he looked at me. "So why do you want to go there?"

"I don't," I said. "But I need to."

"Why need?"

"I'll tell you when we get there."

«»

There was, of course, no coach that went to Olliphract. There were scarcely any roads, though when we asked we were told that there were mule tracks that led up into the hills that finally became the mountains in which the wizards' town nestled, if such a friendly sounding word could be appropriate.

"The easiest approach is from the plains to the east of the hills," said Marbel Khonch, a woman who owned a cartage firm that hauled goods of various kinds in several directions from Wal. "The problem is when you're crossing the plains, you might run into the Azarines."

"I've met some," Farouche said.

"Then you know they can be… tetchy."

"I thought we got along all right," he said.

"The trick is to offer them things they want without implying any obligation on their part," Sera Khonch said. "Their standards are precise and exacting."

"I saw that," Farouche said. "Have you any wagons going out into the plains in the next little while? We could hire on as guards."

She looked him over and I saw her considering the scars on his hands. Me, she gave only a cursory glance. "You have experience?" she said.

"Extensive," said Farouche. When he saw the kind of look she was giving me, he added, "Don't be fooled by my companion's unassuming manner. He was praised for his skills by an adept of the Vindicators Guild."

"If you say so," she said. "The redbeard looks like he could earn his pay."

"He's done caravans and riverboat work."

"Fair enough," she said. "I've got eight wagons heading for Thurm in a couple of days. I'm just waiting for some pottery that's transshipping from Orberine. Do you know where Thurm is?"

I spoke up. "A day and a half's ride east of Ur Nazim." I had passed through it on my way to Exley, in what seemed a lifetime ago.

"That's right," Khonch said. "You can buy good horses there for cheap, if you don't mind that they were only saddle-broken the week before. My advice is to buy your gifts for the Azarines here in Wal. You'll pay a lot more in Thurm."

We took her advice on those issues, and also for where to stay until her train left. I suggested to Farouche that we use the intervening time to learn what we could of what we would find when we reached Olliphract.

"Another visit to the wizards' Guild?" he said.

"No," I said, "there's an academy here in Wal, with experts in all kinds of disciplines. There was an issue here some years ago when the fuglemen imported some disregarded deities. Their gods got to competing with each other for adherents, and things got out of hand."

"How out of hand?" he said.

"Winds, earthquakes, a rain of scorpions, a mass frenzy of eroticism. The thing is, if you want to know about neglected gods, Wal is a good place to ask."

«»

We divided our labors, Farouche and Gashtun acquiring gifts for the Azarines and weapons for the plains, while I sought out the academy. A few inquiries at the campus led me after a short search to a two-story building with pillars at the front and ivy climbing the side walls. Here I encountered Rosh Fadder, whose office door bore a wooden plaque identifying him as an adjunct scholar in the Faculty of Applied Divinity.

He proved to be a small, quick-moving man of advanced age, apparently easily startled. When I appeared unheralded in his open doorway, he jumped up from behind his desk and skittered to the far side of the room, from where he regarded me with a bird-like gaze, turning his head this way and that.

"I am sorry to have given you a fright," I said. "I assure you, I am harmless to all who mean me no harm."

It took him a while to find his voice. His hands still trembled as he said, "My apologies. I've been half-expecting... well, never mind that." He studied me more closely, then said, "You are actually... corporeal?"

"I am." I patted my cheek audibly. "Flesh and blood."

"But you are?" His hand moved in a way that said he was avoiding using a particular word.

"I am," I said again.

He came closer now, peered into my eyes. I knew he was examining my irises, which reveal much to those who know how to look. I refrained from blinking out of politeness.

After a while he stepped back and said, "I've only seen one of you before, and that one was... no longer extant."

"It's all right to say, 'dead'," I told him. "It's one of the commonalities we share with... people like you."

He looked again into my eyes and said, more to himself than to me, "Windows to the soul." Then he caught himself. "I apologize again," he said. "That was rude."

"I am not bothered," I said. "While I will never know the joys of the Overworld, nor will I ever suffer the anguish of the Underworld."

"True," he said, "and an admirable point of view." He seated himself behind the desk and gestured for me to take a chair. "But what can I do for you?"

I sat and told him. The issue naturally engaged his attention and we spoke together for a half hour, during which time I learned much that was useful.

«»

Thurm was a dusty little place that owed its existence to the two roads that crossed there and the prescience of its earliest settlers who dug deep wells to subterranean waters. Sera Khonch steered her wagon train into a mud-walled caravanserai and told us we would be dismissed with pay and a bonus once the goods she was carrying had been collected by their consignees. That took a couple of days and then we were free.

There were several horse copers in the town and their mutual competition meant we were able to buy reasonably good mounts — one each plus a pack horse — with used tack. We also acquired beans, lentils, flour, bacon, and roadbread, along with ground punge and wineskins. We were advised to buy extra waterskins because there were long stretches of dry country between Thurm and the mountains. We took the advice.

We went to the armorers' quarter to get weapons. Farouche sorted through the various available gear with an expert eye, picking out serviceable swords and spears for him and Gashtun and conical helmets for all three of us. I chose my own arms: a slim-bladed saber of good steel and a pair of light javelins. Farouche bought us quick-cocking bolt-throwers and quivers of missiles to hook onto our belts.

The next morning, we set off for Olliphract.

«»

Sometime after noon, out on the plain, we camped for a midday meal near a well that had a windmill-powered pump and watering troughs for the cattle drives that came up from the south and stopped at Thurm. Someone had built a fireplace of stone and though the only fuel was dried dung, there was plenty of it. Gashtun gathered a few chips to start the fire, while Farouche mixed the ingredients for a meal of pottage. Then Gashtun and I went farther afield to find more fuel. We were headed back to camp with armloads of dried, fibrous cowflops when Gashtun said, "Wait a minute. I got to ask you something."

"What?"

He wouldn't meet my gaze, looked first down at his feet then out to the horizon. "In Thurm," he said, "some people were talking..."

"About me."

"Yes."

"And what were they saying?"

He glanced at me then away. I said, "It's all right. I don't get embarrassed and I don't get angry."

Now he studied me. "Don't? Or can't?"

"Can't. It's how I was made."

Which brought us to what he wanted to hear about. So I told him about my origins, about the vats and the seed stocks, and how the developing "person" can be edited to include some characteristics and to delete others. And how the included characteristics can be augmented well beyond the human norm.

"But why?" he asked. "What's the point?"

"Always a good question when it comes to wizards. But there is not always a good answer."

"They make people who are not quite people, give them special qualities," he said. "Are you special?"

"I'm faster than just about any natural-born man. Speed translates to striking power. I also heal quickly."

"So, you could take me in a fight?"

"Yes." He looked doubtful. "I could show you," I said.

I told him to try to hit me. He used the techniques Farouche had taught him, but he couldn't connect. Then I hit him three light blows he couldn't block.

"That was less than half speed," I said.

He shook his head but said he accepted what I was showing him. Then he got to the part that was troubling him.

"Those people, they called you soulless. What's that all about?"

I said, "You know that when the Demiurge created this world, he ordained that all people would have three essences: the *ba*, the *ka*, and the *kra*."

"They taught me that in temple school," he said. "I never really got it. There's just one of me," — he tapped his chest — "in here."

"No, there are three, but they exist as one until death. Then the *ba*, which has absorbed all the evil in your life, goes to the Underworld. The *ka*, which has gathered together all the goodness of your existence, goes to the Overworld. And the *kra*, well it was only a hinge between the two natures and usually it evaporates. Sometimes it hangs around for a while and becomes a ghost."

"Why?"

"Why does it become a ghost?"

"No, why all of this? *Ba* and *ka*, and so on. Why did the Demiurge do it?"

"It is assumed he had his reasons. Scholars and sages have speculated. Nobody knows for sure. He set the world up and then he left it to run its course. That's it. And we just have to get on with it."

I could see it was not a satisfactory answer for Gashtun. It wasn't any more satisfying for generations of scholars and sages. But we were standing with our armloads of dried dung and I suggested we get back to camp.

Gashtun shook his head. "One more thing," he said.

I suppressed a sigh. "What?"

He motioned with his head toward the well, where Farouche was setting up camp. "Does he know about you?"

"He ought to," I said, "considering where he's been. But the knowledge might be part of what was taken from him."

The man shook his head. "This is one strange hoopdedoo," he said.

I set off toward the camp. I could see the first smoke of a fire. Over my shoulder, I said, "It will get stranger yet."

«»

Two days later, we came across a wide trail of hoof prints and wagon tracks heading north. Farouche leaned from his saddle to study them. He straightened and looked northward. "Azarines," he said. "A whole tribe on the move, looks like."

"They'll camp and send out hunting parties," I said. "We should go south a little, put some distance between us."

"We bought gifts," he said.

"Those folks can be touchy," Gashtun said. "Especially when they've got their wives and kids with them." He was looking in the direction the Azarines had gone. "I vote we skirt south."

Farouche looked at him. "Vote?" he said.

I nudged my horse forward so I was between them. "He's right. An Azarine can't overlook an accidental slight with women and children watching. We make one little mistake and..." I traced a finger across my throat.

Farouche frowned. "We'll lose time."

"Are we in a hurry?" I said.

He thought about that. After a moment, he said, "I do feel a... kind of an itch to cover ground."

"But you don't know why."

"No, I don't."

"So, it's not you wanting. It's that 'somebody else' who's nudging you from the inside."

"I suppose," he said.

"You could fight it."

"I suppose."

He sat his horse and looked north again, then west. Then he turned his horse's head to the south and kicked his heels into its sides. I followed, and Gashtun came after me, leading the pack horse.

«»

I thought I knew why the Azarines had been this far west in their territory. My supposition was confirmed the next day when we crested a small rise and I saw a smudge of smoke on the southern horizon. Farouche had been riding in front of us and he stopped and shaded his eyes, then turned to me.

"Azarines?" he said.

"No. Somebody else."

That puzzled him. "Who's out here besides Azarines?" he said.

"You really don't know?"

He got that look that came over him when he discovered he lacked some knowledge that everybody else commanded. "Am I supposed to?"

Gashtun came up, dragging the unwilling pack horse. "If it means anything, I don't know, either."

"If I'm right, it's a place called Sanctuary."

Gashtun frowned. "I've been going north and south on these plains for years, guarding Ser Bernaglio's caravans, and I've never heard of anyplace west of Thurm besides Olliphract."

"It's a recent development," I said. "And its residents don't advertise their presence."

"The Azarines know they're there," Farouche said. "They don't tolerate people settling on their land. They barely tolerate those who cross it and give them gifts."

"They don't consider these settlers to be people," I said.

"Oh," said Gashtun, "I get it."

"I don't," Farouche said. "Explain."

"It will be easier just to show you," I said. I kicked my horse into motion and rode down the slope.

«»

The town was built at a crossing of one of the small rivers that ran down from the mountains now visible to the west and southwest. If it weren't for the smoke from the dung fires, it would be easy to miss Sanctuary from any distance.

There was nothing to build with except the prairie itself, and the settlers had cut blocks of turf then piled them up to make walls, roofing them with canvas they had brought with them.

The place was open to the land on all sides, no walls or towers or gates. We rode toward the town on the wide track the Azarines had left. I could see where they had camped to the east of the huddle of sod huts while they refilled their water barrels and let their livestock graze before taking the long, dry trek.

When we came within sight of the town, I heard a tocsin ringing, hard wood on hollow wood that sounded sharp against the silence of the prairie. Figures came out of the huts and up from the river to form a mass maybe sixty or seventy strong between us and the first houses. I saw spears and swords, some shields and pieces of armor. When we got closer, I could see bolt throwers, too.

We reined in at a distance. Farouche shaded his eyes and studied the crowd. After a while, he turned to me and said, "They're like you."

"Most of them," I said. "A few are identifiable as male or female."

"What are they doing out here?"

"It's in the name they gave the place," I said. "It's where they fled to."

"From where?"

I gestured toward the distant mountains. "Up there."

Three of the townspeople had stepped out in front of the others. They beckoned us to approach. I urged my horse forward, saying, "Better let me do the talking."

Farouche shrugged and followed me. Then the Sanctuary folk got a closer look at him and I saw those who had bolt-throwers raise their weapons. I tugged on the reins to halt my horse, turned in the saddle, and told Farouche to stop for a moment.

"And, whatever you do," I said, over his question, "don't reach for a weapon."

He stopped his horse and put his hands on the forward swell of his saddle. "What is going on?" he said.

"Too long a story for now. Just let me handle it."

We rode toward the three armed townspeople and stopped where they could get a good look at me, and I could see them close up. Two of the men were nearly identical, a type I was familiar with. I was even more familiar with the third. I saw the same face every time I looked into a mirror.

He studied me now, then said, "One of Isphant's?"

"That's right," I said. I rolled up my sleeve and showed him the number and accompanying symbol tattooed on my bicep.

"That the mark of a scout?"

"Yes."

"Same here," he said, touching the spot on his own sleeve where the same symbol would be inked into his skin. Then he looked past me at Farouche and the corners of his mouth drew down. "That's a Kain. We don't let his kind in. They're unstable." A quizzical look came over him. "I thought they'd all been done away with."

I said, "He's not a Kain. He's *the* Kain. The original."

My companion looked a question at me. I turned to him and said, "Once I knew which Minderlanz you were, I knew your story."

The scout with my face was studying Farouche. "The actual template?" he said.

"Just so. And we're not looking to come in. We're just passing through."

That surprised my look-alike even more. "There's only one place to get to, the direction you're heading," he said.

"I know."

"Why?"

"There are things I have to do there," I said.

"What things?"

"My business," I said. "Look, we'll just buy whatever food you want to sell us and move on. Or we'll just go around you now and camp in the foothills."

He turned and talked quietly with the other two, then glanced at the crowd. There were only four or maybe five different types I could see, and they had the intuitive empathy of the vat-born. The consensus was reached in a few moments.

"You can come in," the headman told me. "I assume the norm knows how things are." He gestured with his chin toward Gashtun, who had sat where we'd left him with the pack horse, stolidly observing the scene.

"He knows enough," I said, "though he might stare at you all."

"We've had worse than stares," the man said. "Come ahead."

«»

The low-roofed soddies turned out to be roomier than they looked, because the houses were dug down into the soil. We hobbled our horses and left them to graze on the grass that grew everywhere and went down into the headman's home, which was big enough to double as a meeting hall for the community. I looked up at the ceiling and saw heavy timbers; the man saw my curiosity and said, "We cut them in the foothills and hauled them here. Same thing with the furniture."

He indicated some benches along the walls and a trestle table, and motioned us to sit. Another version of the twins who had met us outside the town brought mugs and a pot of hot punge.

"The foothills. It's safe to go there?" I said, when I'd moistened my dry mouth.

The headman looked at me over the rim of his cup. "If you don't go too far up."

"And if you do?"

He shrugged. "Then it's not safe."

Farouche was looking around without much curiosity. I assumed his lack of interest was part of the drug-enhanced trancer work that had been done on him.

"The Kain," the headman said, then shook his head in wonderment.

Farouche returned his stare. "You know me?" he said. He slid a sideways glance my way. "Or just my 'story'?"

The next shake of the headman's head had a different meaning. "No, I just met a few... like you. Copies. I'd just as soon never meet one again."

Farouche looked a question at me. I said, "It's part of the memories you're missing. I suppose it's time we got it all out on the table."

"All right," Farouche said, "I'm listening."

«»

Olliphract was a city of thaumaturges, scores of them, from masters of the most arcane lore down to mere hedge sorcerers. Wizards vary in temperament and character, but all of them share certain qualities: vanity, narcissism, and an urge toward rivalry. In Olliphract, there being no civic authority to rein in these tendencies, they ran riot.

Thaumaturges competed against each other for precedence and prestige. Singletons were not uncommon, but most practitioners of the hermetic arts, especially those at the mid-level of power and practice, formed cliques and covens. Group competed against group, even as individual members of these coteries jostled each other for increased minims of rank.

"The competitions are divided into disciplines and interests," I said. "Sometimes, there are tournaments in which thaumaturges demonstrate refinements on spells and cantrips, there being little scope in these latter-day times for truly original creations.

"One area of contest was in the staging of limited wars. Six wizards set teams of fighters against each other, devising new scenarios for the conflicts. The participants, for the most part, were not volunteers or mercenaries; they were artificial people, grown in vats and imbued with various qualities that might give them advantage in combat: speed, endurance, strength, improvements to eyesight and other senses. They also bred beasts of war: armored mounts with horns and claws, flying things, night runners."

Farouche raised a hand at this point. "You are one of those grown in vats?" he said.

"I am."

"Exley is a long way from Olliphract. How did you come to be there?"

I told him I would get to that, in time, but for now I wanted to proceed at my own pace. He nodded and sat back on the bench while I continued.

I told him how I was created to serve in the army of a wizard named Isphant. My primary role was scout and skirmisher, sent to discover the enemy's dispositions and assess their strengths and weaknesses. I had fought in a number of individual battles, where the forces of one thaumaturge went up against those of another practitioner.

"But Isphant fancied himself a military genius and craved a wider scope. He persuaded the other five members of the league to join their armies together, three against three, with him in overall command of one of the alliances. It took a great deal of dickering to arrange the order of battle — Isphant's allies did not trust him, of course — but finally the rules were negotiated and a date was set for the war."

"Was I part of that war?" Farouche asked.

"Yes, on the opposing side." I told him he had been a member of a corps of natural-borns — "norms," we vat-born called them — many of them formerly of the Golden Lions, outcasts after the massacre.

"You all served Fatezh the Force, one of the triumvirate Isphant and his two allied wizards contended against. Unfortunately, my master's ambitions exceeded his abilities," I said. "He had never commanded more than a couple of thousand troops and now he was the head of an army of ten thousand. He made his dispositions and sent us forward.

"But Fatezh had an able staff, with many graduates of the Institute and other military colleges. You were one of them," I told Farouche. "You and your colleagues out-maneuvered Isphant. Your army encircled ours, cut us off from supply and reserves, and began to grind us down in a battle of attrition.

"We should have surrendered, but Isphant refused to admit defeat. He ordered the reserves to try to make a breakthrough to relieve us. But the operation was as poorly planned as the mess he had sent us into. Disaster ensued, and massacre."

Finally, the other two thaumaturges in the ill-fated alliance demanded that Isphant give up control. He rebuffed them and, when they pressed him, flew into a spitting, hissing rage. Insults were thrown that could not be ignored. Wands were drawn, spells hurled, and the outcome was not good for Isphant: he ended up shrunken in size, confined to a bottle on a shelf in the castle of one of his former allies.

"We, his army, were abandoned. Some of us found places in the establishments of other thaumaturges. Some came here to Sanctuary. Others wandered out into the wider world to make our way, though we were often poorly received by norms, once they realized what we were."

"What happened to me?" Farouche said.

Throughout my explanation, he had listened with interest, but with his usual air of detachment. He might have been hearing about long-ago events in some distant, foreign land. Again, I wondered what had been done to him.

I told him I could not give him an exact answer. I had heard that Fatezh, after the battle of the six armies, had begun to lose interest in war games. He developed a fascination for a magical artifact: some kind of improbable stone that grew only in the surfaces of stars and required recondite skill to extract and handle, after which it could perform remarkable functions.

"Presumably, you were discharged," I said. "Perhaps you joined the forces of one of the other thaumaturges."

"Malbroch the Omnifacient," Farouche said. "Someone saw me wearing his livery."

The man who had confronted us at the entrance to the town now spoke up. "I can tell you what I know. The two other members of Fatezh's league borrowed him and used his plasm as seed stock for a line of military commanders. Several of them were produced, but they turned out to have an inherent flaw. Bad editing, probably. When provoked, they could fly into murderous rages. And no one knew just what word or deed might set them off."

He spread his hands and looked at Farouche. "So, the line was discontinued."

Farouche took that information in. After a moment, he said, "You mean the copies of me were killed?"

The headman spread his hands again. "Wizards are not given to sentimentality. Their decisions are sudden and their actions brusque."

I watched to see if the thought of his sons — at least, they were such, after a fashion — being slaughtered had an effect on my companion. Apparently, it did not. I decided it was time to tell him the conclusions I had reached, based on what I knew and what I had just learned.

"The picture becomes clearer and more complete," I said. "Nulf Bernaglio desired to punish Exley for the massacre of his family at Drieff. He approached Fatezh the Force with a plan to make himself powerful in the town, offering some disregarded deities as payment. When Fatezh let him know that his erstwhile army included Kain the Butcher, who had led the battalion that carried out the massacre, it must have seemed clear that the hand of fate was working in Bernaglio's favor.

"So Fatezh applied a drug that stripped your mind. He installed inside you a captive demon, or perhaps just the voice of one, then flew you out to where you would encounter Bernaglio's caravan. And so, the plot was in motion. As a bonus, Bernaglio had you rid him of a peculative found-brother who was jeopardizing his relations with the aristocrats of Exley."

Farouche absorbed this with his usual calm. After a while, he nodded. "And now I have this urge to return to Olliphract," he said.

"Probably," I said, "to be destroyed in some awful manner, to complete Bernaglio's satisfaction." I waited a moment, then said, "How does that make you feel?"

I saw my companion's face cloud as he consulted his emotions, then his expression cleared. "Neither one way nor the other," he said. "I know I ought to be angry, fearful, worried, but I'm... not."

"Yet still you want to go to Olliphract?" I said.

Farouche hummed a little two-syllable sound of agreement.

"And when we get there?" I said.

"We'll see."

«»

We overnighted in Sanctuary. In the morning, Farouche, Gashtun, and I rode out in the direction the vat-men recommended. It would take us to a trail that wound up into the highlands and led to a pass that opened into a valley where Olliphract lay, surrounded by peaks and precipices atop which the thaumaturges had built their keeps.

Gashtun was in a more pensive mood than I had ever seen him. We rode three abreast, with him in the middle, and I noticed him turning his head Farouche's way, studying him. When he wasn't looking at my traveling companion, he fixed his gaze on his hands that held his horse's reins and those of the pack horse that trudged along behind us. Other times, he stared out at the endless sweep of long grass, but I could tell that his gaze was turned inward.

After a while, I nudged my mount closer to his, so we rode knee to knee. "You are troubled," I said.

He looked at me. "You're not?"

I showed him a bland face. "I do not have the parts that generate fear. A frightened soldier is a bad soldier. The best I rise to is 'cautious'."

He took that in, then shrugged off whatever thought it raised in him. He said, "He's been lucky for me. I felt I owed him. Plus, I was thinking this was some kind of adventure that would give me tales to tell my grandchildren."

He lapsed into silence and chewed his thoughts again. I said, "And now, how do you see it?"

"As a fool's errand and a damn dangerous one at that." He glanced at Farouche again then lowered his voice and said, "I heard what you said yesterday. He's going back to the wizard that carved up his memories, just riding on into what? Death?"

"Quite possibly," I said. "I can't imagine Bernaglio letting him live."

"Then why are we letting him do it? And why are we going with him?"

"Because we would have to lock him up to keep him from going. But he'd probably escape anyway, and he might harm us if we tried to stop him."

Gashtun's expression was grim. "I don't know what to do," he said.

"Pursue your own best interests," I said.

"I like to think of myself as loyal," he said. "My father always said—"

As we talked I had been looking ahead to where the mountains serrated the western horizon. Now I was sure of what I had been watching. "I believe," I said, interrupting the man, "the decision of what to do is about to be taken out of our hands."

Gashtun shaded his eyes and peered in the same direction I was looking. "I don't see anything."

"You won't, yet," I said. "I was made to be a scout and skirmisher. Enhanced eyesight was one of the... features Isphant designed in me."

I leaned forward to see Farouche and called to him. "Someone's coming," I said, pointing with my chin toward the west.

He did as Gashtun had done, then looked a question at me.

"Flying platform," I said. "You'll be able to see it in a little while."

He reined in, and we all stopped. The speck in the distance was growing larger.

"Not long now," I said.

"Is there anything we should be doing?" Farouche said.

"Nothing that would improve the situation," I said.

The distant object swelled in my vision. After a while, Gashtun grunted something. He reached for the bolt-thrower hooked in its scabbard onto his saddle.

"No," I said. "Fold your hands on the pommel and wait. When he gets here, don't stare too much. But don't ignore him entirely, either."

"I've heard wizards can be touchy," he said.

"The term they prefer is 'mercurial'," I said. "Or capricious, if they're in a good mood."

The object grew until it could be seen as a rectangular flat shape, ringed around with an ornate balustrade. I could make out the two nacelles underneath that housed the pair of imps whose leashed powers lifted and propelled the flying craft. When it descended to hover at knee-height just in front of us, causing the horses to skitter away, I saw that in the center of the platform sat an ornate chair beneath a palanquin of gold cloth fringed with hanging strings of pearls.

And in the chair sat a slim youth with skin of royal blue, decorated with spirical designs of what appeared to be inlaid ivory. He was dressed in the costume of a courtier of the Old Kingdom of Vann, though all such persons and their accouterments had been dust for umpteen millennia. With thaumaturges, I knew, appearances were usually deceptive.

The wizard's mood, however, was unmistakable. He cupped his chin with one hand, the azure fingers tipped in gold, and addressed Farouche.

"I have been waiting," he said, in a voice as dry as the grass that rattled against our stirrups. "I don't care for waiting."

The sound made the horses more fretful. The blue lips frowned and Fatezh the Force gestured with one hand while speaking a soft syllable. Immediately, our mounts became calm. Indeed, I saw that the pack horse Gashtun had been leading was now asleep, standing up. So, no doubt, was mine.

The wizard beckoned in a peremptory manner. Simultaneously, the gate at the front of the platform swung wide. Farouche stepped down from his horse and let the reins trail on the ground. I slipped down from my saddle and followed him toward the platform.

Fatezh's gaze switched from my companion to me. I felt its force but moved forward anyway. He cocked an eyebrow in inquiry.

"I believe," I said, "you may be interested in a proposition I wish to put to you."

"Really?" Fatezh said. "Concerning?"

Farouche had now climbed aboard and stood inert beside the owner's chair. I stood at the gate and said, "I am told you collect small gods."

"What of it?"

"I might be able to acquire one. Actually, of middling size."

He studied me for a moment. I ignored the discomfort and showed nothing but patience. Then he said, "Not all gods are... suitable for my purposes."

"So I understand. This one might be." His other eyebrow rose. I took it as a signal to continue. "It's Efferion," I said.

Fatezh's brows descended but his face was absolutely still for several beats of my heart. Then I saw skepticism, and saw it yield quickly to the anger that coexists with a thaumaturge's vanity, and is never out of reach.

I spoke quickly. "I was one of Isphant's army. He knew of your interest and he conceived a plan to sequester Efferion in his redoubt then dicker with you for certain items he thought you possessed."

That gave the wizard pause. "What items?"

"He did not discuss such matters with me. Instead, he sent me to Exley to prepare for his signal. While I was waiting for word, he was defeated in the battle of the six armies. I was left to fend for myself."

His blue face was still again, the ivory designs standing out in cold relief. "How were you to seize the god?" he said.

I made a soft gesture. "I would prefer to keep that to myself until we have reached an understanding."

I saw the anger rise again and be suppressed again. "You have confidence in Isphant's scheme? His assessment of his own abilities proved to be overrated."

"It seemed... doable to me," I said. "There were risks, but..." I let my voice trail off.

He regarded me for another long moment. Then he said, "Come aboard."

I mounted and the gate closed behind me. I looked back at Gashtun who was watching us prepare to depart with a stricken look.

I said, "The horses and gear and gifts are yours. Go back to Sanctuary and wait for a caravan or cattle drive to come near. Stay clear of Azarines."

He opened his mouth to say something but I indicated Fatezh with a cocking of my head followed by a shake. The thaumaturge was instructing his imps. A moment later, we lifted off, turned in the air, and sped off toward the west. My last view of Gashtun was of him trying to waken his sleeping horse.

Part 3

Efferion speaks

Back before time began, the Demiurge fashioned me to be one of his instruments for creating phenomenality. I was a powerful tool with many functions during the assembling and delineating of the Nine Planes, especially the Second, Third, and Fourth, where I oversaw the laying of the fluxions that tie phenomenality together. I balanced and leveled, set limits and guarded against overlaps. Much of the heterogeneity of time and space was of my doing.

When the great work was done, the Demiurge deactivated some of us. Others he repurposed to play new and continuing roles in the development of his creations. I was one of those who went on. I inhabit the Sixth Plane, because it is more comfortable to my nature, but having played a large part in the making of the Second, Third, and Fourth Planes — the Underworld, Middleworld, and Overworld — I remain *in situ* in them.

In the Second Plane, I am the scouring wind. In the Third, I am a modest pillar of polished basalt. In the Fourth, I am a beneficent spirit charged with providing several varieties of bliss.

As the Middleworlders matured to self-awareness, and as the curiosity I had helped instill in them flowered, some of them became aware of my existence. They sought connection, benediction, and intervention in the mundanities of their lives.

To these importunings I respond as my nature dictates: I extend the edges of my consciousness into theirs, touch them with intimations of the great balance, warm their essences, calm their fears.

As their numbers have grown, I find myself more and more engaged in this occupation. I find, also, that the diversity of my correspondents has spread across a spectrum. Some are less immersed in phenomenality than others. Their imaginations lead them astray. My gentlest touch sears their minds and causes them to exert themselves in ways that harm others.

There is nothing I can do about this. I was made for diffuse purposes, and my nature precludes me from altering objects or events on the Third Plane. I can only infuse and enthuse. And when I am implored in the right manner, I cannot help but respond.

Thus have I become a god, though my powers are muted and constrained. Lately, the pillar that anchors me in the Third Plane was uprooted and carried to a settlement named Exley, where more and more of the Realm's denizens are drawn to its ambit. Their attentions create a kind of tickle in my being that is not unpleasant. Not long ago, I sensed the proximity of a *theropath*, an entity whose natural habitat is the Seventh Plane. It briefly interacted with the local Third Plane denizens, creating an imbalance. I was considering intervening when the disturbance ceased and the *theropath* departed.

I am interested to know where all of this leads. I wonder, sometimes, if my becoming a kind of god is an anticipated outcome of the Demiurge's plans. Or perhaps it is all accident. It was never made clear to us, the instruments of creation, what was his purpose in leaving us extant. Some of us speculated that the Demiurge, himself, was not the prime mover, but was instead acting at the behest of a more significant force. In which case, he was different only in degree from us whom he created to perform his works. Either way, I am almost certain he has moved on to other concerns, his creation having fulfilled its arcane purpose.

The matter is ultimately of no importance, but it gives me something to dwell upon.

——— «» ———

The *theropath* has returned. Or one like it; they have no strong individualities, being more a collection of attributes rather than a coherent personality. When phenomenality was being assembled and refined, they laid down the network of fluxions — red, blue, yellow, green, silver, and black — that hold together the elements of the Second, Third, and Fourth Planes. I was involved with their work, maintaining balance and proportion and often supervised them as they moved across the corporeal worlds like so many spiders spinning their multi-stranded webs.

When they were finished, the Demiurge piled them into a region on the Seventh Plane, where they remain. It seems, however, that some denizens of the Middleworld have discovered how to summon *theropaths* into the Third Plane, there to constrain them and direct their energies. I am puzzled as to the denizens' motivations for doing so. They, themselves, are of very flimsy construction, their *bas* and *kas* barely held together by their *kras*, and those bonds can easily be dissolved by too close contact with entities from the higher Planes.

I am becoming more and more intrigued by the Middleworlders. I am quite sure the Demiurge did not intend for them to interact with *theropaths* — and perhaps not with instruments like me, for that matter — and I wonder what his reaction would be to seeing his creation evolve in such unusual directions.

«»

Something unusual is happening. The basalt eidolon that is my anchorage in the Middleworld has been uprooted once more — this time by the *theropath* — and I am being transported to another location. I am passing beyond the range of the denizens that formerly thronged the fringes of my being. Now I am attended only by one of those *ba*-less, *ka*-less entities that have lately appeared in the Third Plane. Lacking spiritual presence, they are difficult for me to keep in view, but I am curious as to this one's association with the *theropath*. It seems an odd combination, and one I am sure my own creator never intended.

«»

Over the span of my growing engagement with the Middleworld's denizens, I have allowed more of myself to cohere in the Third Plane. Now that I am removed from that association, I will withdraw all but a small fraction of my being to the Sixth Plane, where my comfort is assured.

But, remarkably, I am unable to do so! I query the *theropath*: "Are you constraining me?"

"I am," it says.

For a moment, I am undecided as to whether my next question should be "why" or "how?" I settle for the latter.

"I am drawing force from the argent and sable fluxions," it says.

"But," I say, "the Demiurge hid those from view after he started phenomenality."

"Just so, but the one who commands me intuited their existence, then sought them out and learned how to use them."

Now is certainly the time to ask why. The answer puzzles me.

"He seeks to exert power in furtherance of his appetites."

"What appetites?"

"Mostly," says the *theropath*, "they seem to be for acquiring more power. These creatures are a puzzling breed."

They are indeed. I pick up on a word the *theropath* used. "You said he commands you."

"He does."

"How can that be? You should be far out of reach in the Seventh Plane."

He enters into a convoluted explanation. The "one who commands" is a Middleworld denizen who calls himself a thaumaturge. His name is Fatezh. He has managed to lure another breed of Seventh Plane entity called an *athlenath* through a breach between the Realms. He has then constrained the *athlenath* to corral a number of *theropaths* and put them at Fatezh's service.

"How has he managed this?" I ask.

Again, the answer has to do with the identifying and manipulation of fluxions of various hues, but with the silver and black — argent and sable, in the *theropath*'s archaic vocabulary — playing prominent roles.

"The Demiurge never intended this," I say.

My constrainer makes no response. Consideration of the Great Artificer's intents is far beyond its limited capacity for ratiocination.

I must pause to think, but soon realize I lack sufficient information to make judgments. I come back to the issue of Fatezh's purposes. "What does he intend for me?"

"You possess a great deal of power. He will seek to draw upon it."

The prospect is bizarre. "My 'power' is inherent," I say. "I am its manifestation. It cannot be separated from me."

"Yes," says the *theropath*, "it can. Fatezh has done as much to other deities."

"But that would be like unwinding a ball of thread," I say. "Once it is unwound, its integrity ceases. It no longer exists, except as an unorganized heap of string."

"Just so," says my constrainer, "but then that heap of string has remarkable properties, especially to bind and connect."

«»

I do not remember a time when I did not exist, of course. I was fashioned by the Demiurge before he initiated time. Nor have I ever contemplated a time when I no longer will exist. I am immune to the effects time wreaks upon many beings and, left undisturbed, could expect to go on, largely unaltered, for as long as phenomenality exists. Indeed, it is barely imaginable that the Great Artificer might someday return to dismantle his creation and use me as a tool in the forging of a new universe.

What has never occurred to me is the thought that some actor within phenomenality might diminish or destroy me. It is a disturbing prospect. I am beginning to get a sense of what it must be like to be a Middleworlder, faced with the ultimate prospect of dissolution.

I need to know more. I have exhausted the *theropath*'s limited range of knowledge. There is no point asking the two entities that lift and propel the artifact on which I rest; they are a pair of Second Plane imps whose post-creation purpose is to harass and bring misery to the hapless *bas* consigned to the Underworld. They are nothing but a collection of spites and wickednesses.

That leaves the spiritless denizen who accompanies us on this journey. I cannot contact it as I would a proper Third Plane denizen, as it has no *ba* or *ka* for me to resonate against. I give it some thought and decide that I will have to create a means of vibrating the air in a way that lets it receive the waves as intelligible sounds.

I did so, then had to spend a little more time acquiring an understanding of what various sounds will mean to the creature, and its way of organizing those sounds into language.

Finally, I am ready and I say, "I wish to converse with you."

The results are not as I anticipated. The creature claps its hands to its ears and falls to its knees. I realize that I have not modified the force of my communication. I reduce it substantially and say, "Is that better?"

The little thing, trembling, gets to its feet and takes its hands from its ears. "That hurt," it says.

"I did not mean you harm," I say. "I wish to converse."

"I doubt there is anything we can say to each other that will be useful."

I am not encouraged, but I persevere.

"What is your intent?" I say.

"To deliver you to Fatezh the Force."

"And what will he do with me?"

"I don't know. That's wizard's business, not my concern."

"The *theropath* says he will destroy me."

"I can't comment," it says.

I have established its intent. Now I seek to know its motivation. "Why do you wish me destroyed? Have I incurred your enmity?"

"No."

"Then why?"

"I desire something. Fatezh says he can provide it. You are his price."

"What can he provide?" I say.

I am not adept at interpreting the facial expressions of Middleworlders, especially not the spiritually bereft kind, but I believe I see longing and yearning on the face of this one.

"I want to be real," it says. "I want a life and then an afterlife."

"But that would require a *ba* and a *ka*, and a *kra* to hold them together."

"Yes."

"And this thaumaturge says he can provide them?"

"He does."

"He is mistaken."

The creature makes a gesture as if brushing something away from its vicinity. "I have to believe him. There is no other way."

I am reminded of the Demiurge's concern when we were establishing the Middleworld and its peculiar denizens, with their two contrasting gists. He never did explain why he wanted them that way; indeed, he rarely explained, but just issued instructions, and we who were his tools carried them out. The inhabitants of the rest of the Planes are all, like me, monogistic. We are incapable of what the Great Artificer called "false relation" — we can refuse to speak but, when we do speak, our expressed thoughts have to cohere to reality, at least as we understand it.

I say my captor, "Do you know where *bas* and *kas* come from?"

"No."

"From the Fifth Plane, a Realm far beyond your comprehension. A *ba* and *ka* are automatically generated there whenever a Middleworlder reaches a certain stage of gestation. They travel to this Plane and take up residence in the denizen-to-be."

"How are they 'generated'?"

I tell him that the Demiurge installed a tool there. It is a simple being, not even graced by a name of its own, that maintains a constant watch on the Third Plane, though its perspection only captures the gestation of Middleworlders. At a point where the fetus becomes viable, it generates and inserts the *ba* and *ka*.

"What about the *kra*?" it says.

I explain that the hinge develops naturally from the interaction of the other two gists and acquires its few attributes from the extent that one predominates over the other.

"But what you have to understand is that there is no possibility of entering the Fifth Plane to affect the generation of gists. Traffic can only move in one direction, through the exit. I was instrumental in building the process and saw the Demiurge lock the adits when it was finished."

The creature is stubborn. "What is locked can be unlocked."

"I use the term metaphorically," I say. "The ways in no longer exist. A great many precise and delicate connections that bind the Planes together are established in the Fifth Plane. Entities might disturb those connections. The results would be catastrophic."

"Perhaps Fatezh knows how to take the gists from an existing person and transfer them to me."

"No," I say. "That is not only immoral, it is impossible."

The expression I see now on its face is one I recognize: despair. I have seen it on some of the denizens that came to me for spiritual comfort. I would provide solace to this being — that is my unavoidable nature — but there is no way to make the connection with the gistless. All I can say is that I am sorry for its situation.

"Don't be," it says. "I reject your pity." It turns away from me.

I return my attention to the *theropath*. "How are you constraining me?"

But it does not know. The thaumaturge has applied fluxion-based forces to it that have altered its nature — a thing I would have heretofore considered impossible: the Great Artificer did not fashion us to be mutable. Now I have to consider the possibility that even I, one of the most powerful and versatile instruments of creation, might have change forced upon me.

I am not given to a wide range of emotion, but it occurs to me that anger might be useful in my situation. I wonder if I can generate it. I am also not given to introspection, having been designed to affect phenomenality without being affected in return. But I see that I *am* wondering, something I have never done before.

I find I cannot become angry. I can, however, recognize an inconsistency in the order of things and be motivated to correct it. Fatezh, or at least his actions, represent a glaring departure from the Demiurge's scheme, and I am one of his prime instruments of rectification. I know that the Demiurge was capable of emotions — I often saw him become impatient with processes that did not move as smoothly as he wished — and I can therefore intuit his reaction to what this ambitious thaumaturge was doing. And having done so, I can use his projected outrage as a motivator. I was created to fulfill his will. I find that I can therefore also fulfill what I infer to be his will.

These thoughts empower me. They also raise a question that must be pertinent. I ask it of the *theropath*. It cannot give me an answer: denizen's motivations are beyond its understanding.

So I ask the agistic creature, "What does Fatezh aim to achieve by constraining me?"

"He wants what all wizards want," it says. "To translate himself bodily to the Overworld and live in eternal bliss."

"That is unnatural," I say.

The creature lifts its shoulders and lets them fall. "Thaumaturges are unnatural," it says. "I sometimes wonder why the Demiurge created them."

"He did not," I say. "They came along much later."

"But they were implicit in his scheme of things, or they would not have occurred."

It is an interesting point. For the first time since phenomenality began, I miss the presence of the Great Artificer. It would be useful to know if a Fatezh the Force was part of his grand design or an unforeseen consequence. If the former, my current situation is in tune with the Creator's plan. If the latter, it may well constitute an offense against the correct order.

But, now that the issue has been raised, I have to consider whether my recently evolved role as a deity for Middleworld denizens is also right and proper. Should I have ignored their importunings and remained inactive in the Sixth Plane?

These musings are not pleasant. I was not designed to muse but to measure and weigh, and take action accordingly. I am only a tool, and a discarded one at that. I was created as a self-aware entity, because consciousness made me more effective in my work, but I was not intended to weigh questions of right and wrong, to measure what was proper and what was not, and I have no standards by which to determine what I should do.

I again test the constraints imposed upon me by the *theropath*. Again, they do not yield. I ask the creature how this effect has been achieved.

"Fluxions," it says. "Fatezh diverted their energies through my systems, augmenting and amplifying selected qualities. He has done as much with a number of us."

"Is this acceptable to you?"

"It makes for interesting work."

I say, "I am not sure the Demiurge would approve."

"The Demiurge has moved on," the *theropath* says, "and left us to our own devices. His opinions no longer resonate."

"That is not a judgment for—" I begin, but the creature interrupts me — another thing that would not have happened when I supervised its kind — and tells me that we are about to end our journey. I see that the imps are exerting themselves to bring the flying platform to a landing on a terrace of stone atop a pinnacle of rock that overlooks a closed valley in which an unusual city has been built.

I extend my senses and see that the pinnacle is not a natural feature. It has been created using the force of the fluxions — red, blue, black, and silver — that meet and form a node in the bedrock beneath. The same energies have been harnessed to create a fanciful building behind the terrace on which we have landed: I see arches, cupolas, spires, towers, colonnades, and sweeping staircases, of white and black stone, the windows glazed with bronze-colored glass.

Atop one of the staircases stands a person who has the appearance of a fresh-faced youth, dressed in close-fitting garments of metallic cloth, wearing a broad-brimmed hat of black felt, one side of it pinned up by a gaudy panache of old gold. I look more closely and determine that his appearance is a product of artifice. Beneath the glamor is a man of advanced age, some of his organs supported by energies derived from the subterranean node of four fluxions.

He lifts a hand and arranges its fingers in a precise configuration, then speaks a string of syllables. Immediately, two more *theropaths* sail through a breach in the interplanar membrane that separates the Middleworld from the Seventh Plane. They approach the flying platform and, with the assistance of the one who has been constraining me, they lift and carry the black pillar that is my Third Plane manifestation across the terrace and through an archway.

I am borne along wide corridors cut through the living rock, down ramps and through doorways that swing open at our approach, until finally we arrive at a large chamber lit by floating globes of glass that hover just below the high ceiling. I sense a complex mesh of energies invisibly pervading the space. It soon becomes apparent to me that these forces are deployed to hold in place a number of entities like me: former instruments of the Demiurge's workshop, left to find their own ways after the great labors were finished. Some of them have gravitated to the Third Plane, to become small gods that devoted themselves to some aspect of Middleworlders' existences.

But in this place, they are not engaged in altering some worshiper's luck or assisting in finding some lost object. Their energies have been isolated and confined. Moreover, I sense that conduits now connect the imprisoned deities in series, so that their *mana* can be channeled and directed. I see that a place has been prepared for me, and that a conduit waits to add my powers to the chain of godlings.

The *theropaths* carry me to the spot. Fatezh has followed us down from the landing and approaches as I am positioned and anchored. The *theropaths*, their work done, float toward the ceiling, where they find another breach in the interplanar membrane and disappear back into the Seventh Plane.

Fatezh stands and contemplates me. From within his upper garment, he brings forth a slim tube of pale ceramic, sealed with crystals at either end. He peers at me through the instrument, then reverses it and examines me again. Whatever he sees must bring him satisfaction, because he grunts in contentment. Now he crosses to a workbench backed by a bookcase. He takes down a tome with a tattered leather cover and begins to leaf through its pages.

I turn my attention to the other instruments. I recognize all of them, having directed their work before the beginning of time. But I see that they are no longer the entities they used to be. Their individualities have been diminished. They are faded and weak, and I realize that some of their *mana* has been drawn off and diverted to the matrix of energies that holds them captive.

No doubt that is the fate Fatezh intends for me. I do not approve of his plan. It is unnatural and I doubt the Demiurge would approve. I must find some way to oppose.

The little man-thing that helped to capture me has followed us into the chamber. It approaches the thaumaturge and makes a sound to attract his attention. Fatezh glances up from the book but immediately returns his gaze to its contents.

"Not now," he says. "Go away."

"We had a bargain," says the other.

"We still do. But now I am occupied."

The creature stands its ground. "If not now, when?"

Fatezh looks up again. For all his youthful appearance, his face is now hard. The man-thing takes an involuntary step backward. "I will let you know," the wizard says. "I will have to make preparations for your... conversion. I will need to have my new acquisition integrated into the sequence before I can do that."

The little fellow leaves. Fatezh returns to his studies. I think it is time to address the situation. I remember to moderate my voice.

"Your intent is to translate yourself, as is, to the Fourth Plane," I say. "You would not survive the experience."

He glances over at me, but returns immediately to his perusal of the book. He finishes reading whatever commands his attention there, then closes the volume and addresses me.

"You are mistaken," he says.

"Only a *ka* can abide the conditions of the Overworld. You would unravel and evaporate."

"Not if I change my substance," he says.

"How is that possible?" I say. "Essences are immutable. So the Demiurge has ordained."

"The Demiurge has abandoned his creation. It now belongs to those who can work phenomenality to their own ends."

The concept is bizarre. I say, "By what right?"

"The only right that pertains," says Fatezh. "The capacity to exert axial volition."

"The term is unfamiliar to me."

"In layman's terms, the power of will."

That, at least, is a concept I am familiar with. The Great Artificer imbued Middleworlders with will so they could exercise choice in the development of their *bas* and *kas*. The quality was necessary to the functioning of the Second, Third, and Fourth Planes, that they might fulfill the purpose — whatever it was — for which the Demiurge created them.

"That power was intended to underwrite the operation of the three Planes," I say. "You have gone beyond the Demiurge's concepts."

"Yes," says Fatezh, "I have. That is the natural outcome of his having granted us axial volition."

"It is not natural," I say. "It is an aberration."

"Again, you are mistaken. I could spend the time and effort to try to correct your thinking, but experience with these other deities has taught me that your kind does not learn. Your ideas are fixed. Besides, I have better things to do."

He chooses another book from his collection and begins to read, stooped over his workbench and occasionally jotting down notes with a stylus. I attempt to regain his attention, but he produces the wand once more, gestures and speaks, and my voice is silenced.

I am in a situation I can only describe as unhappy. I am unable to exert myself beyond the constraints Fatezh and his *theropaths* have imposed upon me. Indeed, I do not even understand them, except that they appear to depend on using fluxions as they were never intended to be used. I cannot withdraw most of myself to the Sixth Plane, but am locked within my physical manifestation as a pillar of shining black basalt.

My corporeal form was never a hindrance to me. I could range widely over the Middleworld, effecting alterations to the fluxion network as required, sustaining and balancing the webwork of energies on which phenomenality was based and built up.

But, here and now, I am powerless. I could not lift a speck of dust a minim from the floor. I experience an unpleasant sensation and realize it is frustration. I indulge the emotion for a moment, out of appreciation of its novelty. Then I turn my attention to practical concerns.

Fatezh has imprisoned and silenced me, but he has not blinded my senses. I reach out to examine my surroundings. The first things I examine are the deities, chained together by the thaumaturge's matrix. They are comatose, scarcely aware of themselves and not at all of each other. They exist at a low ebb, and I suspect that Fatezh has already drained them of their energies to draw the power to seize and constrain me.

I explore beyond the chamber, projecting my senses out along corridors and down deeper into the interior of this dwelling. I find other Middleworlders, engaged in mundane tasks. I conclude that they serve the wizard. I come across the man-thing, retired to a chamber, where it sits and reads a book. I detect other beings: the imps in their own den greedily supping a syrup that enhances their powers of lift and thrust; some wisps of humanity — like my captor, devoid of essence, these sylphs exist to flatter and grovel to their master; and one curious anomaly in the form of a man whose essences have somehow been winnowed down, as if his *ba* and *ka* have been partly drawn off.

That should be impossible. But then, so should my capture and imprisonment by a Middleworlder. I make a connection: Fatezh has promised the man-thing a *ba* and a *ka*, and here is a man lacking some of both. Is this part of his plan? Not long ago, I would have said such a thing was beyond possibility. Now I cannot be sure.

I extend myself toward the sleeping man. And find a puzzling condition: not only have his essences been partially leached away, but his mind has also been segmented. An impermeable layer has been established between parts of his mentation. Traces indicate the work of a *theropath*. Clearly, these one-time fluxion-layers have developed far more versatility than they were designed for.

Because he has gist, however diminished, I find I can enter the comatose man's divided mind above the barrier, or I can insinuate myself into the subconsciousness below. The upper portion is placid as an empty room. The lower is a roiling storm of emotions: anger, guilt, remorse, self-hate, despair. I discover memories, grim scenes of massacre and murder. The contrast between the two halves is stark; I wonder if the man has had the layer interposed between them on purpose, to spare himself inner torment.

I withdraw myself. I need to think about what I have learned.

«»

Fatezh is poking at me. Reflexively, I test my constraints and find they remain strong. His importunings cause me discomfort. I respond to him. He notices and removes the restriction on my voice.

"What do you want?"

"I need to test you, then calibrate the responses," he says.

"I do not wish to be tested."

"Your wishes do not come into it. I have you and I will use you to my purposes."

"That is not what I was created for," I say.

"Neither were you created to be a god for humankind."

I consider the issue. "It is possible that the Demiurge did so intend. That would explain why he left me extant after the work was done."

"If he intended that, then he may well have intended for me to come along and do as I am doing."

"That is highly unlikely. I worked closely with the Demiurge, and knew him well."

He makes a peremptory gesture. "The discussion is nuncupative. I have you in my power and will use you as I wish."

"You will not survive translation to the Overworld," I say. "Your *ba* will burst out of you. You may very well ignite at that moment."

"Not if I succeed in restructuring myself as I intend."

He waves away any further discussion and turns to his workbench, from which he takes up the scryer with the two crystals and examines me through it. He makes notes on a pad, then puts down the tube and takes up his wand. He points it at me and utters a string of syllables.

The effect is both uncomfortable and indescribable. I feel that I am being altered in some way. Sensations pass through me. If I were corporeal, I would call them alternating flashes of heat and cold, touches of dizziness, a sense of increased heaviness, followed by a feeling of being weighed down by heavy weights.

He flourishes the wand again, says more non-word sounds. I sense them resonating with the node of fluxions that intersect beneath the floor of the chamber. The sensations cease. He picks up the scryer and studies me through both ends, grunts in satisfaction, and makes more notes.

"Good," he says after reviewing his jottings. "It is working."

"What have you done to me?" I say.

"I told you: recalibration. I need to be able to channel your energies through the other godlings. You will be the keystone of the hermetic arch."

"I do not understand," I say.

"You do not need to." He considers me for a moment. "I will let things stand," he says. "I want to be sure the alterations do not elide. We will resume tomorrow."

He exits and leaves me with much to ponder. I sense that I have changed but I have no system for internal review. I do not know what he has done to me, but I cannot think that his changing of my nature will accrue to my benefit. The other godlings in his putative "arch" are faded and wan. I suspect that his ultimate project, when he executes the final step, will drain them into nonexistence. And much the same may be in store for me.

I must find a way out of this.

«»

My only conduit is to extend myself toward the human denizens of Fatezh's establishment. I brush up against one of his sleeping servants but the fellow reacts with alarm, waking instantly, his gaze darting around his sleeping chamber. I withdraw hurriedly. Fatezh does not know of my ability for outreach; should he learn of it, I am sure he will have the *theropaths* institute another level of constraint.

That leaves only the sleeping man with the bicameral mind. I approach him gently and slip into his being. First I enter his upper mind, but it remains sterile. The kernel of him that exists here is inert. I examine it, and find it is a slimmed down version of the human mentation I am familiar with. The man's psyche has been pared and simplified. I look back along his lifeline and see how this was done. And why.

Fatezh has acquired some remarkable knowledge and skills. He has captured and coerced beings from other Planes and redesigned them to carry out abstruse operations. In the case of the comatose man, he had his demons trim the fellow's *ba* and *ka*, so as to make room for the insertion of a modified *theropath*. Those modifications allowed the *theropath* to emit a particular frequency of sound, augmented by the demon's intrinsic *mana*, to affect the mind-sharing of the residents of the settlement where my temple is situated.

I am aware of this collective-unconscious attribute among the Exleyans, a left-over effect from a conflict between thaumaturges generations before. It has made it easier for me to associate myself into their psychic landscape, to ease and heal and support. I even recall the moment when the shockwave passed through the local noösphere, though at the time I merely watched it happen, since no one of my congregation brought it to me as a problem. I regret now that I have always been merely reactive to my worshippers' needs. Had I been more proactive, I might have investigated. And I might not be in this perilous situation.

The comatose man is my only opportunity. His upper mind is of no use. That part of him does not even have a name, let alone a well-developed personality with which I could associate myself. I withdraw and enter the lower mind.

Here is a different landscape altogether. I see that this part of the man's psyche is engulfed in a never-ending nightmare. It is a dark place, full of pits and shadows, narrow streets and alleys down which rush ill-formed monsters and slavering brutes. I see blood and spilled innards, and shattered bones protruding from flesh, eyes dangling on cheeks, mouths agape with agony.

In the midst of this stands Kain — that is his name, I see — his hands dripping gore, his teeth bared in a snarl. He carries a heavy-bladed falchion, its single edge stained red. In his other hand, swinging by its hair, is a severed human head. He lifts his gaze to a sky dark with roiling storm clouds and roars a wordless sound, the bellow of a beast.

I sense that some of what surrounds me is memory, some of it dreamstuff. But all of it is colored by Kain's *ba*, his dark essence, which had grown to a prodigious size before Fatezh somehow trimmed away perhaps a tenth of its final substance. All of that negative gist has been locked away down here with most of the man's mind. What exists above the barrier is the minimum portion of his *ka* needed to allow the man to function in the human world. I wonder where the rest of his better nature has been put.

I make a detailed examination of his parts and his suppressed memories, paying particular attention to the state of his *ba*, and a plan begins to suggest itself.

«»

Fatezh has coated my physical impetrocation — the pillar of basalt — with a glutinous substance that he has apparently imported from the Seventh Plane.

"What is this for?" I ask him, but he does not respond. Instead, he observes me through his scryer then examines my reflection in what appears to be a mirror of polished metal but is, in fact, another left-over instrument from the Demiurge's workshop. I never worked with the entity, known as a *psurtofere* during the building of phenomenality; it was a tool for preventing time and space from expanding too rapidly at first and for cooling and solidifying the outer edges of reality once it had reached its desired proportion.

Whatever its function in the thaumaturge's plans, it seems to be performing to his satisfaction. He is humming happily to himself as he completes his measurements and turns to me, wand ready for action.

Before he can carry out his next step, I say, "If you made clear to me the nature of your work, I might be able to advise you."

His brows raise themselves to impressive heights. "Am I to believe you will assist in your own destruction?"

"Who is to say that it will be destruction? I have been brought to recognize that conditions and entities I considered immutable may be altered and repurposed. It is possible that, after you have done what you intend — and which I appear to be unable to prevent — I may find myself with different capabilities, even different interests."

I see skepticism in his aspect, but after some reflection he says, "You are unable to lie, aren't you?"

"Subterfuge was never required in my work." I wait to see if he will call my reply inadequate. The truth is, my long association with the psyches of Middleworlders has acquainted me with the art of dissembling, in all its forms. Outright lying is difficult for me, but evasive replies are one of the kinds of mendacity I have learned to encompass in my role as healer of damaged persons.

But Fatezh is one of those who prefer to believe that the world will bend to his dynamism. I believe that is a commonality of thaumaturges. He accepts my explanation and begins to explain his project. It has to do with *bas* and *kas*, as I have surmised. He cannot create them. That was a power reserved to the Demiurge. But he can alter them. The terms he uses are "deflate" and "inflate."

He can reduce or enlarge either of the two gists that animate Middleworlders. He can also isolate the *kra*, the hinge that holds the two souls in place during a Middleworlder's lifespan, then dissolves after death. The tiny few *kras* that do not dissipate remain in the Third World after the *ba* departs for the Underworld and the *ka* ascends to the Overworld. They tend to remain near the locus of death and are popularly known as ghosts or revenants.

By discovering how to weaken the *kra* without killing the person, Fatezh opened the door to manipulating the two souls, even to transferring *mana* between them. He can make the *ba* larger at the *ka*'s expense, or vice versa.

It is the latter process he intends to apply to himself, using my substance as the source of power. But first he must experiment on other subjects to perfect the procedure. Once he has done so, he will transfer all of his *ba* to his *ka*, shed his *kra* and the remnant of his undersoul, and ascend bodily to the Overworld to live in eternal ecstasy.

"What do you think?" he says.

"It is an ambitious objective."

"But feasible?"

Time to dissemble again. "It has not been done before. That, however, is not an argument for its not someday being achieved. Everything must have a beginning."

His eyes flash and he shows a vulpine grin. "Exactly," he says.

I do not tell him that environmental conditions in the Overworld are not conducive to Middleworld matter. His augmented *ka* may fare well there, though it will seem bloated and gross, but the power of the fluxions that bind Paradise together are such that his flesh and bones will dissolve within moments of his arrival.

I ask him how his preliminary experiments have done.

"Excellently," he says. "I have reworked the gists of a human, drawing off some of his *ka* then reinjecting its energy to inflate his *ba*."

"That would make him a monster of evil," I say.

"He was already that. He was responsible for the massacre at Drieff. Do you know of the event?"

"No."

He brushes the matter aside. "The man is useful in other ways. Between assignments, I keep him inanimate."

"And do you intend to 'inject' some of his *ba* into the man-thing that brought me here?"

He shows pleasure at my understanding. "I do. It will allow me to test the redirection of your energies, while calibrating duration and intensity, before I proceed with my own inflation."

I point out that the vat-borne creature will not possess a *kra* to hold the injected soul in place. "It will depart from the host immediately."

"Probably," he says, "but I will have the measurements by then."

"Unfortunate for the man-thing."

The motion of his shoulders and the flick of a hand express his unconcern. "Now," he says, "let us continue with our preparations."

«»

The coating of my corporeal substance does not yield the results Fatezh desires. He declares he will compound a new mixture and make another attempt. I am dismissed from his attention. I return to my only potential means of escape: the comatose man.

There seems no point in accessing his sterile upper mind. I delve into his lower levels and again find his psyche roiled by intense emotions, all of them negative, and dreamlike scenes of horror.

I have gained some facility in dealing with the mentation of Middleworlders through my role as a god. Persons in spiritual need would come to my temple and, after meditation and the taking of a sleeping draft, lie down near my eidolon and slip into unconsciousness. The potion enhanced the vividity of their dreams and helped identify themes of their distress.

I have found I can alter the substance of dreams, enhancing, muting, changing emphases as needed. I can discharge anxieties and reduce the impacts of trauma, preventing the mind from dwelling unhealthily upon past incidents or the repetitive thoughts and images they promulgate. The same qualities that the Demiurge imbued in me — balancing, leveling, intensifying and diminishing — have turned out to be as applicable to the Middleworlder's psyche as to the network of fluxions. When this is all over, assuming I survive, I must devote my thoughts to the question of whether or not the Great Artificer intended this outcome.

But, for now, my concern is with the sleeping man. His state is far beyond that of any worshiper I ever encountered in Exley. Still, he is my only conduit and I set to work. I begin by trying to sort and separate the contents of his undermind: the memories, the dreams, the combinations of both. As I identify one from the others, I apply a color to each category: deep red for the memories, intense blue for the dreamstuff, a rich green for the combinations.

There are a lot of each kind. When I have identified several of each, I turn my attention to the memories first. Exerting my abilities, I begin to leach the brightness out of the image, shading it down from red to pink. I used to do exactly thus with fluxions during the creation.

One by one, I tone down the memories of murder and torture, rendering the scenes of horror in gentle pastels. At the same time, I diffuse the sharpness of the images, blurring and defocusing, rendering the recollection imprecise and vague.

When I am done with the memories, I turn to the dreams and use the same techniques, then I work on the dream-memories. As I work, the man's undermind becomes a quieter place. His image of himself becomes less stark. The weapons and the evidence of murder fade away and he is left standing naked — just a man and nothing more — in a more tranquil place.

There is still more to be done, but I sense that I have accomplished as much as would be useful in one intervention. I do not want to overstress his capacity for change. I learned early on as a god that too much, too soon, can induce psychic shock, which usually presents as catatonia.

A catatonic man will be of no use to me.

«»

I say to Fatezh, "I am curious—"

He interrupts me but continues to coat my surface with a new mixture. "I don't believe curiosity was one of your original qualities."

He is right and I admit it. Not being designed for introspection, I have not noticed that I have changed — or been changed by the new activities I have undertaken.

"I am curious," I begin again, "to know how you came to develop your abilities to work with *bas* and *kas*."

He does not discern the reason for my interest. Like all thaumaturges, he has high self-regard and is happy to demonstrate his knowledge of esoteric subjects.

"It is all about gist," he says, pausing to brush on another damp stripe of the gray and granular liquid he has concocted. "Gist is the underlying substance on which phenomenality is built up. It is the prime ingredient in fluxions, as well as in the *ba*, *ka*, and *kra*.

"As a thaumaturge, I have long studied the nature of fluxions. My ability to apply axial volition — or what the laity call 'will' — to fluxions allows me to create the products of sympathetic association — again, what the common folk call 'magic.' I am proud to say I have myself created new and original products."

He applies another stripe. "One day, when I was constraining a *kra* I wished to use as a door guardian, I noticed that its resonance was similar to that of a green fluxion. Growing interested, I applied to the *kra* one of the simple spells of the Green School. It responded. I then tried a Blue School cantrip. Again, there was a response."

"I never knew any of this," I say.

"You had no need to know," he says. "You were an instrument designed to perform specific tasks. Does a hammer need to know how a nail is made?"

"No," I say. "I am increasingly aware of my limitations." I don't mention that I am even more aware of my newfound abilities.

"It doesn't matter," he says. He completes the preparation of my surface. "Now, we'll see what kind of resonance a spell of the Purple School generates in you."

He gestures with his wand and speaks several syllables. I feel peculiar sensations pass through me, some of them unpleasant but all transitory. I sense no lasting alterations.

Fatezh smiles and says, "I think we're almost there. I'll add a little more kobodium and let it set overnight. Tomorrow, we'll bring in 114 and make the final calculations."

«»

Night time and the wizard's manse sleeps. I have been considering the constraints placed upon me in the light of what Fatezh has said about fluxions. The power of the bonds that hold me in place stem from argent and sable fluxions, the most basic and powerful of the lines of gist-force that constitute the underpinnings of phenomenality.

I did not create those varieties of gist; only the Demiurge had that power. But it was my responsibility to assess their strengths and frequencies and tell *theropaths* to modify their placements and alignments, as necessary. If I had a *theropath* here and under my control, I could free myself in a trice.

But the *theropaths* have gone back to their Plane, and if Fatezh calls them back to manage me, it will be to him that they pay heed. If, however, the thaumaturge were removed from the equation — even if only temporarily — I am sure I could reassert dominance.

I am a tool and a user of tools. Right now, the only tool at my disposal is the comatose man. I have done a fair amount to undo the damage his life experiences have done to him. I have deflated his grossly swollen *ba*, inflated his shrunken *ka*. I see how sits the barrier that separates his under- and overminds, and I am confident I can dissolve it quickly, since it is made of stuff borrowed from his *kra* and pumped up artificially.

The upshot of all this is that I have restored the man's damaged psyche to something closer to the mean, though he will never be "normal." Still, as I say, he is my only possibility for escape.

I do a little more work on him while he sleeps. I am glad to see that his dreams, though still melancholy, are no longer horrific.

Now I must wait and hope to find an opportunity for action. As I think that, it occurs to me that hope was not a faculty included in my original design. I conclude that I must have acquired it, osmotically, from my worshippers.

Part 4

Kain speaks

I am Kain. I realize this as I wake as if from a long sleep and find myself standing in the Master's workroom. It as if someone has whispered my name to me as I come awake. I want to dwell upon this knowledge, because I am aware that for quite a while I operated under the false name Farouche, the character from the old legend, so often a figure in painting, sculpture, story, and at least three operas.

But I have no leisure for such thoughts. Fatezh is in front of me, peering into my eyes. I blink and he nods in apparent satisfaction.

"Good," he says. "Go over there and lie down."

Of course, I obey. I turn and walk toward the indicated couch without volition, a passenger in my own body. I have long since been like this. Fatezh speaks, I obey.

I position myself on the reclining leather, my shoulders and head elevated by the bolster at one end. I have a good view of the Master as he works at his bench. He is putting the final touches to a set of coated fibers — gist conduits, I have heard him call them — coating the ends with the adhesive that will hold them in place.

Careful not to let the sticky stuff touch his flesh or his long robe, figured all over with arcane symbols brocaded into the cloth with wires of gold, silver, and electrum, he carries the conduits across the room to the circle of chained gods.

These are a motley assortment with which I am familiar: idols of gold, bronze, and in one case carved bone; two well shaped stone statues, while another is just a piece of volcanic rock; a woven fetish of jute; one a grinning head in terra cotta; and a new addition, in the form of a waist-high pillar of black basalt, its upper surface covered by a wash of some gray substance that has now dried. Through the thin coating, I can see a line of vertical characters graven into the surface of the pillar that faces me.

Fatezh places the ends of the two conduits against the basalt, holds them in place, and waits. After a long moment, he takes his hands away and grunts in satisfaction as the fibers remain in place. He attaches the other ends to the nearest of the chained gods, a bronze eidolon that resembles an overweight simian with improbable genitalia.

Again he waits, then lets go. The connection holds. The black, gray-painted pillar is now linked to the circle of deities. I cannot see it, but I am assured from what Fatezh has said previously that the entities themselves are now connected to each other, such that their *mana* can be made to flow in a particular direction, at the thaumaturge's bidding.

Fatezh is manifestly happy. He dances a couple of small steps then composes himself. I know he does not care that I have seen his less than dignified display. My opinions are of no interest to him.

Now he turns toward the arched doorway that leads into the chamber, not the one I must have entered by, but the one opposite. He gestures with a hand and speaks an ergophone, and the door opens. He could just have easily told the person on the other side to come in, but he enjoys being theatrical, even before the gaze of a nonentity. I have always assumed he is practicing so that his mannerisms will appear effortless to those — his colleagues and rivals in thaumaturgy — he wishes to impress.

With the door open, the vat-born non-person that called itself Goladry when I was Farouche — but which I now recognize bears not a name but a number, tattooed on its upper arm, 114 — enters the workroom. Its demeanor is as placid as always, but I detect a slight tremor in its step as it crosses the flagstoned floor, at Fatezh's direction, to the second couch. It reposes itself supine, there being no bolster to lift its head.

The thaumaturge measures the distance from me to Goladry, then finds a spot exactly midway between us and marks it with a cross of chalk. He then brings from a cupboard a tripod of gold and positions it exactly over the mark. Next, he opens a drawer in a chest and extracts a blue crystal, the size of a melon and precisely cut to display a hundred and more facets. It reflects the lights from the overhead floating globes so that the chamber's walls are speckled with patches of brilliance.

Fatezh carries the crystal to the tripod and places it snugly into the circle of gold that is its top. He stands back and studies the placement then nods to himself. He turns to me and says, "The process will not take long. There will be some discomfort but you will remain still."

"Yes, Master," I say, as I always do. I am calm, again as I always am in his presence, as per his standing orders.

But I do not have to watch, so I turn my gaze toward the ceiling and follow the gentle drifting of the light globes. I turn my thoughts inward and receive a surprise. Usually, my mind is realm of a calm, colorless and featureless, but now there appears before me, in my mind's eye, a floor. And in that floor is a trapdoor, with a ring to lift it.

Even as it comes into view, I find that I know it has always been there and that I have always ignored it. And suddenly, I know what lies beneath and what will happen if I take hold of the ring and pull.

But, of course, I will not do that unless the Master tells me to. My powers are all separated from me and confined in the darkness below the floor. This is new knowledge to me, though I realize as soon as that thought occurs that I have known these things all along but, like the trapdoor, I have not looked at them.

I turn my gaze back to Fatezh. He is bent over the crystal, touching it here and there with his wand and examining the results through his scrying tube. He projects an air of repressed excitement.

I look over at 114. It lies quietly, eyes closed, hands folded on its belly. But I detect a tremor in those hands.

I look toward the ceiling again and close my eyes, returning to the sterile room that is my mind. But now I find

I am not alone. A dark figure stands beside the trapdoor. For a moment, I think that some part of me has come up from below. But then I realize that I have encountered this person before, in dreams that, until now, I have forgotten.

I examine the figure and see that it is featureless and black from head to sole. It raises a finger to where its lips would be if it had them. I understand that we are not to converse. And I understand why.

I remain calm, but now I am definitely interested in what is to come.

I open my eyes. Fatezh is back at his chest of drawers. He brings out a circle of polished gold, big as a dinner plate, inscribed with a spiral of ideograms from a long-dead language. He carries it to where 114 lies and places the disc on the man-thing's torso, just over where its heart beats.

Then he returns to the chest and retrieves a second disc, identical to the first, except that the spiral of characters proceeds widdershins from the center. Humming a little tune, he carries it over to where I lie and positions it on my chest.

A quiet voice inside me says, *Now*.

Fatezh's eyes go wide and I know he, too, hears the voice. He darts a glance toward the pillar of basalt, and that is his final mistake.

Within me, the dark figure has yanked open the trapdoor. The floor between me and myself dissolves and I am once more Kain, in full and whole.

Fatezh opens his mouth and raises a hand. I know a spell is forming in his mind and he will utter its ergophones, arrange his fingers in a fluxion-caressing pattern, and so unleash some devastating power.

Or he would have, except that I am already reaching up, to take his chin and crown in my scarred and calloused hands, and break his ancient neck.

Part 5

114 speaks

I lay supine, eyes closed, awaiting the great change. The gold disk Fatezh had placed on my chest was heavy. It remained ice-cold and sent a chill through me. I suppressed a shudder.

I could hear the thaumaturge moving about, the sliding of a drawer, then his footsteps crossing the stone floor. There was silence for a moment, then a *snap* as of a large twig breaking. The golden light that played upon my eyelids was suddenly gone and I opened my eyes to near-darkness, the chamber lit only by the light that filtered in through the open doorway.

Something loomed in my vision and I rolled sideways to avoid it. The globes that always floated below the ceiling when Fatezh was in his workroom were falling. The one that had been above me struck the couch as I hit the floor, the gold disk dropping from my torso to spin musically like a top on the flagstones. Other globes were hitting the floor to shatter into puffs of white dust.

I sat up and looked around. The Kain was rising from his own resting place, pushing away a strangely shaped bundle of shining, figured cloth that had somehow come to lie across his legs. In the dimness, I did not make sense of what I was seeing until the object landed on the floor and I saw Fatezh's unmistakable slippers pointing toes up at the darkened ceiling.

The Kain stood up and looked at me. I rose and returned his stare with as much equanimity as I could summon and wondered if I would have to defend myself. The point of continuing to exist, gistless, was questionable, but old habits are hard to break.

But his gaze moved away from me and settled on the circle of eidolons that had been central to Fatezh's ambitions. He went to them, looked them over, then his attention fixed itself on the basalt pillar we had brought from its temple in Exley. It was covered in some gray stuff that had been part of the gist-transferring process Fatezh had intended. The Kain picked at the coating with a fingernail, flaking a bit of it away.

"Now what?" he said. I was going to answer but then I saw he was not speaking to me.

I stooped and picked up the gold disk. I was sure it would have value among the wizardly community. It would probably be a good idea to collect a few other items before the preternatural senses of Fatezh's rivals told them he was no more. They would come, and the conflict over the spoils and remnants, as I remembered from Isphant's fall, would be dangerous to bystanders.

The Kain continued to commune in some way denied to me with the eidolon of Efferion. From his expressions, I could tell that he was taking in information. He reached out and touched one of the fibrous cables that attached to the pillar, but yanked his hand back as if it had been burned.

He turned toward me. "What do you know of this?" he said, indicating the chain of gods.

I saw no reason not to tell him. "It is a compilation of energies, arranged to complement and intensify each other. Fatezh wanted to learn how to focus and concentrate the powers to achieve certain aims."

"What aims?"

"What thaumaturges always want: to go to the Overworld and live in ecstasy forever."

The Kain frowned. "Efferion says it cannot be done."

I shrugged. "He may be right, he may be wrong. Fatezh was establishing new parameters."

"We were not sending him over today," the Kain said. He gestured toward the crystal and the couches. "What was this all about?"

I told him. His frown deepened. "He would have stolen some of my gist and given it to you?"

"Apparently. When I extracted from him a promise to end my gistlessness in return for bringing him Efferion, he did not tell me how he meant to do it."

"You would have been complicit in soul-stealing," the Kain said.

His mouth set in a hard line. I prepared myself for fight or flight. But then his face changed and I knew he was hearing a voice I could not. His attention returned to the chain of gods.

As he studied them, he spoke again to me. "Efferion should be rescued."

"How?" I said.

"I don't know." His gaze went to the books on the thaumaturge's shelves. "Would those tell us?"

"After we spent a score of years learning how to unravel their intricacies and overcome the obstacles they place in the paths of those who seek to penetrate their mysteries."

I glanced over at the remains of Fatezh. "But we don't have much time before a flock of wizards arrive to carry all of this away — and perhaps us as well."

The Kain showed his training and experience as a soldier. He paused to think, then said, "If we are overmatched, we should retreat." He looked again at Efferion and I sensed that he was in some form of communion with the god. "Or can we fight?"

I spoke in answer. "I carried a pair of demons to Exley. They overpowered the god. The restraints they imposed on Efferion remain in place. They did not die when Fatezh expired," — I gestured to the powder of shattered glass globes littering the floor — "unlike his spells."

"Why not?"

I spread my hands to show that I was speculating. "The spells were powered by his axial volition — his will. That does not survive his death. The demons — they're called *theropaths* — have their own powers. Somehow he coaxed or coerced them into using them in his behalf."

"Could we summon them and get them to release all these gods?"

I told him I had no idea how to do such a thing. Besides, *theropaths* did not have any fondness for Middleworlders — gisted or otherwise — and might respond to a summons by amusing themselves at our expense.

"I would not like to be turned inside out," I finished. "Today has been disappointment enough."

"Then we should go."

But I said, "Wait." A thought had occurred. I went to where Efferion was shackled into the circle of gods and examined the cables.

"What happened when you touched it?" I asked the Kain.

"It felt as if something was being uprooted from deep inside me and streaming out through my hand."

"Hmm," I said, then added the thought that had been with me since Fatezh died. "I have nothing left to live for." I reached my hand toward the cable on the pillar's left side.

"That vindicator said you could join his guild."

"Not the life I wish for," I said. I laid my hand on the cable.

Nothing happened.

I took a good grip and pulled. The adhesive resisted for a moment, then gave way. I pulled free the connector on the other side of the god.

"The cables are conduits for gist," I said. "I contain no gist, so I am unaffected."

"Efferion says we should uncouple the others," the Kain said.

"Why not?" I quickly broke all the connections. The circle of idols and stones looked even more forlorn. Idly, I picked some of the dried stuff of Efferion's pillar. I looked at the Kain and couldn't think of anything to say, anything to do.

A motion in my peripheral vision, which is sharper than normal humans', caught my attention. I turned that way and saw an oblong shape that resolved into a road winding among shadows. It grew larger, and as it did so, a small figure appeared, also enlarging as it came toward us.

I recognized the scene. It was what the Purple School thaumaturge had called "the Glooms," a way for wizards to travel from place to place unseen. And now, as the striding figure grew larger, I recognized something else.

"Isphant," I said. "He's coming. Fatezh's death must have freed him from his captivity in a bottle."

"I remember him," the Kain said, and laughed. "He thought he was a natural master of military science."

"I wouldn't mention that," I said.

And then there was no time for conversation because Isphant was here with us, his gaze darting about. He spotted

Fatezh's corpse and went straight to it, bending to feel in the robe until he came out with the dead wizard's wand, then searching more. He pocketed a ring and a small box made of carved wood.

Now he straightened and looked at the Kain then at me. "You're one of mine," he said.

"Yes," I said, "number 114."

He nodded and turned back to the Kain. "You directed the armies that fought against me."

"I did," the Kain said.

Isphant made a dismissive gesture. "I bear you no ill will," he said. "I overreached."

The Kain inclined his head.

Another wave of the thaumaturge's hand took in Fatezh. "How did this happen?"

"I broke his neck while he was distracted," the Kain said.

Isphant quirked his mouth. "I should take action, a noncomp killing a practitioner, but I will not. But for you, I would still be in a bottle on Todl's shelf of curios."

"Speaking of which..." He crossed to the shelves that held Fatezh's tomes and paraphernalia, and made a quick inventory. He moved the wand and said a few ergophones; a capacious leather suitcase appeared and Isphant quickly stuffed it with items from the shelves. Then he closed it and deployed the wand again. The suitcase vanished.

Then he looked at the circle of gods. "And this?" he said.

"Fatezh was conducting experiments," I said, "intended to translate him bodily to the Overworld.

Isphant made a face and clucked his tongue against the roof of his mouth. "Fool," he said, with a shake of his head. "Long ago, I sent my eyes into the Fourth Plane, searching for any sign of success by wizards who had made the transition. I found none. It is a myth clung to by those who cannot abide the unavoidable certainty of their own demise."

I saw a notion occur to him then. He used the wand again and spoke another set of syllables, none of which I could retain, though I heard them clearly. A spectral figure appeared on the far side of the room, almost completely transparent, feeling its way along the wall, like a blind man seeking a door.

"Ahah!" said Isphant. He plucked a stoppered clay bottle from the shelves, opened it and sniffed its neck. Finding it empty, he crossed to where the ghost of Fatezh sought escape and eventual dissolution. The thaumaturge put the bottle on the floor, motioned with the wand and spoke, and the phantom was drawn toward the open container like smoke. It disappeared within, and Isphant replaced the stopper, tapped it with the wand, then scooped up the bottle.

Smiling an unappetizing smile, he tapped the stopper with the wand. I heard a faint wail.

Isphant caused the suitcase to reappear. He put the bottle inside and sent the case away again. Then he looked at the Kain and me and said, "Why are you still here?"

I shrugged. "We have nowhere to go."

Isphant's expression said that was none of his concern.

The Kain said, "I was thinking of returning Efferion to its temple in Exley."

The wizard's aspect did not change.

The Kain went on, "I did some harm there and would like to make amends, for the sake of my *ka*."

"What is this to me?" said Isphant.

"The bottle? Its contents?"

Now it was the thaumaturge's turn to lift and settle his shoulders. But he followed with a roll of his hand that invited the man to continue.

The Kain said, "If you would allow us the use of Fatezh's flying platform, we could make the trip and send it back."

Isphant bridled. "The imps insist on hymetic syrup," he said, "which is troublesome to brew."

I spoke up. "Fatezh has an ample supply."

I saw intrinsic selfishness contend with other sentiments. Finally, Isphant said, "Very well, but take all these other godlings with you. You will recall that I despise clutter."

"There is one other matter," the Kain said. Isphant showed irritation but the man pressed on, "Efferion is under constraints imposed by *theropaths* that Fatezh recruited from the Seventh Plane. It cannot function well under such conditions."

This news only increased Isphant's irritation. "*Thero-paths*? More evidence of Fatezh's idiocy. They are always treacherous. I wouldn't be surprised if they coaxed him toward his Overworld obsession, while they giggled and smirked behind his back."

He took up Fatezh's scryer from the workbench and studied the basalt pillar, then made a sound of contempt. "Simple stuff," he said. He approached the stone, placed his hands on it, and spoke a string of syllables.

I sensed nothing, of course, but the thaumaturge declared the constraints removed. "Now get all of this out of here," he said, "and don't let me see you again."

He summoned a few of Fatezh retainers to carry the thirteen deities up to the terrace where the platform rested. They were nervous in his presence, but quick to comply.

The imps complained of the weight they had to lift, but the Kain mollified them by giving each a beaker of syrup. We lifted off and were soon passing rapidly through the upper air, shielded from wind and cold by an aura the imps projected in return for another round of syrup.

"Efferion expresses gratitude toward you," the Kain told me. We were standing at the forward railing and staring ahead. We had crossed the mountains and now saw the wide plain extending before us into the unfathomable distance. "It wishes it could repay you."

"There is only one thing that I want, and I cannot have it," I said.

"Perhaps you are better off. The good you do does you no good in return, but you are insulated from the consequences of doing evil."

I signaled that the question was nuncupative and changed the subject. "What will you do when you return to Exley and have reinstated the god?"

He was silent for a long moment, gazing off across the plain we were now traversing at great height. Then he said, "I owe Nulf Bernaglio a settling of accounts. I have not yet decided just how much he is owed."

"It was at his urging that Fatezh interfered with your essences, hollowed you out to place the voice of a *theropath* within you, then took away your memories — your very sense of who you were."

The Kain nodded, his face grave. "True enough, but I must consider his motivation: I slew his family, unjustly, in one of my blind rages. He had some cause for revenge."

"Is that true?" I said. "Do you now remember what you did and to whom you did it?"

He ran a hand over his face. "I remember enough. And even if I did not slay them by my own hand, I led and commanded those who did."

We were silent for a while, then I said, "The whole exercise was designed to put him in power in Exley. What do you think we will discover when we get there?"

The Kain signaled that he could not know. "We will just have to see."

"And we will have to contrive an entrance to the town that does not draw attention," I said. "For all we know, we are proscribed persons. The Watch may seize us on sight."

Again, he made a gesture that pushed the resolution of that issue into the future. Another silence ensued.

I left him to his musings and went to sit in the plush chair at the middle of the platform. I could hear the imps in the nacelles below muttering to each other.

I thought about what I would do next. My hopes had been dashed. Gistless I was and gistless I would remain. The end of my life would be the end of everything that was me: no fragment doomed to the Underworld, no soul ascending to the Plane of paradise.

I supposed I would see about working again for Tolderman Ufretes at Chadroyds. They had taken me on as a freelance discriminator and might do so again, assuming I was not a hunted fugitive in Exley. I had found the work interesting and intrinsically rewarding.

I was deciding that would be my first choice when my preternatural visual sense saw something far out on the plain and north of our flight path. I stood and went to the forward rail, and called upon my ability to magnify objects in my field of vision. The Kain, standing beside me, had noticed nothing.

I adjusted my vision further and saw a troop of some thirty horsemen spread around four high-wheeled, dome-topped carts moving in a northeast direction across the grassland. But there was one other figure in the convoy, trailing along in the dust at the rear. His hands were bound before him by a rope that one of the riders held. He stumbled and almost fell when the horseman yanked on the lead. I saw the rider laugh and pull again.

I went to where the Kain stood, brooding, gestured with my chin, and said, "A troop of Azarines, with a captive."

He blinked his way back to the here and now, and looked out over the plain. "That dust?" he said.

I nodded. I took another close look and confirmed my suspicion. "They've got a prisoner. It's Gashtun."

He blinked again, like a man who is reminded of some fact from the distant past that he'd forgotten. Then his jaw set. He went to the chair, above the imps, and said, "Divert to that party of Azarines, off to the left."

One of the imps sniggered. "We are to take you to Exley. No diversions."

The Kain sighed. "More syrup," he said.

"Two beakers," said the imp, while the other one chimed in with, "Each."

"One each," said the Kain. "You'll want some for the return trip."

He winked at me as he said it. I knew there was plenty in the coffer beside the chair. But the deal was struck and the platform swerved and began a rapid descent.

"Faster," the Kain said and our speed increased.

The tiny dots that were the Azarine on their horses grew quickly in size. We were coming out of the westering sun and so we were quite close before someone spotted the flying platform zooming down at them. A horn blew and the formation broke and scattered in several directions, a clump of horsemen forming around each of the wagons.

I saw several reaching for bolt-throwers. The man who had been leading Gashtun was one of these and, as he brought up the weapon to cock and load, he perforce let drop the towing rope. Gashtun staggered and fell to his knees, then dropped prone.

The Kain ordered the imps to set down between Gashtun and the Azarines. The rest of the broken convoy, that had ridden off in their separate clumps, now drew rein and sat their horses, watching us.

"Come on!" Kain said. He vaulted over the railing and ran to where Gashtun lay inert. I pushed open the center gate and followed. We grabbed the exhausted man under his arms and dragged him back to the platform, threw him through the open gate, and leaped aboard. We could already hear the thumps of hooves heading our way.

"Up!" said the Kain and for once the imps did not quibble. Bolts were already landing on the platform's floor, and one struck solidly into Fatezh's ornate chair. Another glanced off Efferion. The platform climbed on an angle in the direction we had come from and soon we were far above the bolt-throwers' reach.

Gashtun was only partly conscious, making croaking noises. Fatezh's retainers had put aboard some basic provisions, so I fetched a canteen while the Kain turned the man over and raised his head and shoulders. Gashtun gulped the water, belched, slumped. His eyes closed and his face went slack. The Kain lowered him to the platform floor and we left him to sleep.

«»

"I think my mistake was, when I saw them, I raised a hand to hail them," Gashtun said, after he finally woke up and tore into a cob of roadbread.

"Probably," I said. "By initiating contact, you took away their sense of agency."

Around a mouthful of bread, Gashtun said, "Well, they took away everything else: the horses, the gifts, my weapons. I'm just glad they didn't strip me naked."

"They're a peculiar people," the Kain said. "I'm glad we came along."

Gashtun swigged some water to wash down the contents of his mouth, then studied the Kain. "If you don't mind me saying, you seem… different, somehow."

"It's a long story," the Kain said. "For quite a while, I wasn't myself. Now I am."

"If you don't want to tell it, that's all right with me," Gashtun said. He tore off another chunk of bread and chewed, looking over to where the pillar of basalt lay on its side. "Is that Efferion?"

"Another long story," I said. "We are taking it back to Exley."

"I went to the temple when they first opened it," Gashtun said. "I felt what they called 'the touch'." He shook his head. "I didn't like it."

"That's why we have different gods," the Kain said. "You get to choose the ones you're comfortable with."

«»

It was evening when we came close enough to Exley to see the smoke haze from its chimneys on the horizon. The Kain told the imps to stop and hover and, after a brief haggle and the dispensing of more syrup, they did.

"We need to think about how we do this," he said.

"I could go in first," Gashtun said, "see how it all smells."

But at that point, Efferion weighed in. I saw both the Kain's and Gashtun's expressions change as the god spoke in their minds.

"Well, that settles it," the Kain said. "We'll fly directly to the temple, land on the roof, and carry the pillar down to the sanctum."

I looked a question at him and he explained that the temple was full of worshippers maintaining a perpetual vigil, calling for the return of their deity.

"Efferion is in touch with them, now that we're within range. It says they're overjoyed."

We moved toward the town, at a height no bolt-thrower could reach. I decided it was time to broach a subject I had been avoiding.

"Fatezh intended to steal essence from you and transfer it to me," I said. "It would have harmed you."

He shrugged. "Possibly, although Efferion said it couldn't be done. But, more important, your deal with the wizard brought the god to Olliphract. If you hadn't done that Efferion would not have repaired me and freed me from bondage. I would still be a slave to Fatezh. Instead, I am free and whole, and able to consider a future. Though I suppose I am now somewhat peculiar and unfit for many occupations."

"You are saying that outcomes matter more to you than intentions," I said.

He weighed that for a moment, then said, "I suppose I am."

«»

We angled in toward Exley from the northwest. The guards on the western gate spotted us. As we passed over, I saw a rider in a Watch uniform spurring his horse up the processional way toward the basilica of the Council of Oligarchs. "Wizards are not wanted in Exley," I reminded the Kain and Gashtun. "We may get an unfriendly reception."

"Nulf Bernaglio is one of the Council now," the Kain said. "I do not expect him to welcome me."

The temple of Efferion came into sight. As we descended toward it, a stream of people emerged from a trapdoor in one corner, many of them carrying glass vessels in which burned votive candles. They formed a crowd around a space left open in the middle of the flat roof.

"Gently," the Kain said to the imps.

The platform eased down and alighted on the tiled surface as softly as a feather's fall. We were surrounded by beaming faces, some with tears streaming down their cheeks, the candle flames reflected and refracted in the teardrops. A woman in a priestess's robe stepped forward and I opened the gate for her. She went to where the pillar lay, made some kind of gesture, bent, and reverently touched her hand to the stone. Some flakes of the stuff the thaumaturge had painted on the basalt came off and clung to her fingers. She frowned and brushed them off.

Straightening up, she called six names and beckoned. Six burly men moved through the crowd and came aboard. After a brief discussion, they arranged themselves into two trios, one to each side, and stooped to lift the pillar onto their shoulders. A moment later, they were passing through the crowd, which parted for them, although many hands reached out to touch the basalt as it went by.

The priestess followed the six bearers and, as they descended through the trapdoor, the crowd followed in an orderly manner. Soon, the Kain, Gashtun, and I were alone on the now darkened rooftop, except for a single figure who approached us.

When she came near, I saw that it was Philaria, the wife of Bernaglio. She looked up anxiously at the Kain and said, "You need to fly away again. You are in danger here. Nulf has gone mad but many people still support him, including all of the Specials and most of the Watch."

"I am not going anywhere," the Kain said. He gestured to me and Gashtun to step down from the platform. Then he gave the imps a beaker each of hymetic syrup and left unlocked the chest where several jugs of the stuff were stored.

"Don't have your party until you're out over the wilderness," he told the grinning creatures.

They laughed and assured him they knew what they were doing. They did not go back down into their nacelles but sat on the chair's plush cushion, which was big enough for both of them. They giggled and toasted each other with syrup as the Kain stepped down onto the roof. Before he could close the gate, they lifted off and the sound of their raucous laughter came back to us.

Philaria said, "The temple cannot offer sanctuary. The Specials have no respect for our cult."

"We will be fine," the Kain said. "The god I have brought back to you is not the god that was taken."

"I don't understand," she said.

"It has grown, in strength and understanding. More to the point, it has discovered it has a will of its own."

Now her face grew concerned. "What does it intend to do?"

"It intends to do good," the Kain said. "And I intend to assist it. I have a lot of evil to make up for."

"You should speak to Rainert, the High Priest."

"I will have to," the Kain said. "I intend to replace him."

She stood with her mouth open as Kain turned and headed across the tiles to where the trapdoor stood open. Gashtun and I followed him. So, after a moment, did Philaria.

Part 6

Efferion speaks

I have learned from the other entities and tools in the circle to which Fatezh bound me. Many of them had memories I could access, and many had experiences with thaumaturges in the past. After I had probed and examined, I came to understand the mania that characteristically infests ambitious wizards, the lust to be more than they were ever meant to be. It has much to do with will and the exercise of will, or axial volition, as they call it.

I was created without will, though some of the semi-inert godlings possessed it to some degree. As I waited for Fatezh to conclude his calibrations, I reached into the cores of the other deities and experimented with the concept of transferring their qualities to me. I found the gist conduits the thaumaturge was using to link us made such relocation not only possible, but easy. I assembled the modest amounts of will in my colleagues into one mass, shaped it accordingly, and installed it in my own composition. It fit quite well.

Now, possessed of a will and bound in a circle of the will-less, I transferred most of the remaining gists of the others to my own core. I experienced a qualitative change in myself, and found it satisfying.

Then I waited for Fatezh to come within reach of the man, Kain, who had entered the chamber internally divided and with his will subsumed by Fatezh's manipulations. At the apposite time, I removed Kain's separation and made him whole again. I knew that I did not have to suggest the appropriate action. His undermind had wanted to destroy the wizard for some time.

«»

Now I am returned to my place in the temple. My worshippers are happy. I see them more clearly now than I did before my experiences in Fatezh's chamber. I see their *bas*, their *kas*, and their *kras*, and know that I can alter their proportions at will. I see the contents of their minds.

Until now, I have always been reactive toward my worshippers. But, having acquired axial volition of mine own — and quite a lot of it — I believe I can become proactive. The issue before me now is: what do I want to do?

I will think about it.

«»

Some time has passed. I have been experimenting. I have seen where the *theropaths* applied their constraints and have altered my conformation to prevent that from happening again. To make sure the change works, I entered the Plane where those beings reside, found the guilty parties, and punished them. They were powerless to stop me. After causing them some acute discomfort, I wrested from them some of their substance and added it to my own.

Then I extended myself toward Olliphract, specifically to the location of my confinement in Fatezh's establishment. Several thaumaturges had gathered there and were contending for ownership of their dead rival's possessions. They immediately became aware of my presence and sought to constrain me. But the *theropaths* they summoned would not come.

I demonstrated some powers to them, then confiscated some of each wizard's axial volition and added it to my own. I found the doing of it to be satisfying. I left them with enough remaining will to feed and care for themselves, but none of them will be casting spells or binding demons from the Seventh Plane for a long, long while.

I am now a far cry from how the Demiurge fashioned me. I still wonder what he would make of the developments and whether or not this was an anticipated outcome of his great plan. But it is not a pressing question to me. I have other concerns now.

«»

My chief priest, Kain, has come to me. A party of armed men are moving toward my temple. They are intent on capturing him and forcibly dispersing my worshippers, whom they consider to be antithetical to the new political regime that emerged after Kain unknowingly imported a *theropath* into the town at a crucial point in the process of selecting their rulers.

The person now in sole authority in Exley is Nulf Bernaglio, who arranged for Kain to be sent to the town in the first place. He also supplied Fatezh with several of the deities that the thaumaturge drained of their powers — a process that I finished. Bernaglio blames Kain for misdeeds of the past in a town called Drieff and wishes to visit painful excesses upon my priest, culminating in Kain's demise.

I find this interesting. The concepts of good and evil are, to me, abstract notions. Of course, I am aware that evil in the Middleworld leaks through into this Plane from the Seventh, where it is a kind of weather condition. It seeps from there into the gist-containing denizens of this Plane and wreaks varying effects. All of this, I am reasonably sure, was part of the Great Artificer's plan. It is not an agreeable situation to think otherwise.

I reach out to the person who has sent the armed force to attack my worshippers. I examine his *ba* and *ka*, both of which are well out of normal proportions. I consider rearranging his inner composition, then decide that it would be better to take a different approach.

I respond to Kain. He listens then makes some objections. I inform him that my decisions are not to be gainsaid. Reluctantly, he acquiesces.

Part 7

Kain speaks

Efferion had reordered me. When I emerged from the temple I was not the man who had landed on its roof along with Gashtun and the vat-born scout I used to call Goladry. And I was not at all the man who had walked the caravan trail, found a patron, and begun a new life in this river town. It would take some getting used to and, though I had confidence in the god, I realized that it was new to its role and still feeling its way forward.

I was not comfortable with the changes, yet had to accept that the god had rescued me from a dire situation and made improvements in my being, for which I ought to be appreciative. And for which I owed Efferion my obedience.

A strong force, sent by Nulf Bernaglio, now styling himself "the Grand Effectuator of Exley," was coming up Idderlond Wynd from the direction of the basilica. Many of them carried lit torches, and in their vanguard marched the men I had selected and trained as Specials, but they were supported by others who wore the uniform of the Town Watch. With them came also another strong contingent who wore civilian clothes but had bands of white cloth, displaying a black symbol, wrapped tightly around their upper arms. All bore cudgels or edged weapons. As they marched, they were chanting a rhythmic count from one to four, though instead of voicing the last numeral, they emitted in unison a guttural "Huh!" and brandished their weaponry.

I was startled to realize that I recognized the cloth emblem. Some of the Justified Celebrants of Drieff had worn just such armbands when they slaughtered Lance-Major Vashonne and his underofficers. The realization raised in me a storm of conflicting feelings. For a long moment, I relived the emotion that had swept through me on that long-ago morning when word was brought to me that my battalion commander had been brutally murdered. My hands clenched then opened as I extended my arms toward the approaching men.

Efferion had told me of the powers I now commanded in his name. He had tied his will — his axial volition, as he called it — to mine. I could draw upon it as if the god were a river and I a side channel connected by a gate. If I opened the "gate," his force would flow through me and rush against the Specials, the Watchmen, and the Celebrants. The results would be devastating.

I must admit, at the end of that long moment, I allowed myself to revel in a vision: my outstretched hands spewing a torrent of power into their ranks, sending them tumbling back from its impact, their bones snapping, their limbs and heads severed from their torsos, their blood erupting in fountains, and their inner parts splattering in shiny strings against the walls.

The old Kain Minderlanz, he who had assaulted the guilty and innocent alike at Drieff, in the fullness of his devotion to the murdered leader of his Free Company, would have unleashed the inferno on the foe, making no distinction between the deluded Celebrants and any others who stood in the path of his vengeance. Indeed, that Kain had done massacre, murdering without discretion, and had paid for it with years of bitter self-aversion.

Efferion had given me a gate to its axial volition, but it was up to me how wide I would throw open that barrier. Now, as Bernaglio's counting, grunting, weapon-thrusting force neared the temple steps atop which I awaited them, I stepped forward into the light of their torches and threw back the cowl of my priestly robe.

The leading ranks, the Specials, saw my face. They broke off their chant and their steps faltered but the men behind them, many of them bearing the mark of the Justified Celebrants, pushed them forward. But then one of the

Specials, a man I had twice promoted for merit, ran a little forward then turned and raised his arms and cried for the force to halt.

The disciplined Specials and most of the Watch responded to the order, though the men in armbands sought to keep moving. The chanting stopped and I heard voices raised in anger, and some expressing confusion. The ordered ranks became a milling mob.

The Special I had made Captain — I remembered now, his name was Boudry — raised his voice. "Company… Shun!" he bellowed.

All of the Specials and Watchmen responded with a simultaneous crash of boots onto cobblestones.

"Arms at rest!" came the next order, and the cudgels and swords pointed at the ground.

"Dress ranks!" The Specials and Watchmen shuffled forward and sideways until they formed orderly ranks and files. The Celebrants milled about unhappily, muttering.

Captain Boudry executed an about-face with parade ground precision and stood rigid. "Commander Farouche," he said to me, "we have orders from the office of the Grand Effectuator."

I kept my voice calm and level. "What are your orders?"

"To enter the temple and subdue unruly elements fomenting rebellion against the common good."

"No such elements exist," I said.

I saw Boudry's eyes go left then right before coming back to me. He said, "I am not sure how to proceed."

Efferion's voice was in my head. *It would please me to make a demonstration of my powers.*

I told him I would not do gratuitous harm and that there were other ways it could amply demonstrate its powers. I quoted the old aphorism about catching more ants with sugar than with salt.

Such utterances do not resonate with me, it said. *I was made to be literal minded.*

"The *theropath* I carried into Exley did damage to their peculiar common undermind," I said inside my head. "I am sure they would be impressed if you were to undo the harm."

Well, the god said, *if you say so.*

I was not affected by what happened next, but the men sent by Nulf Bernaglio were. A blankness took charge of their gazes, then every face showed the same expression: that of a man who has just remembered something once known but since forgotten. A certain common rigidity of posture left them all. Many of them dropped the weapons they were carrying.

"What just happened?" Captain Boudry said.

"You were in magical bondage," I said, "but Efferion has made you free."

His brow furrowed. "To whom were we bound?"

"The Grand Effectuator."

A low sound came out of the crowd. Their faces hardened. I raised my hand before they could put their intentions into action.

"No," I said, "I will deal with him."

«»

The Watchmen who should have been guarding the entrances of the basilica had left their posts. I went into the reception hall and found it similarly deserted, the lamps unlit. From the half-open door into the grand chamber into which Councillor Pavao Cornache had invited me after I disarmed the ill-trained Special came a flickering light, yellow and orange. I crossed the flagstone floor and stepped into the glow.

Nulf Bernaglio stooped over a brazier mounted on a waist-high tripod, feeding pinches of powder into the flaming charcoal and muttering words I could not hear. He looked up as I appeared in the doorway and I saw a succession of emotions in his aspect: startlement, recognition, pure hatred, ending in a mask of mad glee.

He threw the last of the powder into the flames. They turned blood red then a deep black, twisting and rising as if they were made of solid stuff. He pointed a finger at me, said one final syllable, then shouted, "Rend him! Limbs and bowels, then bring me his head!"

I could not see whom he was addressing, then Efferion augmented my sight. Advancing on me was a creature that looked to be made of thick, roiling smoke — like the kind of turbulent superheated cloud of ash and gas that rushes down the slopes of a volcano, enveloping and incinerating all in its path.

Efferion spoke in my mind. *A* theropath. *I will deal with it.*

"No," I said, inside my head, "let me."

I raised my hand, palm toward the demon, and said, aloud, "You will stop."

It was as if the smoke had met a pane of glass. The *theropath* flattened against the barrier. It struggled for a moment, then its motions quietened. I heard its voice, though I did not know whether it arrived through my ears or directly into my mind.

Do not destroy me, it said. *I am compelled.*

"I know," I said. "But no more."

Efferion showed me where the demon was constrained. I used the god's axial volition and broke the bonds. The *theropath* flowed like streaming vapor to a point near the ceiling and passed through into its own Plane. I gestured and sealed the breach.

Bernaglio's eyes bulged in his head. His jaw was moving convulsively. Foam appeared at the corners of his mouth. He looked about as if seeking something to hurl at me.

I kept my voice calm. "It will do no good," I said. "You are defeated."

He stared at me, clearly uncomprehending. I continued to speak in a level voice. "Efferion has come into his full godhood, thanks to you. Your work here has been undone."

Bernaglio was breathing hard, his eyes still full of wildness, his fingers spread like a raptor's claws. I was not sure if he was hearing me.

"He is inclined to be merciful. You will be sent into exile, though not until you have publicly admitted your faults and gone through a ceremony of cleansing."

The oligarch's mouth opened and closed twice. He swallowed and finally found his voice. In a harsh rasp, he said, "No. Not again."

For a moment, I did not understand. Then Efferion entered my mind and showed me the past. I took a step back as if the image that appeared in my mind's eye was solid, concrete reality before me.

I saw the dusty square at the heart of Drieff. Lance-Major Vashonne and his aides came into the space from a side street, the battalion marching behind them, weapons drawn. I saw myself at the head of the cohort, looking about me with an air of puzzlement. I experienced some small surprise at how young I had been.

A gang of enforcers of the Justified Celebrants were clustered together on the opposite side of the square. They glanced over at the incoming troops then returned their attention to the second-story balcony in the big house that occupied most of that side of the plaza. A man was haranguing them and the mob gazed up at him with rapt attention, their jaws methodically chewing katch, dribbles of its brown juice running from the corners of their mouths.

Now the man on the balcony lifted his arms, pointed a finger at the Golden Lions. He said something, and the Celebrants turned as one and hurried over to confront the intruders. Moments later, the tragedy began. I wished I could turn away as a ranting fanatic crushed the Lance-Major's skull with a length of iron, but the image was in my head. I saw the blood and brains spurt, saw my younger self raise my falchion and point it at the murderer, saw my lips form the words, "No quarter!"

And then we charged. We cut down the crazed enforcers, but new Celebrants were already rushing into the square from the big house opposite, their eyes mad with katch. They threw themselves upon us, some of them clawing at us with bare hands. And we, almost as frenzied, hacked and spitted them.

The final image Efferion showed me was of the man on the balcony, regarding the killings with an uninterested mien. Then he stepped inside.

Like mine, his face was younger, but I recognized the saturnine visage of Nulf Bernaglio.

"You were the Anointed," I said.

He drew himself to his full height and thrust out his chin. "I remain the Anointed," he answered me. "Bow down to me!"

"I will not bow to a madman, but Efferion can deliver you from insanity's grip. He did as much for me."

I extended my hand in a pleading gesture. For all the harm he had done me, I wished him no ill. Such was the extent of the god's enlargement of my *ka*.

But Bernaglio's aspect remained wild. "Please," I said, and took a step forward. His response was to seize a heavy piece of brass used for making official seals in wax and hurl it at my head. I ducked and heard the thing clang against the stone wall and, when I straightened, Bernaglio was making for a small door in the inner wall of the chamber. He scuttled through it and pulled it closed behind him.

I crossed the chamber and pulled on the door's handle. Bernaglio had locked it behind him. I consulted Efferion. The god found it an interesting challenge. A moment later, I heard the latch disengage. I opened the door and found a narrow rising stairway.

Axial volition makes a substantial difference, said the quiet voice in my head.

I put my foot on the first step and said, "Do you know what Bernaglio is doing up above?"

The stairs lead to a tower. He is at the top, attempting to wrest an iron bracket from a merlon so he can strike you with it. He is not succeeding.

"Good," I said and began to climb the stairs.

I would not let him strike you, Efferion said. *I wish to study how enlarging your* ka *affects the course of your existence.*

"Whatever your motive," I said, "I am grateful."

As I suppose I must be grateful for your role in freeing me from bondage to Fatezh. Gratitude is a new emotion for me. I seem to have acquired it when I took all the axial volition from the wizards of Olliphract.

"Grateful wizards?" I said. "That sentiment must have been well buried."

I arrived at the top of the tower. Bernaglio saw me and gave over his attempts to wrest the iron bracket from the merlon. He rushed at me, hands ready to strangle, but I held him off with the same force that had resisted the *theropath*.

His face twisted in rage and misery as he struggled futilely to break past the invisible barrier. Abruptly, his expression changed to abject despair. He turned his back on me, rushed to the space between two merlons, and launched himself into the air.

"No!" I cried, reaching after him with my powers. I caught him when he was almost down to the cobblestones in the square. I went to the edge of the tower roof and looked down, to see him struggling without success, suspended helpless just above the ground.

I turned and descended the steps.

I am curious as to your motivations, Efferion said.

"They must be unconscious," I said. "I feel this strong urge to save him, though he did me great harm and has been a bane to thousands."

I do not believe you can 'save' him, the god said. *His* ba *is immense, his* ka *minuscule. He is bound for the Underworld and his* ka *will haunt the scene of his demise.*

"Yet, I must try."

But Efferion told me, as I reached the foot of the stairs, that I was too late. When I emerged from the basilica, I saw that the Specials had followed me from the temple. They had found Bernaglio suspended above the cobblestones and had used their weapons upon him. His corpse was in pieces.

His rule was a nightmare for them, the god said. *He haunted their dreams and drove them to commit crimes that they knew were evil. They will need much healing.*

«»

Time has passed. I have settled into my role as high priest in the cult of Efferion. I am continually learning the work, aided by Philaria and the other clergy. The god itself is exploring the proper use of its powers, sometimes by discussion with we who serve it, sometimes by trial and error. There have been incidences of the latter, some of them comic but fortunately none has resulted in tragedy.

It is a dicey business, this having will, Efferion said to me recently. *It was just as well the Demiurge confined it to you Middleworlders.*

This raised the old question of what the Great Artificer's aim might have been when he created phenomenality. At one point in the discussion, I said it was a shame we could not seek him out and ask him.

It might avail us nothing, the god said. *It is possible that he conducted the work for a deity even greater than he. He may have been just a larger, more complex version of us, his tools.*

"Did you and your kind ever discuss that idea?" I asked.

No. We were not endowed with curiosity. It would have hindered the work if we were constantly pausing to question our situation. Again, that was left to your kind.

⟨⟨⟩⟩

The Exleyans conducted their ratherings and chose new governance. Efferion and we who served him were careful not to interfere, but I went down to Varderon Square to witness the mass singing. I was standing outside Holfman Brothers, watching the electors snake around the great space when I felt a tug on my sleeve.

I turned to find Amalthea regarding me with an expression I could not quite read. She said, "I heard you were back and that you had taken up religion."

"More accurate to say it has taken me up," I said.

Her mouth and eyebrows moved. "Your funds are still on deposit," she said.

I shrugged. "I have little use for them now. I seem to have everything I want."

Again, the brows rose. "Everything?" she said.

Efferion was never far from me. I heard his voice in my inner ear. *I do not require celibacy, even of my high priest,* it said. *Indeed, I am not sure I would approve of it. The Demiurge was quite clear about the efficacy of intimacy in the shaping of the* ba *and* ka.

I smiled at the young woman. "Maybe not quite everything," I said. I took her hand and she let me.

Part 8

114 speaks

I was at loose ends in Exley after Nulf Bernaglio's overthrow. The town's situation did not revert to what it had been before the dictator loosed a demon on the collective unconscious. Instead, Efferion exerted itself to change the overall mood for the better. The result: less crime, less antisocial behavior in general, fewer call outs to the Watch to separate battling spouses and brawling drunkards.

But a happier community brings less business to the doorstep of an inquiries agency, and Chadroyds found they had little need for my services. Laid off indefinitely, I considered making contact with the vindicators' guild but, after a brief moment of reflection, decided that the life of an assassin was not for me.

It seemed the best course was to go to Sanctuary and see what I could find to do among my own kind. It occurred to me that now that Olliphract was cleansed of thaumaturgy, we vat-bred people might make the place our own. It had many amenities and no dwellings made of sod and canvas. Besides, there were several former thaumaturges who could be taught to fetch and carry.

I was packing my few possessions when the Kain came to my lodgings. He now wore the robes and brow circlet of Efferion's high priest. I had heard that he was become a person of prominence in Exley, his god having become the leading deity of the town. People were flocking to the temple and there was talk of the cult moving to larger quarters.

"You are leaving?" he said, seeing my half-packed equipage on the bed.

I told him of my plans. He nodded, then moved his head in another motion that conveyed ambivalence as to the merit of my going to Sanctuary and on to Olliphract.

I paused in my packing. "What?" I said.

"Efferion has been talking to me about you," he said.

"About me? In connection to what?"

"*Bas* and *kas*.

I resumed packing, saying, "I have neither."

Again, the sideways motion of his head, and now his hands expressed ambiguity. "Efferion thinks there is a possibility..."

I stopped again. "Of what? Making me gisted? I would have to be naturally born, and I am too large to fit within the equipment."

"Still, something may be done. Will you come with me?"

"Is there risk?" I said. "I am not yet ready to die."

He smiled. "There is always risk. Just stepping into the street can be fatal if a runaway ale wagon is hurtling past your door. But we do it anyway."

"You are becoming quite the philosopher," I said.

"Comes with the robes," he said, and gestured for me to accompany him.

«»

"Are you serious?" I said, when the Kain showed me the contraption he had built in the cellar of the temple.

"Efferion says the entity that generates and distributes *bas* and *kas* is very simple-minded," he said. "When you think about it, it would have to be."

"Even so." I studied the apparatus. "What is it filled with?"

"Gelatin. And the... lips are made from the same stuff the assassins' guild puts on the wheels of their vehicles so they travel silently."

"Assassins," I said. "Odd that you should mention—"

"It's made from the sap of a tree that grows down south, far below Old Almery."

"All right," I said, waving away further discussion. "How is it supposed to work?"

He sounded like one of the instructors at the Institute, explaining a theorem. "Efferion has been in touch with the entity on the Fifth Plane. It's so rudimentary, it doesn't even have a name. But he tells me that it is a very small Plane and the gist-bestowing entity is its only inhabitant."

"You're not telling me how it works," I said.

"The god has examined its workings and believes that it can be... nudged into bestowing gist on someone it finds in a reasonable facsimile of a womb."

"Nudged," I said.

"The entity has no will. It can't resist if its essential parameters are present."

I cleared my throat. "What do I do?"

"Remove your garments—"

"Part of the reasonable facsimile, I presume."

He nodded in both agreement and encouragement. I said, "This has meaning to you."

"It does," he said. "Efferion repaired my essences, but I still have a lot to make up for. This will move me along the path."

"How will I know if it works?"

"You will be able to converse with the god."

I smiled at that. "Is Efferion's conversation engaging?"

"Try the procedure. You have nothing to lose."

"Not even my dignity," I said.

I disrobed, my back turned to him so that he would not see that I lacked the generative apparatus of the natural born. We vat-men are sensitive about that. Then I slipped between the soft lips of the apparatus and positioned myself in the gelatinous contents.

The Kain said, "Efferion says to curl up into a ball with your head pointing in this direction."

Feeling faintly ridiculous, I did as the god ordered. The goo was not warm and I shivered. Little bumps appeared on my arms.

"Now what?" I said.

"Wait. Efferion is reaching out to the entity." A small silence ensued, then the Kain said, "There, it is done. Slide out through the opening, head first. I will assist you."

I did as he bade me. He helped me to my feet — I slipped a little because of the jelly on my soles — then he handed me a towel. I began to remove the stuff that still clung to me.

"How do you feel?" the Kain said.

I took a moment to examine myself. "No different," I said.

Yet you are, said a voice in my head. *You have gist. You will know the Underworld and the Overworld.*

Tears sprang from my eyes. "I must go to Sanctuary," I said.

Yes. Go and bring them to me. I will make them whole.

Afterword

Back in 1982, I wrote an entry for a novel-in-a-weekend contest. It didn't win, or even make the short list, but later on I expanded the original 27,000 words in a short fantasy novel called *Fools Errant.*

That began the succession of novels, novellas, and short stories that I collectively refer to as the Archonate series. They are set in a universe that, inexplicably and arbitrarily, switches every few thousand years between two contrasting basic operating principles: rational cause and effect on the one hand or "sympathetic association," i.e., magic, on the other.

Some of the tales — particularly those featuring Henghis Hapthorn, the discriminator, Luff Imbry, the art thief and forger, and Guth Bandar, explorer of the collective unconscious — are set in a space-opera milieu called The Ten Thousand Worlds. The rest — including the misadventures of the thief Raffalon and the wizard's henchman Baldemar, and this present volume — are set in my extrapolation of the brilliant Jack Vance's *Dying Earth* milieu, after magic has once more ejected reason from the driver's seat and seized the reins of the world.

Tolkien talked about his great work being "a tale that grew in the telling." My raft of Archonate narratives have undergone the same expansion, as new ideas have popped into my mind when I'm in the middle of telling a new. Gradually, a universe has taken rough shape. Bit by bit, gaps have been filled in and details brought out of the background and into the reader's view.

So here's what you need to know. First, the Archonate setting is not the universe than you and I live in, even taking into account the aeons between our time and the galactic civilization of The Ten Thousand Worlds or the subsequent world of wizards and walled cities that arise after magic has established dominance.

Phenomenality — the Archonate universe — was deliberately created by the Demiurge as a realm of nine Planes. Humanity exists, during life, on the Third Plane. This Middleworld is bracketed by the Second and Fourth Planes, known as the Underworld and Overworld, respectively. More about that later.

The First Plane is an empty, featureless, and infinite realm of nothingness. It was the workshop in which the Great Artificer and his sentient tools constructed Phenomenality, only to be abandoned once the work was done. If you've read the Raffalon story, "Wearaway and Flambeau," you've visited there. It's also the "Old Sea" in the Hapthorn and Bandar tales.

The Seventh Plane is a dimension in which the rules of space-time do not apply. During the space-opera age of The Ten Thousand Worlds, it was the realm through which conduits known as "whimsies" allowed spaceships to cross great distances between star systems. The denizens of the Seventh Plane are able to exert considerable powers if they are drawn into Middleworld. To describe them as demons is not far from the mark. Much of the action in the novel, *A Wizard's Henchman*, and some of the events in the Luff Imbry novella, "Of Whimsies and Noubles," take place in the Seventh Plane.

Also resident in the Seventh Plane, and simultaneously in the Second, Third, and Fourth, are the sentient entities fashioned by the Demiurge to aid in the great work. They were abandoned and left to fend for themselves. Some engaged with humanity and have become various kinds of gods.

The Fifth, Sixth, Eighth, and Ninth Planes are indescribable and play no part in the stories, except that in this novel an important entity is the sole inhabitant of the Sixth.

The fundamental substance of Phenomenality is an elusive material known as gist. A network of gistic conduits

— fluxions — bind reality together. Practitioners of magic have learned how to access the power of these conduits by the focused application of will — the technical term is "axial volition."

Human beings are gistic. Each has two souls — a *ba* and a *ka*, held together by a hinge known as a *kra*. The relative sizes of a person's *ba* and *ka* change over time, depending on how much good or bad the individual does in life. At death, the *ba* descends to the misery of the Underworld while the *ka* ascends to bliss in the Overworld. The *kra* usually dissipates, although in the case of sudden and unexpected death it may remain at the scene as a ghost.

The entities from the Demiurge's abandoned toolbox, now scattered through the Planes, are also highly gistic, giving them extraordinary powers. They generally do not, however, possess axial volition.

The Demiurge, when he departed, left no explanation as to the purpose, if any, of his creation. It has been theorized that he was merely a contractor — or even a kind of ultrasentient tool, himself — for a higher deity. Another theory holds that Phenomenality is actually only a rough draft of a perfect universe, discarded after it had served its purpose. But no one knows for sure. For a fuller treatment of the rough-draft theory, read the Hapthorn story, "Fullbrim's Finding."

And there is no point asking me. I am not a conscious world-builder. I have no grand scheme into which I fit my characters and plots. I am an improviser, relying upon the kindness of my unconscious; I never know, when I start a story, where it will end up or what it will pass through en route. As all the many narratives have unfolded since that busy weekend in 1982, I have added bits of background and pertinent details as they have bubbled up from below.

Nor do I have any overarching purpose to all this storytelling, other than to entertain myself — and, with luck, my readers — and to make a small income. The points of view of my characters, though they come out of me, are not necessarily mine.

If you enjoyed this read

Please leave a review on Amazon, Facebook, Good Reads or Instagram.

It takes less than five minutes and it really does make a difference.

If you're not sure how to leave a review on Amazon:

1. *Go to amazon.com.*
2. *Type in A God in Chains by Matthew Hughes and when you see it, click on it.*
3. *Scroll down to Customer Reviews. Nearby you'll see a box labeled Write a Review. Click it.*
4. *Now, if you've never written a review before on Amazon, they might ask you to create a name for yourself.*
5. *Reviews can be as simple as, "Loved the book! Can't wait for the Next!" (Please don't give the story away.)*

And that's it!

Brian Hades, publisher

About the Author

Matthew Hughes writes fantasy and space opera, often in a Jack Vance mode. Booklist has called him Vance's "heir apparent."

His short fiction has appeared in Asimov's, F&SF, Postscripts, Lightspeed, and Interzone, and invitation-only anthologies including Songs of the Dying Earth, Rogues, Old Mars, Old Venus, The Book of Swords, and The Book of Magic, all edited by George R.R. Martin and/or Gardner Dozois.

He has won the Arthur Ellis Award, and has been shortlisted for the Aurora, Nebula, Philip K. Dick, Endeavour (twice), A.E. Van Vogt, and Derringer Awards.

He spent more than thirty years as one of Canada's leading speechwriters for political leaders and corporate executives. Since 2007, he has been traveling the world as an itinerant housesitter, has lived in twelve countries, and has no fixed address.

Need something new to read?

If you liked A God in Chains you should also consider these other EDGE-Lite titles...

The Black Chalice

by Marie Jakober

Award Winning Novel...

It's 1134. In a bleak monastery somewhere in Germany, Paul of Ardiun begins the chronicle he has been ordered by his religious superiors to write: the story of the knight Karelian Brandeis, for whom Paul once served as squire, who fell prey to the evil wiles of a seductive sorceress, thereby precipitating civil war and the downfall of a king.

As Paul starts to write tale, the sorceress herself appears to him. He is a liar, she tells him, and always has been. She lays a spell on Paul: from this moment, he will only be able to write the truth.

But what is the truth? All his life he has rearranged his memories to suit his faith. Now, against his will, an entirely different story begins to emerge.

About Award winning author Marie Jakober,

Marie Jakober graduated with honors from Ottawa's Carleton University. She has written nine novels. The Black Chalice was awarded the Independent Publisher Book Award and Only Call Us Faithful received the Michael Shaara Award for Excellence in Civil War Fiction.

Druids

(Part One of the Druids series)

by Barbara Galler-Smith & Josh Langston

The DRUIDS Saga begins...

For over 1000 years, Celts rule Europe. The most revered are the Druids: bards, healers, judges, and seers. A special few protect the secrets of ancient Earth magic, including a healer from Iberia, and a seer from Belgica.

Rhonwen, the healer, keeps the Druidic culture and practises alive in a land ravaged by a Roman civil war. Sworn by her Mother to a blood oath of vengeance, she must choose between fulfilling the promise or following her own heart`s path.

Mallec, the seer, is sent from his warrior tribe to the center of druidic learning to become a scholar. His training does not prepare him for an unexpected discovery of an ancient rite for immortality. Once mastered, Mallec must protect the knowledge from those who thirst for its power and are bent on his destruction.

Seemingly separate paths, entwined by dreams and destiny, the DRUIDS saga unfolds.

Grimenna

by N. K. Blazevic

When Courage Finds Hope…

Evil is roosting in the lord's keep, corrupting the land and feeding off its growing despair. When Paiva Ibbie, a young sheepherder's daughter, joins her aunt to work in the kitchens, she brings with her a flicker of hope from a village in the north that remains untouched by darkness. Her good spirit is a threat to the evil's work and it will stop at nothing to ensure that Paiva's hope is turned into the darkest of despair.

About Natasha K. Blazevic

Natasha K. Blazevic lives in St André D'Argenteuil, Quebec. She studied art in college but, after ayear, fled to the countryside of the Quebec Laurentians where she apprenticed as a stone mason and began to cultivate her love of art and animals in earnest. She is a beekeeper and considers herself a student of life with a keen interest in the natural world. She hopes her book Grimenna can not only entertain and enchant readers, but can help to promote a green renaissance.

The Red Wraith

by Nick Wisseman

Magic Awakens in Early America...

On the eve of the Harvest Ceremony, Naysin, a child of the Lepane nation, manifests powers of a dual deity forever torn in two by light and darkness. Cast into exile by his clan for being a spawn of human and spirit, Naysin is lost in a world of change as pale men from the sea arrive to plunder the riches of the Earth. Guided only by the devious facets of his spirit father, Naysin has no choice but to master his powers to survive the destruction of his people. For Naysin, it is a path of darkness and death that will take him from one end of the land to the other and down into the depths of infamy.

About Nick Wisseman

Nick Wisseman lives in Bear Lake, Michigan with his wife, daughter, fifty cats, twenty horses, and ten dogs. (Okay, there are actually ten times less pets than that, but most days it feels like more.) He's not quite sure why he loves writing twisted fiction, but there's no stopping the weirdness once he's in front of a computer.